Christietown

Christietown

SUSAN KANDEL

HARPER

NEW YORK • LONDON • TORONTO • SYDNEY

HARPER

CHRISTIETOWN. Copyright © 2007 by Susan Kandel. All rights reserved. Printed in the United States of America. No part of this book may be used or reproduced in any manner whatsoever without written permission except in the case of brief quotations embodied in critical articles and reviews. For information address HarperCollins Publishers, 10 East 53rd Street, New York, NY 10022.

HarperCollins books may be purchased for educational, business, or sales promotional use. For information please write: Special Markets Department, HarperCollins Publishers, 10 East 53rd Street, New York, NY 10022.

FIRST EDITION

Library of Congress Cataloging-in-Publication Data is available upon request.

ISBN: 978-0-06-145217-8
ISBN-10: 0-06-145217-3

07 08 09 10 11 ID/RRD 10 9 8 7 6 5 4 3 2 1

To Deborah Michel, lifelong friend

ACKNOWLEDGMENTS

Thank you, again, to my friends and family, who never seem to mind when I crib a line or two from them.

Thanks are also due to my brilliant editor, Carolyn Marino, who bears no relationship whatsoever to Cece's editor, Sally; and to the agent extraordinaire, Sandra Dijkstra. Samantha Hagerbaumer of HarperCollins is a delight to work with; ditto Taryn Fagerness and Elise Capron at the Dijkstra Agency.

The literature on the Queen of Crime is vast. Agatha Christie's autobiography proved invaluable, as did the biographies by Janet Morgan and Gillian Gill, and Anne Hart's charming *The Life and Times of Miss Jane Marple*. In researching Agatha's disappearance, I consulted a variety of works, fiction and nonfiction, including Carole Owens's *The Lost Days of Agatha Christie*, Kathleen Tynan's *Agatha*, and finally, Jared Cade's *Agatha Christie and the Eleven Missing Days*, to which I am greatly indebted. Cade's meticulous research and psychological insights provided the basis of my own reconstruction of what Agatha might have been thinking during those fateful days in 1926.

My daughters started off indulging me and wound up Christie fans; my husband is more the hard-boiled type, but he lived and breathed Miss Marple for a solid year. Who could ask for anything more?

CHAPTER 1

The lights sparkled overhead as the man I loved spun me around the dance floor. I could feel my heart pounding in my chest. His was pounding, too.

"'You'd be so nice to come home to,'" he murmured into my ear.

"'It had to be you,'" I whispered.

"'I've got you under my skin,'" he whispered back.

"No way," I said with a shudder. "They played that one at my first wedding."

"Must I remind you that we are dancing the tango, Ms. Caruso?" came a voice from across the room. "Sexy! Earthy! Drama!"

Lou Berman, aka Le Duc de Danse. I tuned him out. We'd found him in the Yellow Pages.

"We've only got one lesson left in the Romance Package, Cece." My fiancé, Peter Gambino, pressed hard on the small of my back. "We have to make a decision about the first dance soon."

"Arms high, Detective! You are a matador!" Lou stomped his feet, then whipped a McDonald's bag out of the trash and whirled it triumphantly overhead.

"'I Get a Kick Out of You?'" I suggested.

On cue, Gambino kicked me in the shins.

"Go with it, Ms. Caruso!" Lou cried. "You are the wounded bull!"

Not exactly the wedding-day scenario I had in mind.

"It's ten o'clock on the nose, people." Lou's wife, Liz Berman, emerged from the back office and flicked the CD player to Off. "Time to hit the road."

Gambino and I disentangled ourselves as Lou folded himself into a ratty metal chair. Liz sat down at her desk near the water cooler and knocked back her regular evening cocktail of antihistamines and acetaminophen. Then, shooting Lou the evil eye, she got up to put the McDonald's bag back in the trash. She was the detail person.

"So what do you think of these kids?" Lou mopped a suspiciously smooth brow.

"They're really coming along," Liz said with no perceptible enthusiasm.

Gambino turned to me. "I told you. We're going to kick butt at next week's lesson."

I patted his arm. "I think we should avoid the word *kick*."

Lou looked dubious, in any case. Next week's lesson was the foxtrot, the most difficult of all ballroom dances, requiring constant shifts in rhythm from slow to fast to medium.

"If anyone can teach you two to foxtrot, it's Lou," Liz conceded.

"You kill me, doll." He went over and wrapped an arm around her waist, lifting her off her feet. Then the two of them—tall, plump, congested Liz and tall, thin, bottle-bronzed

Lou—began to whirl around the room. Gambino and I stared, openmouthed. They didn't need music. They *were* music.

"Married twenty-two years," Lou said, dipping Liz.

"Twenty-two years," she repeated, upside down.

That was about how long it had been since *I'd* last walked down the aisle—young, pregnant, and dumb.

Dumb enough to think winning Miss Asbury Park, New Jersey, would be my ticket to eternal bliss.

Dumb enough to blow off college to put my then-husband through grad school.

Dumb enough—well, just dumb enough.

I wanted to believe I'd learned something since then. I looked over at Gambino. He was kind, smart, funny. He had me, and still wanted me.

Yes, I'd learned something since then.

"While we're on the subject of killing," said Liz, pulling out of her husband's embrace, "get a load of this."

I'd thought we were on the subject of love everlasting but I wasn't about to interrupt Liz, who discouraged that sort of thing. She peeled off her worn leather jacket, took a puff of her inhaler, then wrapped a fuzzy white scarf tight around her neck.

"My dears," she said, "it's truly a mystery to me." Her voice was suddenly frail, her nose longer, her skin pinker. She pulled a pair of knitting needles out of her bag. "But I so often seem to get mixed up in things that are really no concern of mine. Crimes, I mean, and peculiar happenings." She leaned her head a little to one side, like a cockatoo fluffing its feathers. "Nothing, of course, a nice linseed poultice couldn't cure."

"Miss Jane Marple!" I exclaimed.

"Damn straight," she said, then sneezed. "Guess I've got to double up on the Claritin for Saturday."

Saturday.

Saturday was a big deal.

I was dreading Saturday.

But at least Saturday was a distraction from the bigger deals in my life, which for the record would be:

1. Waiting to hear from my editor, Sally, about *Poison Book*, my biography of the mystery writer Agatha Christie. I'd sent the four-hundred-and-two-page manuscript off to her exactly eleven days, ten hours, and thirty-five minutes ago, not that I was counting.

2. Choosing the right ensemble for the upcoming baby shower I was hosting for my daughter, Annie. The champagne-colored, disco-era halter dress I had in mind didn't exactly scream "grandma." But I was barely forty years old. Did I really have to go for double-knit slacks? Or worse yet, a muu-muu?

3. Getting married.

4. Getting married (it merits two mentions).

Like I was saying, thank God for Saturday.

Saturday would mark the opening festivities of Phase 2 of Christietown, a Golden Age mystery-themed housing development on the sun-baked fringes of Antelope Valley, just east of Los Angeles.

I was in charge of Saturday.

In charge of the clotted cream, the scones, and the Cornish pasties; in charge of the yapping Yorkies and stubby Corgis; in charge of the larkspurs, hollyhocks, and snapdragons lining the neat brick path up to the Vicarage (which would be the sales office); and worse yet, in charge of the original, interactive Murder Mystery Tea, starring—yes—Liz Berman (aka

La Duchesse de Danse) as Agatha Christie's beloved amateur sleuth, Miss Marple.

Everyone had a part.

Lou Berman was the butler. He didn't do it.

Wren Abbott, the dance studio's frizzy-haired receptionist, was an eleven-year-old with psychic abilities.

My second-best friend, Bridget, was her governess, Estella Raven, who was rude and spirited and whose studied insolence covered a great fear.

My best friend, Lael, master pastry chef and inadvertent sexpot, was the vicar's wife.

My fiancé, Peter Gambino, was the soldier of fortune.

My gardener, Javier Gomez, was Sir Guy Pilkington of Gossington Hall. He was going to be in a wheelchair for the duration of the play.

And yes, it's true, my neighbors, seventy-year-old twin sisters and ex-showgirls Lois and Marlene—known in their former lives as Hibiscus and Jasmine—would be dancing onstage for the first time in thirty years.

With the exception of Javier, who inexplicably had a Screen Actors Guild card, nobody was being paid. I'd blown my budget on expensive sherry and a large plasterboard facade of Gossington Hall, with real mullioned windows. So instead of hiring actors, I'd called in my chits. It didn't take much convincing. These people were dying to ham it up in front of an audience.

It being tax season, my accountant Mr. Keshigian did not have a part, though I'd been tempted to cast him as Sir Guy's cousin Jasper, the black sheep of the family. Mr. Keshigian, I should explain, was the one who got me the gig in the first place. Mr. Keshigian is concerned about my finances. Writing biographies of dead mystery writers—as he reminds me every time we go over my deductions—is not a lucrative profession. So when he recently found himself attending a real estate seminar where the developer of Christietown was making a presentation, he didn't waste any time. He cornered the guy during cocktail hour and by the time the baked Brie was gone, had me moonlighting as an event planner.

Like I dared argue.

My new boss was named Ian Christie.

Ian Christie was a beet-faced Englishman who claimed (vociferously) to be related (distantly) to the Queen of Crime herself. Fat chance. Agatha Christie was the world's best-known mystery writer and, not counting Shakespeare, the all-time best-selling author in any genre. Christietown, however, was Ian's baby, a master-planned, amenity-packed, Cotswoldsesque cozyland tailor-made for its target demographic: mystery fans, retirees, British expatriates in search of the midday sun. The fact that Phase 1 had been only a middling success (less than half of the 125 existing houses had been sold) had proved no impediment whatsoever to the initiation of Phase 2, which was vastly more ambitious: 500 new houses plus a church and a High Street, with a butcher, a baker, a post office, an apothecary, a pub, and a locksmith.

All this I learned several weeks ago over lemonade and sticky buns at the Vicarage. There were already themed mugs, nightlights, key chains, picture frames, illuminated water globes, and T-shirts, all bearing the logo Ian Christie had designed himself: a white-haired, hatchet-wielding spinster sitting inside a spinning teacup, the word *Christietown* spelled out in dripping blood. But that was just the beginning.

Ian was thinking big: housing developments in similar communities across the U.S., maybe even Europe, and best of all, a Christietown credit card. He salivated at the mere mention of the credit card. His plump hands flew; his pale eyes popped. While waiting for him to settle down, I'd found myself wondering if the chief investors—two Israelis rumored to be ex-Mossad operatives—were equally optimistic. The real estate market wasn't exactly booming these days. And I couldn't imagine there were that many British expats roaming the southern California desert looking for storybook cottages with pseudothatched roofs. But that wasn't my business. I sipped more lemonade. I shoveled another sticky bun in my mouth. "Not my business" was my new mantra. By the end of the afternoon, Ian was congratulating himself for having hired me. Now all I had to do was deliver. That part was my business.

"You hungry?" Gambino asked as we got in his car.

"Starved."

"What do you think about a chili dog at Pink's?"

Pink's, on Melrose and La Brea, was a sentimental favorite of ours. One of our first dates had taken place on its sixtieth anniversary, when we'd waited for four hours in the hot sun for sixty-cent chili dogs. Pink's was famous for them. Orson Welles ate eighteen at a single sitting, which was a record. Orson Welles probably didn't care if he got food all over his pants. But I had on a seventies white jersey dress with bell sleeves, which wouldn't be the same covered in chili grease.

"I'll have fries," I said. "Life's a compromise."

The wrong choice of words, as it turned out.

Gambino took off his glasses and wiped them on his shirt. Then he put them back on in slow motion. I knew what that meant.

"If you have something to say, Cece," he said, not looking at me, "just come out and say it."

We'd been arguing nonstop about the wedding. I was ready to march into city hall and be done with it, but Gambino wanted something more traditional. Thus, the dancing lessons. And the meetings with Father Joe. And the ongoing discussion with my neighbor Butch, who had volunteered his backyard for the reception. I'd thought compromising was a sign of character. Apparently not.

"Orson Welles narrated the third film version of *Ten Little Indians*, did you know that?" It seemed simpler to avoid the issue.

"No," Gambino said sharply. He got onto the I–10 heading east.

"It starred Elke Sommer, the kiss of death," I added.

"Uh-huh." He was doing deep nose breathing now, a bad sign.

"Orson Welles's ghost haunts Sweet Lady Jane." Sweet Lady Jane, our favorite bakery, was located next door to the old site of Ma Maison, where Orson Welles ate lunch every day until he died.

"Cece," said Gambino, "we need to talk."

"Oh, no. I forgot my shoes." Lou had taken one look at my platforms and insisted I change into Liz's dancing slippers before I twisted an ankle. Everyone except me had been excited that Liz and I wore the same size. "They're collectibles. Kork-Ease. From high school. We have to go back."

"You've got to be kidding," Gambino said. But he was already heading for the exit.

Gambino did not understand vintage fashion, but he did understand me. He didn't so much as blink, for example, the time I showed up at a cop pool party in Eagle Rock wearing a Jantzen swimsuit from the forties with boning and Bakelite buckles. Or when I met his sister for the first time wearing an

apricot-colored silk Harlow gown with shirred raglan shoulders and a hint of a train.

Okay, so we did need to talk.

We got off the freeway at Lincoln, and headed back to
Fourth Street. The valet parkers employed by the neighbor-
ing restaurants had gone home, so there were free spots out
front. Gambino came around to open my door for me and we
walked back toward the dance studio, knocking shyly against
each other's hips. That was our way of reestablishing relationship equilibrium. It was a chilly April night. My dress was
thin. Gambino wrapped his arm tight around me and when
that wasn't enough, took off his jacket and draped it over my
shoulders. We arrived at the studio, and saw that the blinds
had been pulled.

"It hasn't even been fifteen minutes," I said. "They're probably still in there."

Gambino knocked.

No answer.

I put my nose up to the glass and through a crack in the
blinds saw the silhouette of a pair of lovers embracing behind
the screen where Lou kept the CD player.

Twenty-two years.

They still had the itch.

It was just as I'd suspected: sexual chemistry trumps all.

"'Fever!'" I suddenly exclaimed.

Gambino put his hand on my forehead. "You're sick?"

"No, I mean for the first song. Peggy Lee. What do you
think?"

"I like it," he said. "A lot."

"Forget about the shoes." I took Gambino's arm. "Take me
to bed."

Chapter 2

My dad, a twenty-year veteran of the force, used to say a good cop never closes more than one eye.

Gambino closes two but still gets the job done.

It was four A.M. when the phone rang.

Detective Tico Soto, Gambino's partner, with his usual impeccable timing.

A body had been found downtown, on Vignes Street, just around the corner from the L.A. County Men's Central Jail. The Seventy-seventh Precinct was in disarray. Two of its men had been shot the day before in a hostage situation that had gone south. So the booking sergeant was calling on the Hollywood Division for help.

Three minutes and thirty seconds later, having pulled on his clothes, kissed me, and retrieved his holster from the hall closet, Gambino was out the front door.

Homicide waits for no man.

I had no problem falling back asleep. That lasted until Javier arrived at eight. Javier always arrived with fanfare: clanging

garbage can lids, overzealous leaf blowing, lusty weed whack-
ing. And the lawn mower. Suffice it to say Javier's lawn mower
is an underrated instrument of torture. I put the pillow over
my ears, then hurled it across the room. Taking that as her
cue, Mimi the cat leapt onto the bed and stalked across the
sheet, eyes on the prize. Now we were face (mine)-to-furry face
(hers). Then, the earsplitting howl: "Fancy Feast or die!"

I'd recovered by the second cup of coffee.

A triumphant Mimi claimed the sunny spot under the
stained-glass window in the living room. I put food out for my
teacup poodle, Buster, who doesn't bestir himself before nine
thirty, and watered the hybrid catmint, which I keep under an
overturned wire basket near the sink so Mimi can nibble on
the tips without devouring the blossoms. Then I went out to
the office to check my e-mail.

I live in West Hollywood in a 1932 Spanish-style bunga-
low with hardwood floors, wrought-iron sconces, Moorish
archways, a turquoise-tiled bathroom, and a toilet that flushes
approximately three times out of four. I won't get into the general decrepitude of the heating and air system, nor the idiosyncrasies of the shower, nor the sloping floor in the kitchen,
not to mention the doorknob that comes off in your hand
every time you try to leave. I've come to realize, first of all, that
neither people nor houses weather more than half a century
unscathed; and second of all, that maintenance is a full-time
job. I don't have the constitution for it. So I use the three and
a half minutes it takes for the shower to heat up to read *Us
Weekly* or *People* or *Star* (there's not much there there) and the
mercurial toilet to scare off unwanted guests.

Also, I improvise.

My office, for example.

It was the garage until I sold my second book and had
enough money to hire one of my best friend Lael's handyman
buddies to transform it into my version of a professorial lair:
walls and floor painted apple green, built-in bookshelves, big
Lucite desk, plush reading chair accented with Pucci pillows,
fresh flowers in coordinating shades, a small fridge stocked
with my favorite snacks.

That was the fantasy, at least.

The Pucci pillows had faded in the sun. I'd never bought
the fridge. The flowers tended to eyeball me accusingly for a
day, then die. This morning, it was twelve gerbera daisies. I
yanked them out of the vase and tossed them into the trash.
Then I dumped the water on the grass, which had pretty much
been decimated by Buster, whose youthful urinary tract the vet
had applauded at last month's checkup.

Happily, my e-mail gave me no trouble. I hit Send and
Receive and in seconds the world was at my feet: Cheap Tickets,
penile enhancement, fake Rolex watches, Sally.

That would be my editor, Sally.

We'd never actually met in the flesh, Sally and I, but I
imagined her spending her days in a sleek corner office of a
Manhattan skyscraper, sipping highballs while eviscerating
manuscripts with her dagger nails. I opened the message.

Hi, Cece! Got your package. Not bad.

Not bad?

In fact, good.

I exhaled.

However—

My least favorite word.

I think you could've eked a little more drama out of Agatha
Christie's mysterious eleven-day disappearance. I would've
thought that was something you'd be dying to sink your
teeth into. So please rework those sections by a week from
Monday, at the latest. I don't want to keep the copy editor
waiting. She's the nervous type. How's the weather out
there, by the way? We're having a glorious spring. Ciao. S.

I stomped into the kitchen to pour myself a third cup of
coffee. I ate a protein bar. Then a cold slice of pepperoni pizza.
Then another slice. What was Sally trying to do, kill me?

I dialed Lael's number, looking for sympathy.

She picked up on the third ring. "You are so lucky, Cece. If
you had called five minutes earlier, I would've had you bring
me more piping bags. My topcoat frosting is incredible. Stop
that, I said!"

"Me?" I asked meekly.

"No, the girls. They're trying to put my sunglasses on the
dog. Do you hear me, girls? Anyway, Tommy came home early
from practice, so I sent him out. Did you need something?
Because I'm kind of busy here."

In addition to keeping tabs on her four children and playing the vicar's wife in tomorrow's theatrical extravaganza, Lael
was creating the edible centerpiece: a teapot-shaped cake with
a sugar-dough leaf handle and a sugar-dough rose petal spout,
accompanied by a twelve-tier tower of actual demitasse cups
on which she was piping delicate frosting flowers: bluebells,

freesia, Queen Anne's lace. The cups were going to be filled with cake and sealed with chocolate butter to resemble strong tea.

"I guess I don't need anything," I replied.

"What do you think for the cake, tiramisu or trifle?"

"Tiramisu." I'm Italian.

"I've decided on trifle."

Next I called my very pregnant daughter, Annie. Instead of a shoulder to cry on, however, I got a diatribe against Pampers, which were not only bad for the environment but also more expensive than cloth diapers.

"Over a three-and-a-half-year period," Annie said, "Vincent and I will have to use over eight thousand seven hundred diapers at a cost of approximately two thousand five hundred dollars. And if the baby is large for his or her age, it'll be more."

Annie wasn't known for non sequiturs. I waited a beat.

"It's a catch-twenty-two, Mom. The larger-size diaper is the same price per package, but the number of diapers in each package is less, making each diaper more expensive. Plus, children using disposables toilet train a year to a year and a half later than their peers using cloth diapers. It's all there at www.tinytush.com."

Before she could continue in this vein, I said I had to go because FedEx was at the door. FedEx was, of course, not at the door, but I did have to go. It was already ten fifteen. My second-best friend Bridget opened her shop at eleven and I wanted to get there before the Friday lunch-hour rush, which occurred when the women of Los Angeles all realized they had nothing to wear for the weekend. It's the same thing at nail salons. Do not show up at noon on Friday.

Bridget is the owner of On the Bias, L.A.'s premier vintage

clothing store. The woman is so knowledgeable that doctoral candidates seek out her opinion on Balenciaga's banner year (1954). So influential she'd received handwritten invitations to the couture showings in Paris three years in a row (she doesn't like to fly). So indispensable that a celebrity stylist once attempted to bribe her with an Hermès Birkin bag (in canary yellow, an affront). We met well before her rise to greatness, working back-to-back shifts at the front desk of an aerobics studio. We bonded over our mutual hatred for exercise, as opposed to our mutual love for vintage clothing. But I can't deny that her inventory has been a plus when important occasions arise or, say, multiple costumes for a murder-mystery play are required.

I tucked a doggie treat in my bag for Bridget's dachshund, Helmut, and was on my way. It was a glorious day, sunny and clear. After more than a decade in southern California, I was still dazzled by the weather. Also by the native flora and fauna: the palm trees, the birds-of-paradise, the old people who looked like young people from behind. I would've made it to Beverly Hills in less than ten minutes if I hadn't been stuck behind a Dodge Dart clocking ten mph in a thirty-five mph zone, which is trickier than it might sound. I'm working on road rage, so I didn't even honk.

Helmut appreciated the treat. It was liver flavored, a splurge. I forgot, however, to bring something for Maximilian, Bridget's new intern, a young man from Austria who favored heavily embellished jackets and smiled only when being offered pastry. Today he was wearing a Russian military ensemble, with epaulets, braiding, and fur cuffs.

"Ms. Sugarhill is presently on the phone," he announced in his heavy accent. "She is being given the nonsense by one old lady in the Palm Beach. Four Charles James gown she is with-holding. The greatest American couturier! Please do you sit until she is coming for you." He pushed me in the direction of the pink mohair chaise at the front of the store.

"Thanks," I said. "I like your jacket, by the way."

"Yes," he said soberly.

After he was gone, I made my way over to the dresses. I still needed something for Lou and Liz's receptionist, Wren, to wear on Saturday. Wren was tiny, with an enormous halo of red hair that she was going to put up in pigtails. She'd been working diligently on her trances. Last week, my son-in-law, Vincent, had rigged a device for her to wear around her waist: with a mere push of a button, it released a plume of smoke, heralding a communiqué from the spirit world.

I thumbed through the racks. Everything at Bridget's was sheathed in plastic, so you couldn't really see it. You had to read the labels on the hangers. This was supposed to deter the looky-loos, not that she got many. Bridget's reputation pre-ceded her.

I studied a couple of baby-doll dresses. Too sexy.

Some geometric shifts. Too hard.

A billowing shirtdress with a Peter Pan collar. Too obvious.

I liked a black-cotton-eyelet bustier dress from the eighties, for myself.

Finally, I pulled a double-knit checkerboard romper off the rack.

"Rudi Gernreich!" cried Maximilian from across the room. "He is like me, from Vienna! His father makes hosiery, then kills himself, boo-hoo! Rudi likes the ladies to wear this with a Buster Brown hat, a school pack on the back, and the little-girl shoes."

Maximilian didn't mention Rudi Gernreich's greatest claim to fame, the topless bathing suit, which he created in 1964 in a panic, convinced that Emilio Pucci was going to beat him to the punch. His last collection, in the fall of 1968, was likewise a doozy: it included a Genghis Khan jumpsuit; a black-and-white bloomer dress based on the art of Aubrey Beardsley; and a Renaissance minidress with ribbon-wrapped tights. In the eighties, Gernreich began a home-based business with a menu of gourmet soups, which he personally delivered in his Bentley to a select list of stores in and about Beverly Hills. Bridget thought he was a genius.

"This could work," I said out loud.

Maximilian instantly snatched the checkerboard romper out of my hands. "So sorry, but don't you see what is the size? Size two! You can count? One, two! It will not accommodate your most big body." He looked with disdain upon my five feet eleven inches and one hundred and forty-four pounds.

"It's not for me," I said sweetly. "But in any case, I'm sure I can do better."

Maximilian looked insulted, so we were even.

Just then Bridget appeared, shoulders sagging. Something was wrong. She looked like one of those saucer-eyed waifs from the cheesy paintings, when in fact, she was an African American woman in a severe black suit and four-and-a-half-inch stilettos.

"What is it?" I asked.

"She's not selling me those Charles James dresses is what." Bridget flopped into the chaise.

"I'm sorry," I said.

"Bitch," said Maximilian with feeling.

"I spent a whole weekend with her," Bridget went on,

"eating cocktail wieners and frozen quiches out of chafing dishes. It isn't fair."

"But you love junk food," I said consolingly.

"Real junk food," she said. "Black junk food. Not the WASP version."

"The woman is going to come around."

"No, she's not."

"Yes, she is."

"You don't know that," she said with a stamp of her elegant foot.

"What is this? You are Bridget Sugarhill!"

"You're right!" Bridget exclaimed, sitting up. "And I want a Big Mac!"

It's a process. Today went more quickly than usual.

Maximilian trotted over to get his man bag from behind the desk.

"One for you, one for me, one for doggie Helmut," he recited. "And perhaps it is better the single patty, no bun, for your friend?"

Ignoring him, I asked Bridget if she could recommend something for Wren to wear.

"All taken care of," Bridget said. "She was in a few days ago, and I gave her a Holly's Harp dress in soft fleece with a lace collar." Holly's Harp was a legendary, now sadly defunct, boutique on Sunset Boulevard catering to rich hippies and rockstar girlfriends. "Wren looked like an angel, with that crazy red hair. But poor Liz."

"What do you mean?"

"She showed up yesterday. We found something perfect. You can take it with you when you go. Stockings, shoes, the whole shebang. But I'm telling you, it took forever! She tried on my entire inventory. Everything made her look like an old frump."

"She's supposed to look like an old frump," I said. "She's playing Miss Marple."

"Whatever. She's taking this whole thing very seriously. Do you know she's been out there, to Aggieworld, three or four times, just to get the lay of the land?"

"Christietown. And you're kidding."

"Nope. Anyway, she's got horrible posture. And needs her nails done desperately. And a decent hairdo. And those allergies." She made a face.

I remembered how beautiful Liz looked in Lou's arms, how graceful.

"Beauty is in the eye of the beholder," I said.

"That's tripe," said Bridget. "Jesus H. Christ! There's lint all over this chaise!" She leapt up in horror. "Maximilian is getting a spanking."

I tried to keep the image from forming in my mind.

"Let me get the outfit for you." Bridget went into the back. I followed.

"By the way," she said, handing me a gray garment bag, which I draped over my arm, "I absolutely adore the governess, Estella Raven. What a mouth she has on her! It's like you wrote the part just for me."

"I did."

"You want to see what I'm wearing?" she asked, her face aglow.

"Surprise me," I said. We chatted for a while, then Bridget walked me to the celadon-and-gold front door. A pair of teen-starlet types with big heads and tiny bodies brushed past us on their way in.

"Welcome," said Bridget coolly. "Have you been here before? No, I don't believe you have. I know my regulars. Please refrain from tugging on the hangers, and don't even THINK about removing the plastic."

At that, one of the girls dropped her Gucci handbag right on its bamboo handle. The other one hastily scooped up the goods and pulled her friend toward the Azzedine Alaïas.

"Do you have to be so mean?" I asked Bridget.

"Believe me, I do."

"It's a miracle anybody comes here."

"Forget about them," Bridget said in a hushed voice. "Listen. I have a theory about who the killer is. In the play. And I'm dying to know if I'm right. So would you please tell me already? I can't wait until tomorrow. Come on, Cece. Who did it?"

I thought about how that old frump Miss Marple might answer the question.

"You don't need me to tell you," I said. "If you've got a theory that fits the facts, then it must be the right one."

CHAPTER 3

Agatha was wearing a fur coat, brown fur-lined gloves, and a small green velour hat on the night she drove away from Styles, her sprawling, mock-Tudor house on the border of Surrey and Berkshire.

It was early December, but there was already frost on the leaves. Winters in this part of England came on early and hard. She wrapped her gray cardigan around her lumpy body. She couldn't even look in the mirror anymore. She was afraid of what she'd see. Shadows, folds, furrows. She was only thirty-six years old. She felt a thousand.

It was at Styles that her marriage had broken into pieces. The house was unlucky. The last three owners had suffered there. She'd wanted to move farther into the country—a cottage, it needn't have been anything grand. There were only the three of them, after all. But Archie had insisted on being no more than a ten-minute walk to Sunningdale Station. She sped past it now, its blue-and-yellow sign enveloped in fog. Monday through Friday, since he'd come back from the Great War, he'd commuted into London for *work, twenty-six miles to the south. City life. How ill it suited him. Mornings were worst. He'd lurch into the station so late he had to run across the lines in front of the approaching train to reach the far platform to board. He had to be more careful. Accidents did happen. She closed her eyes for a moment, envisioning the scene. The screams. The crowd. The sirens. Then her eyes blinked open. She was fooling herself. Work wasn't the reason he needed to be close to the station, not the real one, at any rate. London was where his mistress was. He needed to be close to her.*

It's over, Archie had said. I want a divorce.

What about me? Agatha had cried.

Who are you?

It was not an unreasonable question.

The girl Archie had met all those years ago at a dance given by Lord and Lady Clifford of Chudleigh at Ugbrooke House in Devon—the girl into whose ear he'd whispered such lovely, wicked things—was gone. In her place was a hag as chatty and ridiculous as his mother, fat in her stockingette skirts and staid jumpers. The smell of her repulsed him, the taste of her. No wonder. Agatha tasted like tears now. Her mother was dead. All she could do was cry. And Archie had warned her—had he not?—that he couldn't bear unhappy people.

Her hands clenched the leather-wrapped steering wheel. She looked at them in disbelief. Were they actually hers, the veins so blue and ropy and twisted? Yes, those were her hands, her blood, her veins. Odd that they pulsed so violently when she felt so dead inside.

The road was deserted. It was ten at night. Darkness had fallen like a heavy, woolen blanket. The stockbrokers, the bankers, the gray-haired MPs and their dutiful wives and children were tucked between sheets that had been laundered and starched and ironed by silent servants, gossiping family retainers, indigent third cousins.

All were fast asleep, dreaming of the day ahead.

She no longer dreamed of the future. She dreamed of the past.

Suddenly, something dark passed in front of her windshield. She braked. Was it a deer? She pulled over to the side of the road, switched off the headlights, turned off the motor. She stepped out of the car, a Morris Cowley. It was a four-seater. How she adored that car. She stroked the front bumper absently. Dust. She must speak to someone about that. She'd bought the car herself, for two hundred and twenty-five pounds. She was a successful author now. A wealthy woman in her own right. A wealthy woman alone. A wealthy woman who saw things. A deer! Impossible, of course. She suffered, Archie always said, from an overactive imagination. Worse yet, from an excess of false gestures.

False gestures. False life.

Later that night, back on the road, she threw her wedding ring out of the car window.

What, she wondered, would darling Archie make of that?

Chapter 4

I am a superstitious person.

I believe that you don't toss anything out of a car window, that you don't give a knife as a housewarming present, that cutting your hair on Good Friday prevents headaches, and that the spouse who falls asleep first on the wedding night will be the first to die.

I get it from my mother, which is probably enough said.

So by all rights I should have lost it when Gambino crawled into bed sometime after midnight Friday, armed with a French *Vogue* and a box of See's chocolates and broke the news that he couldn't be my soldier of fortune in the morning. But I was strangely calm—tranquil, even. I thanked him for the presents. I assured him that everything would be fine. Of course, his case came first. Of course, his witnesses couldn't wait. After that, I don't remember anything. I must've dropped off to sleep. The strain of being reasonable had clearly exhausted me. But maybe I'd finally learned to roll with the punches. Dispensed with all that nonsense about omens.

Or maybe I'd had an inkling that losing my soldier of fortune would be the least of the day's disasters.

Saturday morning dawned bright and hopeful. I stretched lazily, then wrapped my arms around my sleeping fiancé. After mumbling what sounded like an endearment, he rolled onto his stomach and started to snore. I tucked the covers around him and glanced over at the clock: 6:19. I'd beaten the alarm by eleven minutes.

Ian Christie's call beat the alarm by five.

"Good morning, Miss Caruso," he said, sounding near tears. "I mean, Cece. I simply can't get out of the habit of 'Miss This'-ing and 'Mr. That'-ing everyone. Shows my age. My, oh, my, it's a big day today. Sun's shining. SPF fifteen for all. Ha, ha! Quite a gamble we've taken with this enterprise. Well, me. Quite a gamble I've taken." He stopped himself dead.

"Good morning, Ian," I said in a voice meant to inspire confidence. "Are you feeling better today?"

"Yes, thank you. You were an angel of mercy yesterday, Cece. By the time I got home, I decided it must've been the flu, which has been going around, you know. My assistant was out four days last week. Of course, bad luck's her middle name; her husband broke his leg recently. But the incubation period for flu was up days ago, so it had to have been food poisoning. I love kebabs, but they don't love me!"

Yesterday afternoon, after I'd left Bridget's, I'd gone out to Christietown to go over some last-minute details with Ian. Poor man had thrown up all over the sales office front desk, perilously close to the $25,000 scale model of Phase 2 that had just arrived from Browning McDuff, the building firm. Even before that, he'd soaked through his festive Tommy Bahama shirt and scratched obsessively at a rash on his cheeks. I think

they call it being betrayed by your body. I shuddered to think
what was going to happen to him if he didn't sell a whole lot
of houses today.

Not my business, I reminded myself.

What was I going to wear? Now there was a real concern.

While Ian prattled on, I lay in bed visualizing the contents
of my closet. Normally, this was a pleasant diversion. Today,
all I could conjure up were tangled piles of mismatched items
and the occasional close-up of a stain. I blinked a few times.
Hmm. Something was coming into view. A toffee-colored silk
blouse cut close to the body and white, high-waisted trousers
cinched with a gold mesh belt. Lauren Hutton in *American
Gigolo*? I liked the concept. Of course, she'd gone braless,
which I could hardly get away with, but at least I didn't have
to hire my lovers.

Speaking of, Gambino had to get up. He was conducting
eleven interviews today, starting at eight thirty. I nudged him
awake. He kissed my shoulder, then squinted questioningly at
the phone. When I mouthed, "Ian," he rolled his eyes, then
staggered into the shower. He never waited the three and a half
minutes for hot water.

Back to yesterday. After vomiting, Ian apologized profusely
then requested breath mints, which I didn't have. His assistant,
however, soon appeared with a toothbrush and a fresh shirt.
While he changed, she poured two cups of strong tea that we
took with us as we strolled away from the Vicarage toward
Lansham Road, where the last houses (Chipping Cleghorn 1
and 2, priced from the low $400,000s, each with four bed-
rooms, three bathrooms, a three-car tandem garage, and 2,346
to 2,981 square feet) were still being built.

Ian drained his cup within seconds, handing it to me so he

could more closely inspect a palm-shaded gazebo, one of nine-
teen in Christietown. True enough, the paint was already chipping. Maybe they should've thought twice about doing things
on the cheap. But that was Browning McDuff's M.O. A film-
production company had recently bought one of their failed
housing tracts in the Mojave Desert for the express purpose of
blowing it up on camera.

Ian and I made quick work of our list.

One: the mailing. A thousand invites had gone out two
weeks ago. Check!

Two: the ads. They'd been placed in the *Antelope Valley
Gazette* and the *Antelope Valley News*. Tour Christietown!
Sample ye olde English fare! Free murder-and-mayhem color-
ing books for the small fry! Check!

Three: the live-radio tie-in; 100.1 the Edge was on board, I
had no idea why. Check!

Four: the food. When it came to food, you could always
count on Lael. Check!

Five: the play. I hadn't known then I'd be down one soldier
of fortune. Check! All good! Ready to go!

On the walk back to the Vicarage, Ian hadn't so much as
blinked at the gazebo. There was a spring in his step, the rash
had faded. I didn't want to take full credit, but I did feel a
warm glow inside.

This morning, as I tore down the Antelope Valley freeway
dressed like Lauren Hutton, I summoned that memory of yesterday: Ian Christie, beet-faced, yet serene; me, organized, effi-
cient, glowing.

Because I'd already screwed up.

Twelve miles outside Palmdale, I realized that my backseat was empty. My backseat was not supposed to be empty.

It was supposed to contain my doddering neighbors Lois and
Marlene, who couldn't get anywhere under their own steam
if their lives depended on it. In a moment of lunacy, I'd told
them they could come with me. And I'd forgotten them. And
it was too late to turn around. And nobody else had room,
which is why I'd gotten stuck with the job in the first place.

Well, that was that. If I could write out my soldier of fortune, I could write out my showgirls. They were comic relief,
really, with those froufrou outfits. It would be fine—better than
fine. There were too many laughs anyway. Death isn't supposed
to be funny. It's supposed to be depressing. And my play was
going to be really depressing now.

Stop, I told myself. Self-pity is not attractive. And I was
almost there. The hop sage and saltbush scrub lining the freeway had given way to the red-tiled roofs—thousands upon
thousands of them, as far as the eye could see, swarming over
the hillside like a Tuscan-village virus.

The housing developments were relatively new. During the
1980s, first-time home buyers, priced out of L.A.'s nearer sub-
urbs, drove farther and farther out to places long considered
too remote for commuters. Lancaster and Palmdale became
large cities overnight. By the 1990s, however, home values had
tanked, foreclosures reaching an all-time high. That's when Ian
Christie stepped in. He bought low and waited for the right
moment. Which was, in theory, now.

I exited at Sagebrush Canyon. Last year, Ian gave the folks
at city hall a good laugh when he campaigned to have its name
changed to "Christie Canyon," which turned out to be the
name of an eighties porn star. Bumping along the unpaved
access road, I tuned in to the Edge, hoping to hear a promo
for my event, but it was somebody giving sex advice to teen-

agers. I'd have recommended they abstain until reaching financial independence, not that I'd followed that advice myself. I hit the Off button. There was some kind of commotion going on up ahead.

Strange. It was too early for the guests to be arriving.

I pulled into the lot across from the Vicarage, cut the engine, and grabbed Liz's Miss Marple costume out of the trunk.

What was this?

A news van from a local TV affiliate.

Cars parked willy-nilly.

People milling about.

This was not our target audience.

These people weren't waving checkbooks.

They were waving signs and posters and placards:

TEN LITTLE INDIANS NO MORE!
CHRISTIETOWN CELEBRATES RACISM!
DON'T BUY INTO IT!
TRIBAL LAND SULLIED!

Where was the huge Christietown welcome banner I'd strung up yesterday?

I couldn't see it.

All I could see was a reporter holding a microphone in front of an indignant-looking man with a bullhorn.

And Ian Christie—wringing his hands and ruing the day and probably losing his shirt, which was already dripping wet.

CHAPTER 5

Ian came running over the minute he saw me, right through some freshly planted beds of lovage, foxglove, and clematis. But that was the least of his troubles.

"Oh, Cece," he wailed. "This will be our undoing! It's a disaster of epic proportions!"

In the background, we could hear a chorus of children chanting, "One little, two little, three little racists."

"Take it easy, Ian," I said. "Maybe it's not as bad as it seems." It was obviously worse.

"Whatever shall we do?" His sweaty hand was clutching mine now. "Oh, dear. They've brought coolers and blankets."

"I think we should start by finding whoever's in charge."

"That's a fine idea," he said without conviction. "Of course. It's just a big misunderstanding. We'll have these good people on their way in no time. Only logical thing to do."

We made our way over to the man with the bullhorn. He was Native American, very tall, with a shaved head. The bones in his face looked sharp enough to cut glass. He'd finished his interview. The camera crew was packing up. But he wasn't done, not by a long shot.

"Can you imagine," he bellowed to the rapt listeners, "two thousand years ago, Roman families teaching their kids to sing 'One little, two little, three little Christians' when they were throwing them to the lions?"

It didn't seem like such a stretch.

"No!" he cried. "Even the Romans had more decency!"

Ian Christie piped up, "I beg your pardon, sir, but that particular children's rhyme is not the one Dame Christie was referring to in her book title."

Oh, no.

The man put down his bullhorn and gave Ian a radiant smile. "This gentleman is quite right," he said.

Ian looked pleased for half a second.

"We should clear up a few things," he said, looking Ian straight in the eye. "First of all, 'Dame' Christie's book has had three different titles. The original title was *Ten Little Niggers*—"

Ian blanched.

"Which was derived from an unforgettable ditty recited to African-American children as a bedtime story. A story of their annihilation enacted for the amusement of others."

"Shameful!" came a cry from the crowd.

"*Ten Little Indians* was next. It was supposed to be less offensive. And what do we say to that?"

A chorus of boos.

"But the book is no longer published under either of those titles," Ian protested. "It's published as *And Then There Were None*, the last line of the rhyme. Nothing offensive there."

"Does everyone know that line?" the man asked. "'One

little Injun living all alone / He got married and then there were none.' What does that sound like to you?"

"Death by assimilation!" shouted a youngish woman with a baby in her arms.

At that moment, one Yorkie and two Corgis wearing kilts sprinted toward the man with the bullhorn.

"Alice May, Jenny, Scout!" A woman with a platinum blond bob was following in hot pursuit. "Heel! Stay! You are better than this!"

"They're setting the dogs on Joseph!" an elderly man cried. "Where is the camera now?"

Ian turned to me despairingly. God help us, I was the authority figure.

"Please say you're Linda," I called out as the woman barreled past us. Meanwhile, the man with the bullhorn—Joseph, I'm assuming—had gotten down on one knee to pet the dogs, who were licking him all over the face.

"Yes, I'm Linda," she said, struggling with her fanny pack. "We spoke yesterday. Are you Cece?"

It seemed like a trick question.

"Nice dogs," Joseph said to Linda with a rakish smile. Linda blushed, and handed him some treats to distribute to the dogs, who didn't deserve them, if you asked me.

"So are you or are you not Cece?" Linda repeated.

At that point, I had no choice but to acknowledge that I was indeed the person who had selected Alice May, Jenny, and Scout from the worldwide database of purportedly well-trained dogs at the Hollywood Animal Actors Agency. The dogs were not there to attack the protesters—whom I obviously hadn't anticipated—but to enhance the English country ambience. Dogs were ubiquitous in Miss Marple's hamlet of St. Mary Mead—real ones, little china ones on mantelpieces. Anyway,

Linda was supposed to be wearing a mackintosh and dark green wellies while trotting them around—not a faded wraparound skirt, Birkenstocks, and oversize white sunglasses. And the dogs were supposed to be well-behaved and unclad—not in *kilts*, for god's sake, which were Scottish, not English, and therefore entirely inappropriate.

But Linda had lost interest in me. She much preferred basking in the warmth of Joseph's attention. They were fussing over the dogs, chuckling at the lamb-chop-shaped treats, probably exchanging phone numbers. Maybe I'd get invited to the wedding. Linda must have decided to spread the love because just then she turned to Ian—who no longer knew which way was up—and complimented his shirt, which was now dry.

"It's a guayabera," he said. "In addition to Dame Christie, Ernest Hemingway is a great passion of mine. His Cuban years, in particular."

"Did you say Hemingway? Ernest Hemingway was a great friend to the Native Americans," Joseph began, drawing Linda and Ian into a huddle.

"Joseph?" the woman with the baby ventured timidly.

"I'm busy right now," he replied without turning around.

With Joseph otherwise engaged, the mob—which I realized consisted of no more than fifteen people, some of whom were now making faces at their erstwhile leader behind his back—began to disperse. It seemed like an opportune moment to duck into the Vicarage to drop off my things.

We were in the middle of a desert, but the Vicarage was the apotheosis of Cotswold kitsch: faux stone with a thatched roof, Canterbury bells spilling from window boxes, ivy climbing the walls. On Ian's ecologically unsound orders, the front garden was to be overwatered daily so there'd always be flowing rivers of mud. Visitors were invited to don one of the pairs of wellies lined up outside the timbered front door, but by the time you got that far you were already a sodden mess, so I never bothered.

Inside was the latest in high-tech sales paraphernalia: wall-to-wall plasma-screen monitors showing the happy denizens of Christietown taking sunset walks on the nine miles of nature trails; three offices separated by acrylic walls which provided natural light without reducing privacy; and two separate conference rooms with state-of-the-art video-conferencing facilities so people around the world could watch Ian Christie perspire in situ.

Ian's assistant wasn't there yet, so I made the executive decision to commandeer his office. It was the first one you saw, on the right. Unfortunately, the door was locked. The door to the next office was unlocked, so I let myself in, but it looked like it'd been set up to hot-box prospective buyers, with a framed black-and-white photo of Agatha Christie on the wall, a tin of butter cookies on the side table, and a sheaf of Christietown high-gloss brochures on the console. The third door was the charm. It was empty, or so I thought until I sat down at the desk practically on top of somebody's half-eaten bagel and cream cheese. It seemed an odd place to stow your breakfast. I found a Ralph's grocery bag under the desk. Inside was the offending tub of cream cheese, two plastic knives, and a Tropicana juice box, along with the fleecy white minidress from Holly's Harp, crumpled into a ball.

I shook the dress out and hung it on the hook behind the door. Wren had obviously arrived. Good. The whole thing went bust without my psychic eleven-year-old.

Just then, my cell phone rang. It was Lael. She'd arrived half an hour earlier and stationed herself in the Blue Boar Pub. She said the plasterboard facade of Gossington Hall had been set up in the dining area and that she'd seen Lou, who'd gone outside to stretch his legs. Wren was with him. She was doing a trial run with the smoke device. The caterers were heating up the food, which smelled wonderful, and the edible teapot centerpiece had been unveiled to gasps all around. Javier, my gardener, was rolling around in his uncle's wheelchair, which he refused to get out of because he was a method actor. He and Lael were about to run through their lines. That was Lael's delicate way of letting me know they'd be making out in the corner.

Sir Pilkington (Javier) and the vicar's wife (Lael) were having a torrid love affair. Sir Pilkington I'd invented. Lael's character I'd based on Reverend Leonard Clement's young wife, Griselda, from *Murder at the Vicarage*. Griselda had chosen her middle-aged husband over a cabinet minister, a baronet, three subalterns, and a ne'er-do-well with attractive manners, but I sensed in her a latent lust for power. Thus the allure of Sir Pilkington.

I checked my watch. Still an hour to go, and no Bridget in sight. And Liz—where was Liz? I needed my star. I grabbed her costume and Wren's and closed the door behind me just in time to run into Ian, who was salivating like a fox with two bunnies on his radar.

Lois and Marlene, my errant showgirls.

"Hello," Marlene said.

I opened my mouth to respond, but Ian interrupted. "Things have settled down. And can you imagine? After bidding adieu to my new friend Joseph I found these two lovely ladies wandering around the parking lot."

Lois looked down demurely.

"We've become quite well acquainted," he said.

Marlene beamed.

"And I have learned something very important. Like so

many of us, they have wearied of city life. They are seeking something more idyllic, something with personality and charm and, most of all, the company of other like-minded souls."

"Oh, Ian," Marlene cooed.

Ian tapped his temple and nodded, as if he'd just solved the riddle of the Sphinx. "I am suggesting our Sittaford Two residences."

With three bedrooms, two and a half baths, two-car garages, and approximately 1,784 square feet, the Sittaford 2 residences were priced at just over $300,000, meaning Lois and Marlene were only about $300,000 short.

"So, if you'll excuse us, Cece, I'll just escort Lois and Marlene into our beautifully appointed office here"—Ian pushed past me toward door number 2—"where we can go over the numbers in privacy."

"Ladies," I began.

"Oh, do you know these charming creatures?" asked a wide-eyed Ian.

"I certainly do," I said, narrowing my lids.

"We've known Cece for years and years," said Marlene. "She's had some very bad haircuts in the past, but she's looking lovely today."

Lois bobbed her addled head up and down.

"How did you get out here?" I asked.

"We took a taxi," said Marlene. "We didn't want to disappoint you."

"Here you go," said Lois, handing me a receipt from Yellow Cab in the amount of $179.00. "You can reimburse us later."

"We hope you don't mind," said Marlene. "He was such a nice young man we left him a twenty-five percent tip."

I explained the mix-up to Ian, who looked stricken until his assistant arrived, accompanied by some *actual* prospective buyers, a couple in their sixties who'd seen the ad in the *Antelope Valley News* and were very interested in the new homes in the vicinity of the High Street. Ian whisked them away, while Lois and Marlene followed me out the door.

People seemed to be arriving in droves. The parking lot was almost full. The valets were at their station, ready to take overflow cars to an empty field just over the hill.

"Ian told us all about Agatha Christie," said Lois, struggling to keep up. One of her heels was held together with Scotch tape. "Her play, *The Mousetrap*, holds the record for the longest run ever in London. Since 1952."

"That was a good year," said Marlene, sighing. "I was in the full flower of my youth then."

"Agatha had a picture-perfect Edwardian childhood," Lois continued. "She was from Devon, home of mariners like Sir Francis Drake and Sir Walter Raleigh."

"The sea, the sea," said Marlene.

They could go on like this forever. I'd seen it.

"Sea air promotes the regeneration of brain cells," said Marlene. "Maybe that's how she had the energy to write over eighty novels and plays. Living inland, I don't believe I've had the energy to even *read* eighty."

"You have," said her sister. "You adore the Harlequin romances, remember?"

"Oh, yes," Marlene said, smiling. "I do prefer love to murder. What about you, Cece?"

At that moment, I stepped into a mud puddle. So much for my white pants. I bent down to assess the damage.

"Cece—" Lois said.

"Not now," her sister interrupted. "Cece knows the rule about white after Labor Day. But she's under a lot of pressure today."

"You're so forgiving, Marlene," I said.

Lansham Road was a riot of testosterone: men in hard hats carrying piles of lumber; men in green coveralls planting trees; men with walkie-talkies; men with sandbags. The ladies could barely contain themselves. A pickup truck filled with freshly painted street signs kicked up some dirt as it rolled past us. After giving the driver a wave, Marlene stopped to flirt with some muscular specimens unspooling a bolt of wire-mesh fencing. That ended when she spied a short man with a shock of black hair getting out of a dark green Lamborghini and swooned.

Lois asked, "Are you all right, Marlene?"

"Who is that?" Marlene was gasping for air. "He looks exactly like Omar Sharif."

Lois made exasperated noises. "Omar Sharif, Omar Sharif! I ask you, will it never stop?"

Marlene had a faraway look in her eyes. "We met backstage at the Flamingo in Vegas. I was married at the time. It was tragic."

The Omar Sharif look-alike was Dov Pick, known in the business section of the *Los Angeles Times* as the Icepick. I wasn't surprised he was here today. He was one of the two principal investors in Christietown. Dov hopped around to the passenger side to open the door for a voluptuous brunette, in an oversize sweater and short shorts, who resembled Gina Lollabrigida. Most men would look happy to have a girl like that on their arm. But Dov didn't look happy. He looked miserable.

Which must have been how I looked when I walked into the kitchen of the Blue Boar a few minutes later, only to be ambushed by Lou, who cried, "Where is Liz? She's disappeared!"

CHAPTER 6

"Bridget's disappeared, too," Lael said calmly. "But if we keep stuffing people's faces with scones and clotted cream, they won't know the difference. Are you familiar with carbohydrate-induced cognitive impairment?"

"I'd love a scone," said Lois to Marlene. "Wouldn't you?"

"Quiet!" I said, pointing them to the dressing area. "Now is the time to get dressed."

Lou, already in his butler costume, was frantic. "Liz can be so difficult. She said she wanted to drive out herself. She wanted time to get into character without being distracted. I thought it was crazy, but you don't argue with Liz. So okay. I came out with Wren. But we left an hour after she did, and there's been no sign of her. And look!" He pushed his Velcro rip-away tails out of the way and grabbed something from his pocket.

Liz's inhaler.

"She lost hers a couple days ago. I picked this one up for her at the pharmacy on the way over. What if she needs it? What then?" He ran his long fingers through his shoe-blacked hair.

I collapsed into a chair.

After a moment, Javier said quietly, "Bridget did not disappear. She went to fix her hair."

"Bridget's hair is cut into a tight Afro," I said. "There's nothing to fix."

"He means the Estella Raven wig," said Lael. "Bridget's been in the bathroom for half an hour. That's all I was trying to say before."

"Maybe she's fallen in the toilet," said Marlene.

"A person can drown in two inches of water," her sister added.

"Change! Now!" I commanded them.

"Temper," cautioned Lois.

"Did you try Liz's cell phone?" I asked Lou.

"I just get voice mail. She's either been on the phone, or it's out of juice."

"I'm sure she's stuck in traffic, that's all."

Unconvinced, Lou took a seat next to Wren, who was too busy chewing on her nails to offer much in the way of comfort. I handed her the dress she'd crumpled up and sent her to the dressing area, along with Lois and Marlene.

"The freeway is a nightmare," I added, mostly for my own benefit. "I know Liz is going to be here any second." She had to be. The play was supposed to start in fifteen minutes.

"Ta-dah!"

We all turned around. There was Bridget in a long blond wig and some sort of sheer, gray-tinted garment that clung to her every curve like a second skin.

"I know. It's fabulous," she said, running her hands over her hips. "A Vionnet dress from the twenties. It's one of the rarest things I've ever had in the store. Some poor schlub in Port

Saint Lucie, Florida, didn't realize what kind of wardrobe his mother had. The thing is, it probably looked like nothing on the hanger. No darts, no decoration, no nothing. Like an old rag. But when you put it on, the body and the dress are one. As Madame Vionnet said, 'When a woman smiles, her dress must smile with her.' Do you think my nipples are too prominent?"

"You are supposed to be a *governess*," I cried. "What part of that do you not get? A proper, British governess!"

"Those types can be very kinky," she replied breezily. "FYI, the shoes are by René Mancini. Cobbler to the couturiers. Jackie Kennedy used to order twelve pairs of pumps from him every three months."

"Make way!" The caterer came through the swinging doors with an empty tray in each hand, tossed them in the sink, grabbed two full ones. "They're eating Cornish pasties like there's no tomorrow. And the sherry was gone twenty minutes ago. These people are animals. By the way, you're on, dude. Anybody ever tell you you look like George Hamilton?" She directed her last comments to Lou, who grabbed one of the trays, which I grabbed back, saying, "He's not a waiter."

"I'm a butler," said Lou.

"That's right," I said, looking at the motley crew I'd assembled. "And you will take your cues from me. All of you. Do you understand?"

Only Javier nodded.

Five minutes now.

Lois and Marlene came out in matching red swimsuits and fringed caps.

"We put the rhinestones on ourselves," said Lois.

"There's a gun you use," Marlene said. "We got it at a garage sale last year. And look," she added, "Isadora Duncan scarves."

Lois did a twirl with hers and stumbled, landing directly in Javier's lap.

Two minutes.

The caterer bustled back in.

"They're all seated. Am I supposed to keep feeding them? I'm down to the rejects." She held up a tray of misshapen pasties.

At that point, I had no choice.

I ran into the bathroom, tore out of my Lauren Hutton outfit, unzipped the gray garment bag, and put on a faded tweed skirt, a wool sweater, a baggy cardigan coat, a felt hat, thick stockings, well-worn brogues, and a steel-gray wig.

"Oh, Miss Marple," said Javier, wheeling himself to my side. "Thank goodness you've arrived. We've all been so distraught since the untimely demise of my father, the duke of Chislebury, late last night. Maybe you can help us find the culprit." He grinned in delight. It was his longest speech in the play.

"The last anyone saw of the good duke was in bed," said Bridget, turning to give the audience an optimal view of her assets. Several of the men hooted appreciatively.

"Good Mr. Griffiths"—Bridget continued, gesturing extravagantly toward Lou—"brought the good duke his sleeping draft. Normally, it's a cup of chocolate at eleven, but the good duke had been having trouble sleeping these last few nights. So good Dr. Haycock prescribed something."

What was with the "goods"? They weren't in my script. I shot Bridget a warning glance.

"Perhaps if my father hadn't started all this nonsense about changing his will, he would've slept better," said Javier. He was cruising Lou's way when his right-front wheel caught on the rug. "For Christ's sake," he burst out, immediately clapping his hand over his mouth.

Lois tiptoed over to the fireplace, cleared her throat, and started to weep. At least someone was taking this seriously.

"The duke and I were to have been married tomorrow!" she said, blowing her nose. Then she smiled questioningly at me, and when I made the mistake of nodding, wedged her hankie inside one nostril and dug away.

"Really?" drawled Bridget, who was, as I'd predicted, brilliant at being insolent. "How very amusing."

"Not so, my dear woman! The vicar was to have presided. We fell in love, you see. He saw me onstage. The duke, not the vicar." Lois did an attractive little two-step. "And he so desperately wanted an heir."

I was counting on the audience not to notice that Lois was well past her childbearing years. Luckily, most of them were busy eating.

"*Qué rico!*" said a woman in the front row, stabbing her fork into a meat pie like she really meant it.

"The duke was such a dreamer," said Marlene, striding toward center stage. Inspired by a Luis Buñuel film I'd seen on a bad date years ago, I'd cast both Lois and Marlene in the same role. It had seemed like a good idea at the time. "Ah, the patter of little feet on Aubusson rugs."

"So what if I couldn't produce an heir," said Javier angrily. "It's this disability. And I'm tired of hearing about it."

With that, everyone turned to look at me. Of course they were looking at me. I was supposed to say something. What was it? I'd written the damn thing, but I had no idea. I felt my knees start to buckle.

"Miss Marple," said Wren, twirling her pigtails dementedly. "You should sit down. You don't look very good. Does she look good?" She turned to face the audience.

"No!" they cried in unison.

"Have you had your tea today?"

"No tea," I said. The room was spinning now.

"Estella, bring Miss Marple some tea," Wren said.

Bridget ran back into the kitchen as Wren sat me down in an easy chair.

Bridget came back out with a paper cup of water, which she practically poured down my throat.

"Feeling better, Miss Marple?" Bridget asked.

"Yes," I managed.

Wren said, "Now that you're refreshed, didn't you have something you wanted to tell us?"

"It is true, of course," I recited, "that I have lived what is called a very uneventful life, but I have had a lot of experience in solving different little problems that have arisen."

Javier interrupted me. "That's not it."

"When I was a girl, nobody ever mentioned the word *stomach*."

Bridget shook her head.

Finally I said, "It really is very dangerous to believe people," at which point Marlene, ever supportive, cried out, "Yeah, baby!"

And that was only Act I.

Act II went more smoothly. Lael and Javier got carried away during their love scene. Lou, the closest thing we had to muscle, pried them apart. Wren's device was a big hit. She detonated it just before informing her governess that Sir Guy Pilkington's late wife, Lady Donata Pilkington, was attempting to contact her from the great beyond.

Coughing through the smoke Wren closed her eyes and said in a high, squeaky voice, "He is a ... a ... malevolent ... force."

"Who?" Bridget asked.

"He is ... the ... the ... personification ... of evil." Wren pressed her fingers to her temples.

"Who?" Bridget insisted.

"Beware the false face!" Wren cried, then fell to the ground in a faint.

At that point Lou entered stage left and Bridget gasped (which she was not supposed to do).

"I knew it," Bridget muttered loud enough for me to hear from inside the mahogany wardrobe where I was hiding. "The butler did it." I rocked the wardrobe to signal her to shut up, then stopped for fear of tipping over.

Lou stood there lamely, waiting for the doorbell to chime offstage, which was where he was supposed to be. When he finally heard his cue, he said, "I believe it is the retired Anglo-Indian colonel from next door to see you, Miss Raven." He peeked behind the curtain. "Indeed, it *is* the retired Anglo-Indian colonel."

I couldn't breathe inside the mahogany wardrobe. Plus, my head was itching like crazy under the wig. I was probably allergic to the pomade I'd used to make my hair fit.

"Come, dear child," said Bridget. She picked her psychic charge up off the floor and they exited just as the phone began to ring.

Javier launched himself onstage and said, "Where in the blazes is my manservant whom I pay so handsomely? That I should have to pick up his slack is lamentable."

Okay, folks, this is it.

Javier spun around a few times, popped a wheelie, and, seeing no one, rose from his wheelchair to answer the phone.

At which point, I—Miss Jane Marple—threw open the doors to the wardrobe and exclaimed, "You, Sir Guy Pilkington, remind me of a parlor maid I once employed! She was always breaking my teacups and then hiding the pieces!"

"Are you calling me a liar?" Javier asked.

"No," I said. "A murderer!"

A few people in the audience started to applaud, like they couldn't wait for the thing to be over with, at which point the entire cast emerged, smiling and bowing, along with a young man I'd never seen before in my life.

"Is it over already?" Marlene asked. "We didn't get to do our dance."

"Cece," Bridget whispered to me, cocking her head in the direction of the stranger, who had floppy blond curls and rather resembled an angel, "in case it escaped your notice, he doesn't look like a retired Anglo-Indian colonel. They're fat, with mustaches."

"He's not an actor," I hissed. "I have no idea what he's doing onstage."

"Sorry to bust things up here," the stranger said, addressing the room, "but I'm going to need everyone to remain calm. I'm afraid there's been an ... incident."

"Well, duh!" said Lois, putting her hands on her hips.

I was suddenly cold all over. "What do you mean, an incident?"

The audience was starting to stir now. Several people stood up. The stranger exchanged glances with an older man across the room, who locked the front door of the pub and pocketed the key. The second guy had on schlumpy pants and a jacket with big pockets. The bags under his eyes reached halfway to his chin.

Unfortunately, I recognized the look.

He flashed his badge as he joined his partner onstage.

"I'm Detective Mariposa," he said. "You've met Detective McAllister." The stranger smiled, but caught himself before waving. "We've got a body in the sales office," Mariposa said without emotion. "White woman, middle-aged, brown hair."

Out of the corner of my eye, I saw the color drain from Lou's face.

"Don't exactly know what happened yet. We're working on an ID. So I'll be asking the questions from here on in."

"This sucks," yelled someone in the audience. "My kid didn't get his coloring book."

The other one, McAllister, said, "Right now, we're looking for a Ms. Caruso. Is there a Ms. Caruso here?"

"I'm Cece Caruso," I said, my voice shaking.

Someone else called out, "I thought you were Miss Marple."

No.

Ms. Caruso was alive.

And Miss Marple—it appeared—was dead.

CHAPTER 7

When Agatha took her hand away from her forehead, she saw that there was blood on it.

She quickly wiped it away with her napkin and finished the last of her coffee, which was as cold and as bitter as the previous night had been.

She left the station in a hurry. It hadn't been easy to make it even that far. The walk to Guildford from Newlands Corner, where she'd abandoned the car, was at least four miles, which would have been hard to manage even in proper shoes. The penny bus that came over the ridge at breakfast time had been her salvation. From there, she caught a milk train to Waterloo Station, where there wasn't so much as a bun left at the buffet. She was hungry and tired but she could hardly stop now.

The taxi driver took her to Whiteleys.

William Whiteley had founded the place back in the 1850s. "Everything from a pin to an elephant" was his motto, eventually earning him an unsolicited Royal Warrant from Queen Victoria. A few years later, the old man had been killed in the store by someone claiming to be his illegitimate son.

Agatha had always been perversely attracted to murder scenes.

This morning, Whiteleys betrayed little of its scandalous past. The righteous hum of commerce filled the lobby. She felt comforted by the crowds, comforted by her anonymity. She selected a heavy winter coat with fur at the cuffs and collar, some night thing, and a small traveling case of brown crocodile.

She was ready.

She glanced up at the large clock over the perfume counter. She had to hurry. The Pullman train to Harrogate left King's Cross at a quarter past eleven. And there wouldn't be another until Monday.

Harrogate was a fashionable spa, frequented by everyone from people who'd made something out of nothing—poor William Whiteley came to mind—to foreign dukes and duchesses. The names of visitors, as well as the local amusements available to them, were published weekly in the Herald.

The week of December fifth, her name would be among them.

The train whistled as it pulled away from the station.

She smiled to herself as she saw her face reflected in the glass.

CHAPTER 8

People talk about falling apart, but after making an official ID of his wife's body, Lou Berman *fell apart*, sinking to the floor as if his bones had turned to dust.

Wren went to him, but he shoved her aside. The rest of us looked away as his cries tore through the room.

Liz Berman had been born with a weak heart.

It had finally given out.

Lou covered his face, but the tears slipped through his fingers and ran down his arms. They kept coming for a long time. Afterward, I knelt down beside him and found his hand. He let me hold it until we saw the truck pull into the driveway through the Vicarage's front window.

LOS ANGELES COUNTY CORONER'S OFFICE

They spelled the words out in stark white letters so you couldn't miss them, even in the dark.

Lou got up, wiped his eyes, straightened his clothes.

"I'll be fine," he said.

"I know," I said, though I didn't.

Casting a glance back at the small office where his wife of twenty-two years lay dead, he walked out the door.

Nobody wanted to be the first one to speak.

"Well, shit," said Detective Mariposa, breaking the silence. "That was something. I've seen a lot of messed-up people in my time, but nothing like that. Not ever." He twisted his mouth into a smile. "No way my wife would cry like that if I keeled over. Hell, she'd probably celebrate." He looked at Detective McAllister, who was staring at his shoes, hoping his partner would give him a break. No such luck. "You think so, McAllister?"

McAllister raised his head and said, "Yeah, I think she'd celebrate. She'd have a party and invite the whole department. Okay?"

Mariposa snorted. "I love you, too, Pretty Boy."

McAllister said, "That about covers it. Sorry to inconvenience you with all the questions. We won't be needing anything more."

Mariposa added, "Yeah, like we say in the business, no harm, no foul."

"What he means," McAllister said wearily, "is that we're very sorry for Mr. Berman's loss." His blond hair glowed like a halo. It wouldn't have surprised me if Mariposa, on the other hand, had a tail tucked into his pants.

I drove back home with the windows open and the radio blaring. Lois and Marlene were in the backseat being uncharacteristically quiet. For that at least I was grateful. I couldn't bear the thought of their chatter—not now.

While I'd been playing the fool in the Blue Boar Pub, Liz had been dying. No one to hear her, no one to see her, no one to save her.

I kept going over the events in my mind.

Sometime after eleven, Ian's assistant went into the office. She was looking for a pen. When she saw the woman's body behind the desk, she let out a shriek that sent Ian running. Ian's shrieks interrupted Dov Pick and his girlfriend, who followed suit. None of them, however, had any idea who the woman was or how she'd gotten there or who had done whatever it was that had been done to her. So they'd called the police and screamed bloody murder.

Detectives Mariposa and McAllister had shown up within minutes.

She might have been there like that for hours, they'd speculated. Only the autopsy would tell. But there was no sign of foul play, which was convenient since half a dozen people had trampled the scene.

At that point, Ian had suggested it might be a good idea to find me.

I was afraid to go into that office. I was afraid of dead bodies. Panic-stricken. Superstitious. But everyone in the room was counting on me. I was supposed to clear things up. I was hoping—praying—I wouldn't be able to, that the dead woman wouldn't be Liz, that she would be some poor soul none of us had ever laid eyes on before.

I pushed open the door.

The office had no windows.

No air.

It smelled like a sickroom, thick and rank.

The acrylic walls gave off a dizzying glow.

The woman's body was lying behind the desk, a chair toppled next to her, a phone in her hand.

The detectives told us later that she'd been trying to call 911.

I remember her hair spilling down her back in thick curls, her skin as white as snow, her lips and nails as red as blood.

She was wearing a black dress and black high heels. I didn't recognize her right away. She looked so beautiful. But there was no doubt. It was Liz.

When I came out of the office, I looked straight at Lou. His arm brushed mine on his way in. Where he'd touched me, I felt the kind of cold you feel a split second after you've been burned.

"Cece! Oh, Cece!"

I shook my head like I was coming to.

Lois was bellowing at me from the backseat. "Can you hear me above the music?"

"Unfortunately, yes," I said under my breath.

"What did you say? We can't hear you," said Marlene.

"Well, I can hear you," I shouted, then snapped off the radio. "What is it?"

"I'm just so sad for that sweet man," said Lois.

Oh, Lois, I am, too.

Out of my rearview mirror, I saw the Christietown sign retreating in the distance.

Damn Ian Christie.

No, I couldn't blame him. It was my fault. I'd gotten Liz into this. I'd taken her from Lou.

Twenty-two years. What did he have left?

The dance studio.

His memories.

Would he remember her the way she'd looked yesterday, or the way she'd looked today, so beautiful, so still?

Of course, Lou had always been the pretty one.

Like Archie Christie. Too handsome for his wife, people said. Agatha should have known.

You can't trust a handsome man.

At their first meeting, Agatha had been thrilled when Archie encouraged her to cut several partners so she could dance with him. Several days later, he'd turned up at Ashfield, her family home, on a motorcycle. What woman could have resisted?

Lieutenant Archibald Christie, member of the elite ranks of the Royal Air Corps, decorated war hero, recipient of the DSO, the CMG, and the Order of St. Stanislaus Third Class with Swords.

I'd never really had much sympathy for him. But maybe that wasn't fair.

People are entitled to change their minds. Entitled to fall out of love. But history means something. Sharing a child means something.

I wondered what went through Archie's head during those eleven days when his wife, Agatha, disappeared and was presumed dead.

What did he think when the authorities informed him that a Morris car was found not far from their home, at the edge of a chalk pit?

And when he was told an initial search of Newlands Corner had yielded a black shoe covered with mud and a brown glove lined with fur, what then? Did he see the look in her eyes when he'd told her he was through with her?

When a local landmark, the Silent Pool, was dredged with a pump, did he remember how distraught she'd been, that she'd been sleeping badly, working poorly, not eating?

My editor, Sally, had generously given me until a week from Monday to figure it out. Glad my mind was so uncluttered.

After dropping off Lois and Marlene, I pulled into my driveway, cut the engine, and trudged across the grass to my front walk. And then I stopped short.

Because standing there on my doorstep were two blondes I didn't know from Adam, and one dark-haired man I knew like the back of my hand.

CHAPTER 9

"Richard," I said to my ex-husband, trying—failing—to stay calm. "Richard, Richard, Richard!"

He looked at me as if I was crazy. Just like old times.

"Cece," he replied. "Cece, Cece, Cece."

Bastard. "It's just that this is such a surprise. What a surprise to see you!"

"I don't know why it should be a surprise," he said impatiently. "You knew we were coming for Annie's baby shower. She is my daughter, after all."

"But you're early. You weren't supposed to be here for days." The house was in a shambles. I had nothing to spread on crackers except Fancy Feast.

"We're so sorry to spring ourselves on you like this," said the younger of the two women, whose age I'd put somewhere between twenty-five and thirty. She was unnaturally dewy. I hated her. "I've heard so much about you," the woman said, extending her hand. "It's a thrill to meet you."

Richard cleared his throat and adjusted the knot on his tie. It was striped, orange and black. Princeton colors. He threw his arm around the woman's delicate shoulders and said, "Cece Caruso, my fiancée, Jackie Dehovitz."

A flush spread becomingly across Jackie's milky white cheeks. I remembered that Richard had always loved strawberry Quik.

"And I'm Jackie's mom, Dot," said the other woman, who'd positioned herself on her daughter's other side, closing ranks so as to better confront the enemy.

"Aren't you going to invite us in?" Richard asked.

"Well, of course. That's what I'm doing," I turned the key in the lock. "After you."

Richard looked skeptical. "You sure it's safe?"

"Watch out for falling objects," I said with a laugh, which died in my throat as I glanced into the entry-hall mirror and caught sight of a wizened, lipstick-less, pomaded crone in tweed and orthopedic shoes, who turned out to be me. At least I'd taken off the wig.

"I don't normally wear my hair like this," I said, foolishly throwing myself on their mercy.

In perfect syncopation, Jackie and Dot stroked their matching bobs, whose brilliance rivaled the afternoon sun.

"And I'd never buy a baggy cardigan coat." I ripped it off my shoulders and let it fall to the floor. "It doesn't belong to me. It doesn't even fit."

Richard picked an imaginary speck of dust off Jackie's cream-colored suit. "You were always eccentric about clothes."

"Richard," cautioned Jackie. "We talked about this."

Oh, she didn't know the half of it. He looked like Cary Grant, sure—even at twenty-two, he'd looked like Cary Grant, with those prematurely graying temples. But underneath, he was pure Chucky. Which made her Bride of Chucky, poor thing.

I picked up the cardigan and shoved it behind a pillow, tossed Buster off the couch, and grabbed a couple of empty Diet Coke cans from the coffee table. "I'll be back in a flash. Please make yourselves at home."

"I'm allergic to cats." Richard was sniffing around the big easy chair under the window. "In case you've forgotten. But that cat must be dead by now."

"Richard!" said Jackie.

I'd gotten Mimi immediately after the divorce. He'd always hated her.

"She's alive and well and around here someplace," I said, racing into the bedroom and slamming the door shut. I could do this. I could definitely do this. In a personal best, I emerged four minutes later in an improvised French twist, red hooker mules with poufs, and a sexy, floor-length silk wrap with kimono sleeves.

I went overboard. In retrospect, I can see that.

"Drinks, anyone?" I launched into my best hostess imitation, despite the fact that all I had to offer was half a bottle of cheap Chianti and tap water.

Nobody wanted alcohol except me. Desperately.

Dot won me over when she found a jar of pimiento-stuffed olives and a tray I didn't even know I had somewhere in the recesses of my pantry.

"Richard can't stop talking about your work," she said, arranging the olives in the center of a plate.

"Oh?" I set the glasses down on a chipped Mexican wood tray, all ears.

"I must admit—but please don't mention it—I haven't read his book yet."

His five-hundred-page analysis of the collected works of

James Fenimore Cooper, published by a third-tier academic press? I couldn't imagine why not.

"So he talks about my books?" I pressed her.

"Oh, yes, nonstop."

"Hmm."

Dot pulled the leaves from some lemons I had sitting in a bowl and placed them in a circle around the olives. Then she sliced the lemons into half-moons and placed them around the circle of leaves. The olive plate now looked like a Busby Berkeley act.

"Of course, it could be because he knows I'm a mystery buff," she said. "And Agatha Christie, well, she is my absolute favorite. The thing I love best is the tea! Imagine, a perfect world where people have tea all afternoon and chat. People like Miss Marple and Hercule Poirot." She tapped her forehead. "I love that he solved crimes using nothing but his little gray cells. When you come down to it, I should've married him, though I think he was probably a homosexual." She blushed, then threw up her hands. "I wouldn't have cared, to tell you the truth. We could've cultivated marrow roots together, traveled the world, nabbed evildoers. Anyway, I've been rereading Christie's autobiography—in anticipation of meeting you, Cece." She smiled. "And after I'm done with that, I'm rereading the whole kit and kaboodle. Even the romances."

Agatha Christie wrote six semi-autobiographical romances under the name Mary Westmacott, which she tried—unsuccessfully—to prevent from being traced back to her.

"How do you find the time?" I asked.

"I was an executive secretary for thirty-one years but I retired last year." Dot rinsed off her hands and adjusted the jacket of her nubby pink-and-white-tweed pantsuit. "These days, I have too much time. That's why it's so nice to have Jackie and Richard here for a visit. Three whole weeks! Gives me a chance to fuss over them. I love having people to fuss over, I truly do. Oh, is this your cat?" she asked, spying Mimi, who'd come out of hiding. "She's absolutely beautiful."

Richard did not deserve a mother-in-law like this. My mother, he'd deserved.

Back in the living room, the happy couple was seated on the sofa, poring over some glossy hotel brochures. I caught a glimpse of palm trees and crystal chandeliers.

"We're getting married right here in Los Angeles next June," explained Jackie, curling her long legs up under her. She looked like a white-chocolate pretzel, which Richard also loved. Dot caught me staring.

"Double-jointed," Dot whispered. "I had a hip replacement last year. I can barely look at her."

Jackie heaved a sigh. "It may be silly, but this wedding is all I can think about. Falling in love is magical, don't you think?" Bet she believed in fairies, too. "Richard and I met in Chicago, but I grew up here, in Glendale. Mom's getting ready to sell the house, but I wanted Richard to see it. The room I grew up in." She hugged herself at the very thought.

"Unchanged," said Dot. "All her medals are still there, the trophies, certificates, banners."

Jackie looked at me, smiling expectantly. No. I refused to ask. No way. Then I looked at her mother and sucked it up.

"What was your sport, Jackie?" I asked.

"Cheerleading."

Of course it was. "So it's going to be some big shindig, this wedding?"

"We're thinking the Beverly Hilton," said Jackie. "And I hear you're getting married, too."

"Yes, we're thinking Buckingham Palace."

Richard glared at me.

"Kidding! I'm kidding!" I said.

"This is exactly what I'm talking about," Richard said to Jackie. Then, turning to me, he said, "The shower is a wonderful occasion, to be sure, but not the sole reason we're here." He smiled at Jackie. "There's the wedding to plan, of course." Jackie looked pleased. "But," he said, turning back to me, "we also thought it extremely important to spend some quality time with Annie. This is a difficult moment for her. After all, she and Vincent just won custody of Vincent's son, little Alexander, now she's having a baby of her own, and both her parents are remarrying, to boot. She's going to need some extra emotional support. We thought we could model healthy coping behaviors for her."

The doorbell rang just as I was about to gag.

"Excuse me," I said to the group, yanking my hostess gown into place.

It was Detectives McAllister and Mariposa, who let themselves right in.

"You can't do that," I said. "Not unless you have a warrant. I'm entertaining."

Dot looked excited. "A warrant! Are you cops?"

"I can't believe this," Jackie whispered to Richard. "You were so right."

"We see you've got company," Mariposa began, "but this is urgent business." He circled around the living room, like he was sniffing for bombs.

"What exactly is so urgent, Detective Mariposa?"

"Liz Berman."

I held my breath for a second, then asked, "What about her?"

McAllister pulled a Baggie out of his pocket. There was a small bottle in it, with a handful of dark capsules inside. "This was found at the scene. The lab did a rush job."

"Stop beating around the bush, Pretty Boy," said Mariposa. He got right up in my face, so close I could see every pore. "Liz Berman didn't die of natural causes. Liz Berman was poisoned."

CHAPTER 10

It was evening by the time Agatha's taxicab pulled up in front of the hotel.

The Harrogate Hydropathic.

Last stop for widows, hypochondriacs, and foreign dignitaries.

Such an interesting name, the Hydropathic.

For most, one imagined, it conjured up visions of healing. But not for Agatha. For her, it conjured up psychopaths and sociopaths and pathologies.

Not pathos, however.

She'd wearied of emotion.

She was learning to appreciate logic.

The valet led her up to her room. It was clean and simply furnished. The chambermaid, a dark-haired young woman with an overbite, introduced herself as Rosie and commenced an endless narration.

Queen Mary often visited her daughter, the princess, and her son-in-law, Viscount Lascelles, at nearby Goldsborough Hall. She enjoyed browsing through the Harrogate antiques shops with her comely ladies-in-waiting.

The Russian royal family often appeared in late fall. They liked to travel incognito, which was hardly a problem as everyone who worked at the Hydro employed the utmost in discretion when it came to the hotel's guests.

On and on Rosie the chambermaid went, stopping only long enough to gape at Agatha's black handbag, which boasted the latest fashion accessory, a zipper (Rosie had only seen handbags with zippers in the magazines), and to frown at Agatha's lone traveling case, which perturbed her until she was assured that more luggage would be arriving shortly. Only violent yawning deterred the girl from her apparent goal of chattering nonstop until daybreak.

Once she'd gone, Agatha lay down on her bed and thought about the mistakes she'd made.

That note she'd left for the servants to give her secretary, Charlotte. She'd asked Charlotte to cancel rooms that had been booked in Beverley for the weekend. My head is bursting, she'd written, I can't stay in this house.

Dreadful.

At least she could count on Charlotte for discretion. Agatha was certain of Charlotte's loyalty.

But the note Agatha had left on the hall table for Archie—no, she couldn't think of that anymore. She leapt up from the bed in a panic and stood in front of the mirror.

She turned this way and that. She looked a wreck. She'd brought no evening clothes. But she could certainly go downstairs and have a refreshment. There was no harm in that. Archie was always after her to watch her weight, but he wasn't here to slap her hand away.

The Happy Hydro Boys played nightly in the Winter Garden Ballroom. There was a colorful poster in the lobby vitrine: "Enjoy the inimitable Harry Codd on violin, Frank Brown and Bob Tappin on drums, Reg Schofield on piano, Bob Leeming on saxophone, and Albert Whiteley on the banjo." A Miss Corbett accompanied the Hydro Boys as a singer.

The ballroom was half-filled. Agatha took a small banquette in the corner and picked up a newspaper crossword someone had left behind.

Two across: synonym for "discerning," nine letters.

Oracular? No, that was eight letters.

Sibylline?

A perfect fit.

In Roman mythology, Sibyl was the prophetess who dwelt near Cumae, in southern Italy. She became immortal, but after refusing Apollo's advances, was condemned to endless old age. Oh yes, thought Agatha, I could write a story about that.

She watched the couples on the dance floor over the top of her Herald. *Enough wallowing. She'd loved dancing ever since she was a girl taking lessons at the Athenaeum Rooms, over the confectioner's shop. Now the band began to play, "Yes, We Have No Bananas." What fun! She put down the paper and found herself among so many others, all dancing the Charleston.*

It was a lovely evening.

The loveliest evening she'd had in so long.

Back in her room, she undressed and arranged her things.

A comb.

A hot-water bottle.

A small photograph of her little girl.

And a bottle of laudanum, which bore the label of a Torquay chemist and a picture of a skull and crossbones.

CHAPTER 11

"Poisoned?" I sank down on the couch, bewildered. "How can that be? I don't understand."

Mariposa chewed on the back of his pen. "Here's the general scenario: perp gives bad juice to victim, bad juice kills 'em. That make it any clearer?"

"For Pete's sake!" McAllister shook his head in disgust, then turned to me. "There was foxglove in Liz Berman's allergy pills."

Jackie's milky face fell. "Richard, didn't we talk to the florist about foxglove centerpieces?"

Mariposa said, "Bad idea. The toxin's located in the sap, flowers, seeds, and leaves."

Richard stood up abruptly. "We have to go now. Jackie?"

She leapt to her feet like an obedient puppy.

"Do you need us, Detective?" Dot asked hopefully.

"I don't think so, ma'am," McAllister replied.

I was actually sorry to see them go.

"So where were we?" Mariposa asked. Now he was flipping his pen around like a majorette with a tiny baton.

McAllister closed his eyes. "We were about to question Ms. Caruso about Mrs. Berman's activities this morning."

"Please, sit down," I said to them.

They sat down, then McAllister prompted, "You were saying?"

"Me?" I asked. "I wasn't saying anything. I have nothing to say about Liz's activities. I never even saw her this morning."

"But you were expecting her, is that correct?"

"Yes," I replied. "She was the star of my play. I was upset that she wasn't there, like she was supposed to be, mostly because I was counting on her. It never dawned on me that something could be wrong."

McAllister cocked his head to the side. "Where was Lou all this time?"

"He was at the Blue Boar. With the other members of the cast. By the time I got there, he was frantic."

"What time was that exactly?" he asked.

"I don't know. I wasn't wearing a watch. Maybe ten?"

"Go on," he said, nodding.

"He was shouting. He was upset."

"Why?"

"Why do you think? Because his wife had disappeared!"

"Why would he have thought that?"

I got up and started pacing. "She'd left their house before he had, so she should've shown up at Christietown long before he arrived. But she hadn't shown up. And she wasn't picking up her phone. And he had her inhaler." Just then something occurred to me. "I wonder why nobody thought to check the parking lot for her car."

McAllister and Mariposa exchanged glances.

"That's a good question, Ms. Caruso," Mariposa said. "It

was parked just in front of the Vicarage. You must've walked right past it when you arrived at"—he paused and flipped back through his notes—"eight thirty this morning."

"I have no idea what kind of car Liz drives," I said. "Drove. Anyway, how was I supposed to recognize it? Lou's the one who should've recognized it." I stopped short.

Mariposa stood up, a gleam in his eye. "Yes," he said. "Exactly."

"That's not what I meant to say," I protested, turning to McAllister. But he wasn't going to help me out of this one.

Mariposa cut to the chase. "What can you tell us about Mrs. Berman's relationship with her husband, Mr. Berman?"

"I can't believe this. Why would you be asking that?"

Because the husband is guilty nine times out of ten.

"Why do you think?" Mariposa asked, throwing my words back at me.

"Now you listen," I said. "Lou Berman was in love with his wife. He had nothing to do with this. My god, you saw what happened to him."

Mariposa started sucking on his pen, then pulled it out of his mouth with an obscene *thwack*. "People can put on a good show when they need to."

McAllister changed the subject. "Ms. Caruso. Did Mrs. Berman have any enemies that you know of?"

"There were protesters there all morning," I said. "They have some kind of ax to grind with Christietown. One of them could have been responsible." But I didn't believe that for a second.

"Anyone with a more personal interest in Mrs. Berman?"

"Look, I barely even knew the woman. I took dancing lessons from her husband. You never saw them dance. They were amazing together." Tears pricked at my eyes. "Are we done yet?"

McAllister was quiet for a moment, then he rose to his feet. "I think that's all I need right now. You?" he asked Mariposa.

Mariposa looked around, then patted his pockets to make sure he wasn't forgetting anything. "I'm okay."

They thanked me. McAllister gave me his card and asked if I had any questions before they left.

I could think of only one.

I wanted to know if Liz had been in pain.

"No pain," said McAllister, looking straight at his partner. "The heart rate increases, and brings on heart failure. It happens very fast."

He was a nice man, and a liar.

After they left, I changed into a pair of old jeans and a sweatshirt and went out into my garden. It was early April. The spring flowers were blooming. Narcissus, hyacinths, a pair of tall sunflowers. Last summer, I'd watched, riveted, as the stalks moved in thrall to the sun. There were dandelions, too. Some people thought they were weeds, but that wasn't true. Dandelions provided nectar for the bees after the fruit trees were tapped out.

I stopped in front of a terra-cotta pot at the edge of the garden. It was bursting with tall spikes of bell-like flowers in pink, mauve, and blue. The dark spots inside looked like they'd been drawn on with Magic Marker.

Foxglove.

Also known as ladies' thimble, fairy finger, lion's mouth, and throatwort.

Last winter, Javier had wanted to toss the seeds into the same bed as the potatoes and turnips. He'd explained that foxglove helps root vegetables grow. But I'd been adamant about the pot. The first year, the plant had produced only leaves, finely toothed and furry. When the flowers first appeared a few weeks ago, Javier instructed me to cover them in cheesecloth for a while. They needed special care. They'd grow to four feet, maybe more, if I didn't cut them first.

But I wasn't going to cut them.

I got down on my knees.

No, I was going to yank the poisonous things out by their roots, one by one, until they were gone.

CHAPTER 12

It was close to seven by the time I was done. The sun hadn't gone down yet. It was too busy turning the clouds all sorts of crazy colors: cherry red, purple, tangerine. I watched, transfixed, as the colors vanished into the darkening sky.

Afterward, I took a long, hot shower—as long and hot as my plumbing would allow. After drying off and wrapping myself in my white terry-cloth robe, I took to my bed with an Agatha Christie novel.

Appointment with Death.

Hercule Poirot goes to Jerusalem for a much-needed vacation. It's the little Belgian detective's first night in the holy city. It's hot, so he's left the shutters open. The words drift into his room, out of the still desert air. The voice is male, nervous: "You see, don't you, that she's got to be killed?"

I closed the book. This wasn't working. I wanted an escape from real life, not a reminder of it. Then I opened the book again because I had to know who did it.

A family terrorized by a cruel and selfish mother. A schizoid daughter tearing her napkins to shreds. A romance. And a trip to Petra, capital city of the ancient Nabataeans, to see the ruins surrounded by sandstone cliffs. There, in her tent, the evil mother meets up with a hypodermic syringe containing a fatal dose of digitoxin, derived from *Digitalis purpurea.*

Foxglove.

I sat up with a sudden realization.

I had notes on this.

Twenty minutes later, I was seated at my desk with my poison file.

In more than half of Agatha Christie's sixty-six novels, the corpse is a victim of poison. This was no accident. During World War I, Christie worked as a dispenser at the Red Cross hospital in her hometown of Torquay, where she learned everything there was to know about the chemistry of murder.

Foxglove was one of her old standbys. It appeared in her writings in the form of digitalis, digitoxin, digitalin, and the closely related strophanthin. Cyanide, strychnine, and arsenic were other favorites, but not nearly as accommodating. The digitalis family of drugs has been used for the treatment of heart disease for centuries. If you want to kill an elderly heart patient, it's the way to go.

Christie occasionally took liberties, like putting a packet of strophanthin in the victim's gin and having said victim perish within minutes. Generally speaking, however, it is only when given by injection that foxglove-derived poisons work that quickly. When administered by mouth, death tends to occur more slowly. Symptoms—which include convulsions and vomiting—appear from one to twenty-four hours after ingestion, with death delayed for up to one to two weeks. But to give Christie her due, the margin of predictability when it comes to

digitalis is extremely low. Anything can happen if the murderer
mixes up a strong enough cocktail.

I closed the file, then went back into the house.

Who put foxglove in Liz's medicine? When did they put it
there? It could've been yesterday morning. It could've been two
weeks ago. Was there any way to know for sure?

It was after one when Gambino crawled into bed.

"Liz is dead," I said, still half asleep.

"I heard," he answered, wrapping me in his arms.

"Also, Richard came early."

"I'm really sorry," he replied.

Sometime in the middle of the night, I had a bad dream I'd
dreamed many times before. I'm behind the wheel of a car. I
don't know how to drive, but the car is moving forward, faster
and faster. I'm flying up hills, racing around corners, plunging
down embankments, but no matter what I do, I can't make it
stop. I woke up in a cold sweat and reached out for Gambino.
He wasn't there. I went to the bathroom and splashed cold
water on my face, then pulled on my robe and walked into the
living room.

Gambino was sitting on the couch with something in his
hand.

I could see the L.A. Sheriff's Department logo glowing in
the dim light. Detective McAllister's business card.

I'd left it lying on the coffee table.

Gambino gave me a look.

"What?" I asked.

"You know exactly what," he said. "You are to stay out of
this. You had nothing to do with Liz Berman's death. You are
not responsible in any way. Please don't make me say it again.
You've heard the lecture."

I had.

More than once.

But even half-asleep I knew—we both knew—that it was going to take a lot more than that to stop me.

We didn't talk much in the morning, just "Excuse me" and "Please pass the butter" and "Have you seen my watch?" We'd talked enough the night before, not to mention that we were both pressed for time. Gambino had had a break in his murder case. There was an emergency meeting downtown. And I had a condolence call to make.

Lou was standing outside his house, smoking, when I pulled up.

He took one last drag on his cigarette, then tossed it onto the sidewalk and crushed it underfoot.

"Liz wouldn't let me smoke inside the house," he said, opening the car door for me. "I know it doesn't matter anymore, but old habits die hard, you know?"

The Bermans lived in a modest English Tudor house in Carthay Circle, a middle-class enclave developed in the twenties in the shadow of Wilshire Boulevard's Miracle Mile. I'd once seen a photograph of Norma Shearer on the red carpet at the Carthay Circle Theatre, where *Gone With the Wind* made its world premiere. She looked glamorous in an Adrian gown with big shoulders and a fur collar. David O. Selznick had originally cast her in the role of Scarlet O'Hara, but she received so many letters from fans who felt she was wrong for the part that she bowed out. In any case, the theater, an art deco masterpiece, was torn down in the sixties to make room for an office building. I'd passed it on my way over. It already looked like a ruin.

The house smelled like old people.

"I think we could use some fresh air in here, don't you?" I opened a louvered window. Through the narrow panes I could see the rotary sprinkler on the front lawn spinning in circles, spraying droplets of water everywhere.

"Sure," said Lou. "Okay."

I moved the newspaper—yesterday's—and sat down on the couch, which was in dire need of reupholstering. The cushions were ripped and the stuffing was starting to come out.

"Can I get you anything?" Lou took a seat opposite me in a plastic chair that resembled a wedge of coconut.

"No, thank you," I said with a smile. "Have you been all right?"

"Oh, sure," he said, pressing the back of his hand against his unshaved cheek. Without the usual gel, his black hair looked coarse and unruly.

"That's good to hear."

He fingered an unlit cigarette then stood up, yanking at his gray sweats, which had lost their drawstring. He disappeared into the kitchen and came back out with a tray of cold cuts.

"Have some deli meats," he said. "Somebody brought them over. I'll never eat all this myself."

He hovered over me as I made myself a pastrami on rye. Then, satisfied, he sank into a black globe chair on casters. Above him was a huge *Barbarella* poster. It looked like Jane Fonda was aiming her ray gun directly at his head.

"You have some great chairs," I said, taking a bite of the sandwich. "Um, good."

"Liz liked to go to the Rose Bowl flea market."

"I go every once in a while," I said. "When I remember."

"Liz went religiously."

"That's how you find the good stuff," I said, wiping my mouth.

"They think I killed her," he said.

"I know." I put my sandwich down.

"I didn't do it," he said.

"I know."

"Did you hear the story about how we met?" It was the first time he'd smiled since I'd been there.

"No, tell me."

A small black cat appeared and leapt onto his lap. "I was taking this drama class," he said, scratching behind the cat's ears. "I already knew how to dance, thought maybe I could make Broadway if I could act, too. Liz was in the same class. I never really noticed her. She was shy, never said much, not all that good-looking, not the kind you'd pick out of a crowd. One day we had to roll around on the floor and be animals. I was a lion—king of the jungle!—because I'm that kind of idiot."

I laughed.

"Liz was a tabby cat. And she blew everyone away. She purred, she stretched, she licked her paws with her little pink tongue. Every guy in the room wanted her. But she picked me. I'm the one who taught her to dance. She wasn't much technically, to be honest with you, but she knew how to throw herself into it. It was a gift, you know? When she waltzed, she was a Viennese princess. When she tangoed, she was a Latin spitfire." He stopped and stood up. The cat hit the floor with a thump. "What the hell. It's a good story, isn't it?"

I nodded.

"Except for the ending. Good story, bad ending." The cat shot out of the room, its nails skittering across the bare wooden floor.

"I wish it could've been different," I whispered.

Lou finally lit the cigarette he'd been holding. He sucked hungrily, then blew out a ribbon of smoke. "I was okay last night. I read the paper, I watched some TV. I was fine until I saw this."

He picked a piece of paper off the coffee table and handed it to me.

"From the desk of Liz," it said at the top.

"It was a to-do list," he said. "It was in the glove compartment of the car. All the things she meant to get done this week." He stubbed out his cigarette, put his head in his hands. "Listen"—his voice was muffled—"could you just go now?"

I didn't want to leave him like that, but he insisted.

On the way out, I ran into Wren, who was getting out of a white VW convertible. She was carrying two Ralph's grocery bags and a pink bakery box dangling from a pretty ribbon.

How thoughtful she was. How big and sad her eyes were.

We said hello, then I got in my car and pulled away from the curb. I couldn't find a good song on the radio, so I drove home in silence.

I spent the rest of the day in the kitchen, doing dishes, reorganizing the cupboards, and baking Gambino a conciliatory apple pie.

CHAPTER 13

The water was boiling.

Agatha had always felt that anything important one person had to say to another could be said in less time than it takes to make a pot of tea.

I love you, for example.

Or: *I hate you.*

Entire universes of meaning in a few short words. She admired such economy.

Not Rosie the ubiquitous chambermaid. Rosie didn't understand economy.

This afternoon's conversation came just as Agatha was attempting to relax with a piece of the hotel's good apple pie. It revolved around Rosie's family woes, which were legion: a wayward cousin, a father with gout, an unwieldy tax bill, a cuckolded brother. After what seemed a decent interval, Agatha shooed the girl away. She was eager to settle down with the books she'd borrowed from the Messrs. W.H. Smith library in Parliament Street the day before. Among them were several adventure thrillers, a selection of myste-

rie, and a book of romantic poetry by Charles Caverley entitled Fly Leaves. *Not half an hour later, however, the latter volume slipped from her fingers as sleep overtook her.*

She dreamed of the icicles on the front porch at Ashfield. When she was a small girl, she'd beg the gardener to break them off so she could pretend they were spears and she was a mighty warrior. She'd do battle until her spears melted and she was just Agatha again.

Upon waking, she bathed and dressed quickly, then made her way to the offices of the Times, *which were almost ready to close for the day. She wanted to take out an advertisement. She inquired as to rates, then spent some time on the wording.*

The clerk behind the desk peered at her shamelessly, finally commenting upon her resemblance to the missing novelist, Agatha Christie.

Paying him his fifteen shillings, she informed him that he had overstepped. Then she closed her purse and turned on her heel.

He ran after her, abashed. He hadn't meant any harm. He was clearly mistaken. Why, he asked laughingly, would Agatha Christie have taken out an advertisement in the name of one Mrs. Theresa Neele of Capetown, South Africa?

Indeed, she murmured, turning her back on him once more. It was almost dark now, but she had to be certain he couldn't see her eyes.

CHAPTER 14

Would you please stop yelling?" I begged my mother. "The people in the parking lot can hear you, for god's sake. Hold on."

I clicked over to Annie. "Honey, please don't cry. Hang on a second."

I clicked back over to my mother. "I have a headache. I have to go."

Before I could click back over to Annie, the elderly gentleman sitting next to me touched my arm. "If you don't mind my saying so, dear, you're going to get indigestion that way. Take it from me. I'm the king of acid reflux." He wiped some egg salad from his mouth, then asked for the check.

Monday, twelve noon. The lunch counter at Jan's, on Beverly Boulevard. Waitresses with bouffant hairdos were serving patty melts and rice pudding to a stream of happy, busy people. I was busy but not happy, thanks to my ex-husband Richard, who'd apparently spent the night informing my nearest and dearest that I was a person of interest in a murder investigation and quite likely to face jail time.

I kept reminding my mother, when I could get a word in edgewise, that Richard was not to be trusted, but she wasn't buying it. After all these years she was still enamored of him: Richard from the good family, Richard with the good education, Richard who looked like Cary Grant. She'd done his colors and his numbers and was well aware of what kind of head he had on his shoulders. Richard would never lie to her. I was another story.

Annie, who had a better grip on reality, let it go. She said how sorry she was about Liz. And that I shouldn't get so upset. And that I should eat more tofu and whole grains. Before hanging up, we made a date for the six of us—Richard and Jackie, Gambino and me, Vincent and Annie—to meet at the baby store Thursday night to pick out a crib.

Call me psychic, but I predicted it wouldn't go well.

In the meantime, I was on my way to Christietown. Ian's assistant had left a message saying my check was ready and I could pick it up after two. That gave me just enough time to have a cup of coffee in peace. I couldn't bear the thought of choking down more tea with a frantic Ian. Liz's murder was all over the Sunday paper and still making headlines this morning: "Mystery Cult Death!" "Slaying at Murdertown!" They made the place sound like Jonestown. Ian was going to be beside himself.

But everything seemed just ducky when I got there. A convoy of flatbed trucks and cement mixers made their way down the access road, sounding a rousing chorus of honking horns. Red-and-orange banners blew merrily in the breeze. The birds were chirping, the jonquils stood at attention. And lining the brick path up to the Vicarage were brand-new topiary rakes plunged headfirst into the mud, each with a handle in the shape of a different murder weapon. Best of all, the parking lot was packed with Fords, Lincolns, and old Hondas with new paint jobs. I even saw a well-preserved Nash Rambler with a bumper sticker reading WORLD'S SEXIEST GRANDPA. I heaved a sigh of relief. These were Ian's people.

Inside, it was quiet. Maybe everybody was out giving tours of the model homes. I walked to the reception desk and picked up a flyer promoting tomorrow's big event, the first meeting of the Tuesday Night Club.

The Tuesday Night Club was Ian's homage to Agatha Christie's stories of the same name. In the earliest of these, Miss Marple—hoping to amuse her condescending young nephew—assembles a group of St. Mary Mead's wittiest conversationalists. The talk turns to crime. All are aficionados. They decide to meet until each of them has presented a mystery for the others to solve. Inevitably, four of the five miss the boat. The fifth is the estimable Miss Marple. After digressing about the idiosyncrasies of Inch's Taxi Service, the benefits of camphorated oil for a cough, or the virtues of an upright armchair for those with rheumatic backs, Miss Marple blithely, infallibly, nails the culprit.

Agatha Christie had the utmost respect for women of a certain age. Then again, she'd never met my mother.

I peeked over toward the offices.

"Anybody here?"

No answer.

I plopped down on the sofa and flipped through the latest issue of the *Antelope Valley News*. Then I went through *Good Housekeeping*. I ripped out a recipe for "Easy Beef Bourguignon" and pocketed it. Gambino loved red meat.

"Hello?" I called out. "Ian?"

Still no answer.

I went back to *Good Housekeeping* and read an article about the dangers of childhood vaccinations and another about organizing your closets. I hadn't realized that all my problems could be solved with boot sleeves. Sounded like something a pirate would wear. Then I meandered back up to the reception desk. Ian's assistant had left her handbag in full view. Louis Vuitton. Pretty pricey for an assistant. I poked at it. Felt like she had bricks in there. I walked around to the other side of the desk, opened the bottom drawer, and put the purse inside for safekeeping. Then I took a seat in her chair. Nice. Ergonomic. Nobody was going to get carpal tunnel syndrome in a chair like this. I spun around a couple of times, then idly plucked a piece of paper from her printer and read it. Ah. A memo to the wayward Christietownspeople: all window coverings visible from the exterior of any and all houses *must* be white or off-white in color upon pain of death.

Control freaks.

I was putting the paper back in the printer when I first heard the yelling. I leapt back to my spot on the couch. Not my business. I put my nose back where it belonged, in the classified section of the *Antelope Valley News*. Cars, motorcycles, jobs, lost pets.

You really couldn't help listening, they were so loud. The voices were male, but I couldn't make out what they were saying. Suddenly, I was overcome by a burning desire to stretch my legs. I started walking in the direction of the offices.

"Idiot! I trusted you to ..."

Lost the rest of that sentence. I tiptoed farther on. By now, I was standing right outside the door.

"You think they are going to ..."

"Cumulative-stress bullshit ..."

"Far enough ..."

"I suppose we'll have to ..."

"Fine!"

I jumped back as Ian threw open the door and walked out with a life-size cardboard cutout of the Christietown logo (old lady wielding a bloody hatchet) under his arm.

"Cece!" he said, dropping the murderous biddy to the floor.

"I didn't mean to interrupt," I sputtered, bending down to help him. The fall had bent the biddy's elbow back at an unnatural angle.

"What are you doing standing here at the door?" he asked. "Surely you weren't eavesdropping?"

I turned beet red. "I didn't hear a word of what you were saying. That's good, solid construction for you." I pounded on the wall, praying it wouldn't fall down on our heads.

Dov Pick came slamming out of the office next. He glared at Ian and elbowed past me without saying a word. Ian didn't pay him much mind. He was busying himself with the old lady. He unbent her elbow, stood her up next to the assistant's desk, then, frowning, moved her in front of the scale model of Phase 2.

"Is everything all right?" I asked.

He broke into a freakish smile. "Since you ask, it couldn't be better!"

"Pardon?"

"Oh, that Dov," he said, waving his hand dismissively. "Don't give him another thought. He's such a dramatist. My goodness, how he makes a fuss. He's upset about some con-

tracts with Browning McDuff. They want to charge us over-
time for something they should've finished ages ago. It's nothing at all. Codswallop."

"Codswallop?"

"Nonsense. Cece, dear, I need your discerning eye. Do you
like this over here?" He moved the biddy next to the potted
palm at the entrance and stepped back to appraise his handiwork.

"Looks good," I said. Then, "What exactly 'couldn't be
better?'"

Ian wheeled around to face me, hands on hips. "Sales, you
ninny!"

"Sales?"

"Yes, sales. They're through the roof."

"They are?" I asked. "Despite what's happened?"

"*Because* of what's happened."

"But—"

"Dear Liz Berman. I will forever be grateful. It's as if she
sacrificed herself so Christietown could flourish."

"My god, Ian!"

"Of course I'm sorry she's dead, where are my manners?
Tsk, tsk. But the publicity has been amazing. The hordes are
flocking to Murdertown. They come like vultures to feast on
the poor woman's remains, and I reel them in. It's perfect."

He raced over to the front desk and pulled out a stack of
papers.

"These are contracts, Cece. I've signed seventeen in the last
four hours. Yesterday, before the police had even removed the
crime-scene tape, I sold eleven Sittaford Two residences. The
ones with the double garages!"

Ian handed me my check and I walked back out to the car
in a daze.

He'd struck me as so benign, with his rashes and his splotches and his codswallop. But he was hardly that.

I suddenly wondered how far he'd go to make Christietown a success.

It's not every girl who has an adept in the black art of high finance on speed dial.

I had my accountant, Mr. Keshigian.

His big blonde of a secretary answered the phone with a kittenish hello. When she realized it was me, however, she turned cool, pleading ignorance about her employer's whereabouts. I knew, of course, that he was sitting on the other side of the wall, playing fast and loose with the tax code. She just wanted to keep her boss out of harm's way—though anyone could see it was actually the other way around. I bullied her into putting him on.

Before I could say a word, Mr. Keshigian delivered the news that the assets of any person serving prison time are frozen. "Not that it matters in your case," he finished, "there not being any assets to speak of."

"Hold your horses," I said. "I'm not going to prison. I'm just a witness. Not even."

"Look, my job is to make the information available, that's all. You know I'm a big advocate of planning."

"Yes, I'm aware of that. But that's not why I'm calling you. I need to know everything you can tell me about Ian Christie— with whom *you* got *me* involved, remember?"

"Ian Christie, Ian Christie," he mused, ignoring the last part of my question. "Well, this is his first big project, this Christietown. And he was very impressive at the symposium, very impassioned. Talked a lot about his illustrious ancestor.

She was made dame commander of the British Empire in 1971. Her books have been translated into over a hundred languages, and have sold in the billions. Billions! Like McDonald's hamburgers! Lots and lots of money there." Mr. Keshigian's voice quieted to a hush.

"Do you think he's really related to Agatha Christie?" I asked.

"Who knows and who cares? He's funded for the next couple of years, and that's what counts."

"That's what I wanted to ask you about."

"I'm all ears."

"What happens to Ian Christie if nobody buys his houses?" How desperate was he? That was my real question.

"It depends on how the deal was structured. If he got the money up front, which he probably did, nothing happens except that he doesn't get any more."

"What about the developer, Dov Pick?"

"Don't mess with the Icepick."

"Oh, come on."

He sighed. "Dov Pick and his partner have a lot at stake. They've already shelled out the money to the builders, to the architect, the city, the permits, the lawyers, the water experts, the structural engineers. They're in to the tune of millions. They're the ones who really need to get their money out."

"Is there any reason to think they won't?"

"Hey, why don't you develop some land and see if you can sell five hundred houses? It ain't that easy."

"What I mean is, have you heard of any business-related issues they might be having?"

"Nope."

"Personal crises?"

"Nope."

I swear the big blonde was giggling in the background. They were conspiring against me. Mr. Keshigian put his hand over the receiver for a minute, then came back, saying, "Listen, everybody's got problems. It's a rule of thumb. If you look hard enough, you're going to find 'em. I suggest you go through the business section of the *Times* with a fine-toothed comb."

"Great."

"Hey, I'm just an accountant. A lowly toiler. You're the one with the creative gifts."

I expect the guys at the IRS would find Mr. K. a tad disingenuous.

CHAPTER 15

When I got home, I made a pot of coffee and headed out to the office to do some research. I was looking for anything that might qualify as a red flag: bankruptcies, criminal investigations, mysterious fires, big insurance payouts, missing wives with family money. I didn't need a conviction and/or hard time. Murky circumstances would be just fine.

I shooed the cat off the top of the monitor and opened Google.

First up was Ian Christie.

Turned out there were lots of those guys.

One Ian Christie was a film scholar in Australia with a particular interest in Peruvian cinema.

Another was a life coach whose advice about mentoring struck me as extremely sound.

Yet another Ian Christie lived in Milwaukee and hosted a local talk show entitled "Christie for the Mill," which had been canceled recently. That Ian Christie had a blog and a vast number of hobbies.

There were also MP3 downloads of several Ian Christie videos, sadly unavailable. The musical Ian Christie was an oboist and the surviving half of a pair of brothers from Manchester, England. I thought I'd hit pay dirt with him, but realized after reading his bio that he was too old by at least thirty years.

My Ian Christie was a slippery devil.

For a while there it looked like he'd managed to fly in under the radar, not counting all the Christietown hoo-ha, which relayed nothing compromising about the project and nothing *whatsoever* about its creator's background, only the official party line that he was "very distantly related" to the lady in question (ha)—that, and a mention of his name among the attendees of the world Hemingway Conference in Cuba in 1999. I was pretty much ready to pack it in when something jumped out at me: an Ian Christie listed in the index of *They Fly Through the Air*, published in Britain in the 1970s.

It was a history of the circus.

I chewed on that one for a minute.

Yes, I could imagine my Ian in a clown suit, with big red shoes. Or with a handlebar mustache, corralling folks over to see the bearded lady. I did a more detailed search. The author of *They Fly Through the Air* was a former ringmaster of a small traveling circus from Cheltenham, and for more than a decade, one Ian Christie had been his right-hand man. The latter was described as "jolly and ruddy and excellent at wringing a quid out of the balkiest granny."

It had to be the same one.

My Ian was no murderer.

My Ian was an old-fashioned hustler.

Dov Pick was next. No, I'd save the best for last. Next was Dov's silent partner, Avi Semel.

Avi Semel migrated to Los Angeles in the early eighties. After reading an article citing the five most successful businesses to be in, he opened his first dry cleaner's, Stars and Stripes, on Hollywood Boulevard. He hooked up with his wife—a customer, as well as an actress who played the sexy mom in a run of teen films—when he asked if he could post her head shot above the cash register. Four shops followed in quick succession, then he sold the lot of them when he partnered with Dov to form the SP Group, an "integrated, full-service real estate investor with in-house acquisition, development, finance, leasing, and management capabilities" (as per their Web site). No mention of any Mossad background. No intelligence collection and no paramilitary actions, unless you counted the divorce from the actress, the multimillion-dollar settlement, and the second marriage to the nanny. The last time he was quoted in the *Los Angeles Times*, Avi said that his adopted country had been good to him.

The same appeared to be true for Dov Pick, the fourth son of a podiatrist and a manicurist from Tel Aviv. Dov started off in the import/export business, which was vague enough to mean almost anything. Jeans? Hookah pipes? Automatic weapons? He hung around Coffee Bean and Tea Leaf on Sunset Boulevard in West Hollywood, schmoozing with the regulars while studying to become a real estate broker. Within a week of getting his license, he'd purchased the property next door, fondly known as the minimall of death. Everybody thought he'd bought it for land value, but within the month he'd slapped on a coat of paint, planted fifty palm trees, and leased every last space. When he sold the mall two years later, he quintupled his initial investment. That was the Icepick for you.

I read on.

Now it was getting interesting.

As it turned out, Christietown was peanuts to these guys. The big thing they had going was Dusk Ridge Ranch, a planned community in the hills west of Palmdale, which abutted Christietown to the east. Dusk Ridge Ranch had lain dormant since the original developer went into foreclosure, but Dov and Avi had negotiated with the lender to assume its debt and go forward.

Seven thousand two hundred homes, along with parks, schools, and recreation facilities. It was practically a city.

They'd broken ground last month. There was a nice picture in the *Antelope Valley Press* of Dov and Avi in hard hats sticking their shovels into a pile of dirt. There was also a Native American (not Joseph) waving something in their faces. The caption read "A tribal leader fanned sprigs of burning sage with his ceremonial eagle feather and blessed the dedication of the Dusk Ridge Ranch development." The article was reprinted on someone's blog under the heading, "Even the Injuns Done Sold Out." Many comments and questions followed.

Nancyblueshoes@earthlink.net asked, "Are you sure that was a blessing going on?"

Nineteenthhole@aol.com asked, "Is a golf course in the plans for Dusk Ridge Ranch?"

Econmajor@ucla.edu asked, "Are all of the former pledges regarding infrastructure to be honored?"

The latter struck me as a very good question, though I had no idea what it meant, much less what the answer was.

So I did what any logical person would do. I called my ex-husband's fiancée's mother for help.

CHAPTER 16

The next evening Dot was waiting for me outside her house, located on a quiet street in Glendale, a middle-class suburb just adjacent to the ritzier Pasadena. She was ready for action in a pink cashmere warm-up suit, pink terry-cloth headband, and pink sneakers. She matched her well-maintained, Tudor-style house, which was also pink.

"Definitely your color," I said, smiling.

"You bet," she said, pirouetting, which couldn't have been easy with a hip replacement. "When I turned sixty, I swore off black. Would you mind, dear?" She gestured toward a small suitcase on wheels.

"Oh, sure," I said, grabbing the handle and dragging it down the front walk behind me. "What's inside?"

"Supplies."

"Supplies?" We stopped at the rear of my car.

"Tools of the trade," she replied gaily. "Reference materials. Laptop. Paper and pen. Tape recorder. Camera. Handcuffs."

Maybe I hadn't quite explained things.

"Also, a travel alarm, short-wave radio, and—"

"May I interrupt for a moment, Dot?"

"Of course."

"Tonight is actually supposed to be a lighthearted kind of event. Nobody's going to solve any real crimes or apprehend any real criminals. I mean, it's fine to bring your stuff if you really want to." Why did I bother? Of course she was bringing her stuff. "But all that's going to happen is that people are going to have a glass of sherry, get to know one another. I thought you'd enjoy it."

I'd also thought ferrying Dot to Christietown would give me one last excuse to snoop around. When I'd called Ian earlier in the afternoon with the news that I might have a prospective client for him—which was barely a white lie since Dot *was* planning to sell the Glendale house—he invited us both to the inaugural meeting of the Tuesday Night Club. God bless him, he wouldn't take no for an answer.

As I'd suspected, the same went for Dot.

I hefted the suitcase into the trunk, and she slammed it closed. Off we headed into the sunset, admiring the plumes of fuchsia and orange streaking across the sky. Well, we would have if my windows hadn't been so filthy. I turned on the windshield wipers and four tiny Japanese-made geysers sprayed water, then wiped it away.

"Much better," said Dot. "It's important to know where you're headed."

I hoped she hadn't meant that metaphorically.

Dot settled into her seat and pulled some knitting out of her bag, explaining that she was making a hat for Jackie's cousin's new baby boy. The yarn was pink, which suggested the extent of her obsession. We drove for a while in silence, broken only by the soft hum of the freeway and the click of knitting needles.

The hat looked so small. Babies' heads are in fact proportionately huge compared with adults' heads. Little hands, though. Also feet. Also little toes, like kernels of corn. I was halfway to that trippy state of vehicular bliss—your mind and body have parted ways, though you're still vaguely aware enough to contemplate baby parts at sixty-five miles per hour—when Dot asked how my new book was coming along.

I crashed back into consciousness.

Not a question I was prepared to answer.

I tried to ask about her, but on that subject she was strangely mum. Instead, I got the unexpurgated story of Jackie's cheerleading triumphs, from her humble beginnings as a USC Song Girl to her two-year stint as an L.A. Rams cheerleader to the moment she eclipsed all other rivals to become the L.A. Clippers spirit captain, and, finally, director of the Seattle Sonics/Storm dance team. Naturally there were disappointments along the way; Jackie injured herself during tryouts for the Atlanta Falcons dance team when she was twenty-two and had to have emergency knee surgery, which she came out of with flying colors, thanks to a gifted surgeon and her own spectacular genetics. Two years ago, she'd opened a cheerleading camp for underprivileged youth in Chicago (motto: "Little Feet . . . Big Dreams"), but then she'd met Richard at an Art Institute of Chicago fund-raiser (Richard's mother was a longtime docent) and abandoned all those little feet and their dreams—well, Dot didn't put it precisely that way.

Though I was loath to admit any common ground between Jackie and myself, I did find it interesting that she was a former cheerleader. And unrepentant about it. One look at her and you knew she had all her little outfits hanging in the front of her closet, cleaned and pressed so she could see the sequins and fringe every time she opened the door. Richard was insufferable on the subject of my teenage years on the pageant circuit. I'd always thought that if he had it to do over again, he'd choose somebody who wouldn't know a spirit stick if it hit her over the head. I still remember the day he made me throw out the gold lamé dress I'd worn the night I twirled my baton on the stage of the Asbury Park Civic Center, took out a spotlight, and won the crown in spite of it. Why did we have to keep carting that thing around from apartment to apartment? he'd asked. It's not like you even fit into it anymore. In those days, I didn't have the nerve to question him. Poor Jackie.

As I exited Highway 14, Dot powdered her nose in anticipation.

"Are we there yet?" she asked, like a little kid.

"This is it," I answered, pulling into the lot.

There were twinkling lights strung across the trees and under the eaves of the Vicarage. Ian's theory was that holiday decorations, regardless of the time of year, provided people with subliminal encouragement to open their pocketbooks. Dot was unmoved by the colored lights, but when she saw the wooden sign with the hatchet-bearing biddy spinning around in the teacup, she let out a gasp. It made me feel a little guilty, but only until I realized I was actually doing her a service by saving her from having to spend yet another boring evening with Jackie and Richard.

I convinced Dot to leave her suitcase in the car for the time being and we headed over to the Blue Boar. We were early, and only a handful of people were there. Some were standing close to the fireplace, which had a single Duraflame log in it. The rest were clustered around the large oak buffet.

"Can I get you something, Dot?" I was impressed by the lavish spread.

"Try one of those," said a burly older man clad in a green version of Dot's warm-up suit. He gestured toward a platter of what looked like fried wontons. "They're personal steak and kidney pies. Very authentic."

"Mmm," said Dot, who downed one, then grabbed another. "Absolutely delicious! Oh, and look at those savories over there. They look so appetizing. I'm always amazed by what a sprig of parsley can do."

"Maybe I'll try one of these." I picked up a tiny ramekin filled with something I thought might be crème brûlée.

Just then, Ian came over, making happy noises. "I'm so glad to see everyone tucking in. The stomach rules the mind, as Hercule Poirot tells us. Wouldn't you agree, Cece, that food makes an event? Cece, are you all right? Doesn't the soufflé au kipper agree with you?"

"Love it," I said, searching for something to wash away the vile taste in my mouth. "Excuse me for a moment."

I found the beverages and poured Diet Coke down my throat. I imagined the tiny bubbles irradiating the evil kippers.

"Agatha loved good food," Ian was saying when I reappeared with a glass of sherry for Dot. "Do you know that even when she was living in the Arabian desert in a tent with her second husband, she dressed for dinner? She imported Stilton cheese and chocolate truffles for her and Sir Mallowan to enjoy, and prevailed upon local cooks to produce éclairs with cream from water-buffalo milk and walnut soufflés cooked in a square tin can."

"According to her autobiography, Agatha had a very happy childhood, with no end of delicious treats," added Dot. "She writes beautifully about the hot buns made by Cook, and the French plums that were always in a jar in Auntie-Grannie's cupboard."

"The French plums," exclaimed Ian. "Why yes!" He suddenly looked at Dot as if she herself were edible.

"Stop that," said Dot, sipping her sherry. "I'm here for the intellectual stimulation."

At her rebuff, Ian turned redder than usual. Then he remembered she was a potential client. He collected himself and approached the podium. After surveying the room, he clinked his glass a couple of times with a handy Christietown button. "Ahem! May I have everyone's attention?"

All eyes—that would be ten sets of two—turned his way.

"Welcome friends and mystery lovers! I am your host, Ian Christie."

"Is he actually related?" whispered Dot.

I rolled my eyes.

"Please find seats in the circle while you can," Ian said with a fluttering motion of his hands.

Everyone looked back. The circle was vast in diameter. Unless a busload of seniors arrived in the next few minutes, seats were not going to be a problem. While Ian nattered on from the podium, I quietly removed a dozen chairs from the circle and pushed the remaining ones closer together. The burly man in the green warm-up suit helped me move half a dozen more. We put the extras in the kitchen.

Dot sat herself nearest the fire. The others, several of whom were using walkers, moved slowly. Once everyone was seated, Dot raised her hand. Still wounded by her rejection, Ian tried not to notice her, which worked until she started waving her knitting needles in a menacing fashion.

"Yes?" Ian said, ever wary of a lawsuit.

"I'd like to go first, if that's all right," said Dot.

"Works for me!" shouted the burly man.

The idea, Ian explained for the benefit of the uninitiated, was that somebody in the group would spin a mystery yarn, ripped from the headlines or invented whole cloth, and the others would attempt to unravel it. And yes, Dot could go first.

She cleared her throat and the others leaned forward in anticipation. Turned out she was like Scheherazade. Her audience listened intently as she spun a labyrinthine tale involving the heist of an armored car, a shootout between rival gangs, and the kidnapping of the no-good son of a deposed mob boss. When she got to the part about the Baccarat crystal chandelier in the $2,000-per-night Las Vegas hotel suite crashing to the floor, it was time.

I doubled over coughing, and slipped into the night.

CHAPTER 17

First things first.

I consulted my glow-in-the-dark Swatch watch, which I'd won at a West Hollywood Bastille Day Fair for guessing how many condoms were in the jar. The watch was ugly, with a green-and-brown Eiffel Tower on the face, but it kept perfect time.

Five minutes past eight.

I had half an hour max before Dot sent a squad car to find me, or, worse yet, came looking for me herself. I needed to get to the Vicarage as fast as possible and didn't want to be spotted. I decided to bypass the brightly lit streets of Sittaford 2 in favor of the empty field just past Lansham Road, where the last of the Phase 2 houses were still being built. Nobody was going to see me out there, with the possible exception of a bobcat. And bobcats weren't interested in large mammals in vintage orange-patent-leather Courrèges coats. They were interested in rodents.

The moon was no more than a sliver in the sky, the stars as tiny as pinpricks. They say it takes five minutes for your eyes to adjust to darkness once you get away from the white lights, but I wasn't sure about that. It was 8:11 now and I couldn't see a thing, unless you counted the half-framed houses, which looked like something left over from a fire. Some vaguely hulking forms in the middle of the street turned out to be cement mixers, abandoned for the night. I thought about climbing aboard one, but the good citizen in me prevailed.

The newly paved sidewalks were littered with construction debris. I did my best to steer clear of broken glass and stray ball valves. As I crossed from one side of the street to the other, a shaft of moonlight illuminated what looked like a key, just in front of an overflowing Dumpster. A key! Agatha Christie loved keys. They always turned out to be important clues. When I bent down to pick it up, however, it turned out to be nothing but a rusted piece of metal. I tossed it into the Dumpster, disappointed at having found nothing instead of something.

By the time I left Lansham Road, my eyes had begun to adjust. I could see the clumps of lupine and prince's feather growing wild in the foothills. The Kitanemuk Indians had once roamed those hills, hunting for berries, feasting on brown snakes. But that was hundreds of years ago—before the missions, before the stagecoach, before the railroad, before Christietown, before Dusk Ridge Ranch.

Now the vacant field lay before me, a barren stretch of weeds and gnarled roots. I kept moving, ignoring the pebbles that had lodged themselves in my shoes and were cutting into my feet with every step. I checked my watch again: 8:14. I started running. Almost there. I briefly stumbled over something—a blown-out tire? a rusted steel sprocket? a dead rat? But I caught my balance, sighing in relief when I saw the lights of the Vicarage parking lot just ahead.

Then I heard the dead leaves rustling behind me.

CHAPTER 18

Agatha gazed outside her window. The Hydropathic's elderly gardener was raking the dead leaves. There were three boys playing nearby, biding their time until the poor man turned his back and they could dive headfirst into the pile, spoiling his hard work.

The thing about people was that they were always testing you. They wanted to know how far they could push you. But the gardener was too smart. He was watching the boys out of the corner of his eye. And he was the one holding the rake.

Agatha opened the window. The air was cold, but sweet. She closed her eyes for a moment, then turned over the sheet of paper in front of her and began writing.

The words came easily. But then they always had, even that first time, ten years ago now, when she'd holed up for two weeks at the Moorland Hotel at Hay Tor, on Dartmoor. That time, it had been her sister, Madge, who had tested her.

"I bet you can't write one in which I can't guess the ending," Madge had taunted. Oh, but Agatha knew she could. She would write all morning, until her hand ached from the strain. Then she'd have lunch, read a book, go out for a walk on the moor. She'd learned to love the moor in those days—the tors, the heather, the wild part of it away from the roads. As she walked she'd talk to herself, enacting the chapter she was next going to write.

The moor was haunted. There was the place where the Coffin Stone lay, cleft in two by a thunderbolt, forming the sign of a cross. Dartmoor was often struck by lightning. Unusual terrestrial magnetism, so science explained it. But legend explained better than science why clocks and watches ran backward on arriving there.

Her favorite spot was in the highlands, at the foot of Mount Tor, where a ridge of stones, the granite hounds, could be heard baying at twilight, warning that the shadow of death was hanging over some moorland dweller. Conan Doyle had surely had that spot in mind when he wrote The Hound of the Baskervilles: "The longer one stays here the more does the spirit of the moor sink into one's soul, its vastness, and also its grim charm."

Conan Doyle was such a brilliant man. But she'd come up with something all her own.

The broken coffee cup.

The stain on the carpet.

The candle grease on the floor.

The burned pieces of paper in the fireplace.

A lost key.

The homely details.

The family squabbles.

And a Belgian detective whose head was shaped like an egg.

Madge had dared Agatha to write a detective story and she'd done it. The book had been accepted and would appear in print. There, as far as she'd been concerned, the matter had ended. At that moment, she hadn't envisaged writing anything ever again.

But life steers its own course.

The boys outside were whooping and shouting now.

Agatha watched with satisfaction as the gardener escorted them back inside, his pile of leaves untouched.

Archie had tested her, too.

Poor man hadn't understood she could be pushed only so far.

CHAPTER 19

I stopped in my tracks—not moving, not breathing.

The wind howled. An owl hooted.

"Who's there?" I called, the words catching in my throat.

Silence hung on the trees like a lead weight.

I turned around slowly. "Is anyone out there?"

There was no answer. It was so dark, so cold. My legs were shaking, my heart pounding, my palms sweating. This is crazy, I thought. Just my overactive imagination.

But then I heard it again.

Someone was out here. Someone was following me.

I whipped my head around in time to see him emerge from the shadows. The moonlight illuminated his eyes, which were hard. I saw something glint in his hand, and as I opened my mouth to scream he raised it and pointed it at me, and then everything dissolved into a hot white circle of light.

And she lives to tell the tale.

Oh, man. I put my hand up to shield my eyes. "Would you mind turning that flashlight off?" I asked, embarrassed.

"You fucking bet I'd mind," the man replied. "This is private property and you're trespassing."

I recognized the accent: Dov Pick. The devil you know.

"I'm an employee," I said.

Dov lowered the flashlight and looked me in the eye. "You sure about that?"

"Well, I actually work for Ian. You saw me the other day, in the Vicarage. Don't you remember?"

He squinted at me. "No."

Flatterer. "You and Ian were having a sort of misunderstanding. Does that ring any bells?"

"No." He pulled a cell phone out of the pocket of his jeans. Shoot. He was calling Ian. I started babbling incoherently, which at the time seemed like a plan.

"Who'd have guessed you liked to hang out at Coffee Bean and Tea Leaf on Sunset? I go there all the time! I'm addicted to the iced blendeds with extra whipped cream." Apparently, I couldn't stop myself. "Did anyone ever tell you you look like Omar Sharif?"

Dov hung up the phone.

"Real estate is absolutely fascinating," I continued without taking a breath. "My cousin is a broker. He failed the test six times. His first sale was to my aunt. A condo in Leisure World. Agatha Christie was obsessed with buying and selling houses, did you know that?"

He put up his hands. "Okay, okay. I surrender. You can stop now. I remember you."

"Thank goodness. I'm exhausted."

He did something with his mouth, which may or may not have been a smile. "But you still haven't explained what you're doing out here in the middle of the night. It's dangerous."

You're telling me. "I had an errand to run."

"What?"

He was relentless. "Ian needed me … to find a lost key."
That piece of metal I'd just seen by the Dumpster. It was the
first thing that came to mind. Too bad.

"God damn it," he yelled, shaking his fist. "This is the shit I
can't believe. After I told him, and told him! Jesus, that stupid
piece of—"

"I didn't find it," I blurted out. "I looked for that key everywhere." Whatever you say. Just don't shoot me with your flashlight.

"Where'd that dickbrain tell you to look?" There was no
mistaking Dov's frown. His entire forehead crumpled, making
a beeline straight for his nose.

"Nowhere. I don't know."

Dov grabbed my arm and started walking me in the direction of the Vicarage. That could've been a good thing. It was
where I wanted to go anyway. Only I was supposed to be alone,
not alone with a man known as the Icepick.

Inside, the air-conditioning was up full blast.

"Assholes think I'm made of money," muttered Dov, flick-
ing the switch to Off. Still holding on to my arm, he marched
us past the scale model of Phase 2, past the wall-to-wall plasma
screens showing imaginary Christietownspeople enjoying riot-
ous good times in the as-yet-unbuilt Victorian-themed music
hall, past the desk where Ian's assistant sat, into Ian's office. It
smelled awful, thanks to a dying hydrangea swathed in green
foil with a card sticking out of the dirt reading, "Good Luck!" I
needed it. Dov kicked the door shut, then sat me in the upholstered swivel chair and spun me around so I was facing him.
He could've used a shave.

"About that key," he said. "I don't want to talk about it. Tell me your name again."

"Cece Caruso."

"Cece, you are going to forget you ever heard about it. Do I make myself clear?"

I bit my lower lip involuntarily. "Crystal clear."

"Thatta girl," he said, patting my thigh. Then his cell phone rang. This had to be Ian. And Dov was going to tell Ian that he had me sitting here and how angry he was that Ian had sent me to look for the key, which of course Ian had not because there was no key. No key that I knew about, at least. As Dov stood to take the call, I sprang up from the chair with every intention of getting out of there, but then I remembered that I was in Ian's office because I was hoping to find something incriminating about these people's business operations, and how was I going to do that if I left? So I sat back down while my captor, ear glued to the phone, became increasingly agitated. After a few minutes of mute scowling, he flung open the office door, stormed into the hallway, slammed the door shut behind him, and started yelling at the top of his lungs in what sounded like Hebrew.

As far as I knew, Ian Christie didn't speak Hebrew.

That was a positive.

Still, I had to hurry. Dov wasn't going to leave me alone with the family jewels forever. Hands trembling, I eased open the top drawer of Ian's desk. It contained several file folders. The top one was marked "Browning McDuff." Inside were miscellaneous invoices. Screens. Fire extinguishers. Lumber. Not very interesting. Another envelope marked "Petty Cash." A bottle of pills. Viagra, speaking of the family jewels. Another folder containing bills of sale for the Sittaford residences. I stopped to listen. Dov was still screaming, so I started flipping through them, but the tiny numbers and letters were impossible to decipher under this kind of pressure. Also, my contacts were dirty. Also, I had no idea what I was looking for. Shit. Dov had hung up. He was coming back. I shoved the folders back in the drawer and, desperate for something—anything—to take away from this whole sordid experience, grabbed the small stack of pink "While You Were Out" slips sitting on the top of Ian's very full trash can and shoved them in my purse—this, at the very moment Dov was opening the door.

"You're back!" I said like a lunatic.

Dov walked toward me, stroking his stubble, taking his time, as cool as a cucumber. I was sweating bullets. "Orange," he finally said, "is a good color on you."

"Thank you," I said, mentally calculating the distance from the chair to the door.

He stepped closer. "Not everybody can wear orange."

"Correct," I said. "Tough color."

He looked at me some more.

"I can't wear beige," I stammered.

He circled around me, stopping where he started. "I hope you don't mind me telling you that you're a good-looking woman."

My bad karma had finally caught up with me. The Icepick didn't want to kill me. He wanted to have his way with me.

"Thank you, but I'm engaged." I showed him the emerald ring Gambino had given me as proof.

He took my hand in his. "A woman like you should have a bigger ring." He squeezed, too hard.

"I did, the last time," I said, pulling my hand back. "It didn't make any difference."

He spoke slowly, like he was talking to a child. "That's because it wasn't big enough."

And then his phone was ringing again, and the screaming started again, and he was pacing the room like a caged tiger, and suddenly I didn't matter anymore. Gingerly, I got up from the chair and, as I made my way toward the door, he stepped aside to let me pass.

Our bodies touched slightly, but as if by mutual agreement, our eyes didn't meet.

CHAPTER 20

I slipped back into the Blue Boar and took my seat as unobtrusively as I could.

"You okay?" whispered Dot.

Not really. As if Dov wasn't bad enough, the "While You Were Out" slips were a wash. Ian's mother was as bad as mine, calling day and night. His shirts were ready at the dry cleaner's. His gym membership was about to expire. The Agatha Christie memorabilia he was interested in would be available after two on Friday at a store on Sunset Boulevard.

"Cece?" Dot's voice was low. "Where were you all this time?"

I pointed to my tummy.

"You're pregnant!" she exclaimed. "How wonderful!"

All heads turned my way.

"I'm not—"

"Congratulations!" said an elderly woman, clapping her hands.

The burly man wagged his finger and said, "You should be sitting down, young lady."

Dot said, "That is so adorable. You and your—"

"I am not pregnant!" I broke in. Then, in a quieter voice, "I have indigestion."

Everyone looked disappointed, and vaguely disgusted.

"I think that about wraps it up," said Ian, scowling at me. "See everybody next week. And thank you for coming. We will be having many more such events. Concerts, performances, book groups. Life at Christietown will never be dull, I assure you!"

Dot stood up and linked arms with a large, middle-aged woman standing next to her. She reminded me of a Slavic Jackie Collins. Naturally, she, too, was wearing a warm-up suit, only hers was fully loaded: fringe, studs, designer insignia, shoulder pads. Her frosted mane complemented her pale snakeskin boots.

"No worries, dear," said the woman, taking big steps toward me. "There'll be other babies. Let me introduce myself. I'm Silvana Holtzman. Formerly of Farmer's Insurance, currently self-employed. And you're Cece." She stuck out her hand. I wasn't sure if I was supposed to shake it or admire her nails, which were long and bejeweled. I shook—carefully. "You and Dot are coming to my place for a nightcap, and I'm not taking no for an answer."

The theme of the evening.

"Cece?" queried Dot. "Do we have time?"

I owed her. We headed outside, where Ian, juggling a copy of *Burke's Peerage* and a Lladro figurine of an English bulldog, cut us off at the pass. I knew that he was desperate to get Dot back to the office, so I took him aside and told him she wasn't the type to go for the hard sell.

"Horses for courses," he said stoically.

"You win some, you lose some?" I asked.

"More or less."

The man was nothing if not a realist. I promised I'd work on her, and that we'd talk in the morning. Once he left, I gave the ladies the go-ahead. The whole way there, they had their heads together like teenagers. Occasionally, a giggle erupted into the night.

"Ridgeway Lane, Otterbourne Road, de Bellefort Avenue." Dot was reading off street signs. "Why, those are all the names of characters from *Death on the Nile*."

"What a memorable movie!" exclaimed Silvana. "My second husband and I made love in the back row of the theater on East 86th Street in New York City. We'd just come from the King Tut show at the Met."

"Mum's the word," said Dot, cracking them both up.

"Anthony Powell was the costume designer," I said, trying to keep it clean. "He had Lois Chiles wearing a pair of shoes with diamond heels that came from a millionaire's private collection and Bette Davis in a pair of reptile shoes made from the tiny scales of twenty-six python skins."

"Python is cheap. Like my second husband," Silvana said, tossing her hair. "Not to mention Larry. The burly man in the green warm-up suit?" She rolled her eyes, which were gorgeous. Aquamarine. "We had a thing for a few weeks. But he believes you can get more than one use out of a paper plate. Disgusting. Here we are, darlings. Home sweet home!"

We stopped in front of one of the modest, cookie-cutter residences of Phase 1. These had gabled roofs, attached single-car garages, rows of scraggly impatiens lining the faux-brick paths, and brass door knockers shaped like tabby cats. Silvana, however, was no conformist: her house had a tin

Santa sleigh on the lawn and billowy crimson-colored curtains in the window.

"Has Ian seen your curtains?" I asked her, remembering the memo I'd come across the other day in his office.

"Oh, Ian Schmian," she said with a wave of her hand. "Dov and I have an understanding."

Before I could press her for details, she led Dot and me inside and seated us both on a strange red velvet settee, with tufts, mahogany scrolling, and a high, asymmetrical back.

"It's a fainting couch," she explained, turning on various light fixtures. All the bulbs were pink. "You don't see them much anymore. In the old days, ladies used them when they wore corsets because they couldn't bend at the waist."

I could see the continuing relevance of the fainting couch. Silvana's warm-up suit was so tight I was surprised she could bend anywhere.

"I love your aesthetic," said Dot, who hadn't struck me as a devotee of the bordello look.

"I like a room to exude sexuality." Silvana picked up a remote control and clicked it. Flames filled the fireplace. "Instant romance. You, me, a bearskin rug? My first husband had no taste at all for that sort of thing, more's the pity. Impotent! But you should see the Seligmans go at it. They're around the corner, on Medenham Wells? Old people. He was a jeweler, went bankrupt. She makes her own bagels. They never close the drapes. So what'll it be? Champagne cocktails? Digestives?"

Dot and I both chose champagne, which Silvana served in margarita glasses embossed with red chili peppers. She poured herself some Bailey's Irish Cream, dropped three ice cubes into the tumbler, and topped it off with a voluptuous mound of whipped cream, which she consumed accordingly.

Silvana was a gossip. Maybe she could shed some light on the situation. "You know men," I said.

She licked some whipped cream off her upper lip by way of response.

"What do you think of Ian?"

"Ian?" Silvana looked surprised. "I don't think anything of Ian. Befuddled?"

That was the problem. He was one way on the outside, but nobody knew what he was like on the inside.

"Is he really related to Agatha Christie?" Dot asked.

"What do you think?" Silvana snorted.

"Do you think Christietown is the big success he'd hoped?" I asked.

"How am I supposed to know?" In the mirrored-tile fireplace, I saw the reflection of a dozen Silvanas dropping ice cubes into drinks.

"You're savvy," I tried. "A businesswoman, someone who's been around the block. At least that's how it looks to me. Am I right?"

Her eyes met mine. "Why are you asking?"

"I'm asking because I brought Dot here, and I don't want her to get involved in any shaky financial situations."

Dot started to say something but, to her credit, didn't.

Silvana was silent for a minute. "Have you been talking to Dov?" she finally asked, setting her drink down on the gold-leaf-rimmed coffee table. Dot gave a start at the sound of glass hitting glass.

"Sorry, darling," said Silvana.

"Dov and I chatted earlier," I said, not untruthfully.

"Dov's the one who's in trouble."

Now we were getting somewhere. "How so?"

Her hands flew up to her heart. "His lady friend left. It about killed him. I'm telling you, a person needs a liability policy for love."

Great. Now I had the story of Dov's love life from an insurance perspective. I excused myself to go to the bathroom, which had a white fur toilet-seat cover and excellent lighting over the sink. I looked about twenty-five years old. No wonder Silvana seemed so confident. But I had a feeling she knew more than she was saying.

"Cece? Everything okay?" Dot called out. Somewhere in the back of her mind she still thought I was having a difficult pregnancy.

"Fine!" I turned on the faucet, then sat on the edge of the tub to go through the "While You Were Out" slips again. In addition to the mother and the dry cleaner and the memorabilia and the gym, Dov had called twice, wanting to know the second time why Ian hadn't called him back the first. That message was dated yesterday. Then there was something from a Dr. R. that read "Failure to Perform, 1200/3800, A.V. East Kern W.P." Between that and the Viagra, it looked like Ian had personal issues I was extremely sorry I knew about. Why would a doctor leave a private message like that with a secretary? Tacky. Of course, this was all completely pointless. I wasn't going to find out anything about Liz's death this way. I turned off the faucet and hit the lights. I needed to get Dot home, I needed to mind my own business, I needed to believe Gambino when he told me none of this was my fault. Only I didn't believe him, so where did that leave me?

I came out to find Dot and Silvana huddled over a lobster, which appeared to be living in the kitchen sink. Silvana said it reminded her of her second husband, the one who was cheap, not the one who didn't like sex. The second husband did like sex, a lot.

"Isn't he virile? I bought him three days ago, but I can't bring myself to eat him," she said. "I keep telling myself he's taking the waters."

"He must be dying," I said. "Are you feeding him?" I was immediately sorry I'd asked because Silvana got defensive about her new pet, at which point even Dot started to lose patience with her. Which made me think of my pets. They'd probably destroyed the house by now. We had to go.

On the drive home, Dot worked on Jackie's cousin's baby boy's hat, then dozed off. I was a little worried she might stab herself with the knitting needles if we hit a bump. Then the needles fell off her lap onto the floor and I stopped worrying. Dot talked in her sleep, mostly mumbo-jumbo. But at one point, I did make out, "Give me a nice two-pounder, with extra drawn butter."

She was amusing, that Dot.

Chapter 21

A little after eight the next morning, Gambino and I grabbed our *L.A. Times* and walked up the street to Hugo's, a breakfast spot favored by Hollywood screenwriters who eat mung beans. Others are also welcome. Hugo's has philodendrons in pots, nice waitresses, good southern exposure, and a vast number of choices when it comes to oolongs, which are teas. Both of us ordered bacon and eggs. We're L.A. transplants. Our lives are consecrated to keeping it real.

"Honey! There's Robert Downey Junior," I said, peeking over the top of my sunglasses. "He's on his cell."

Gambino took a slug of coffee. "Yeah, we're old friends."

"Ha-ha. Did you see Rob Reiner paying his check?"

"Missed him," Gambino said. "I would have liked to see Meathead."

"Next time." I cut into my egg. Yolk oozed onto the plate. I sopped it up with my toast. Delicious.

"So what are you up to today?" Gambino asked.

Not sneaking into anyone's office. Not stealing anyone's phone messages. "Just work. What about you?"

"Solving this case would be good," he answered.

Ditto.

"Can you pass the butter, please?" Gambino asked.

I handed him a pat. He was the only person I knew who didn't bother unwrapping it first. He cut straight through the foil, then squeezed.

"So," I said. "Did you find the victim's business partner yet?"

"Nope," he said, slathering his toast. "Jelly?"

I passed it over. "What about the ex-wife?"

"Not actually an ex. They never divorced. But yeah, we found her. She's a counselor at a halfway house in the city of Orange. Tico and I have an appointment with her this afternoon. She says she hadn't seen him in almost two years. He left her and the kid. He never sent money. Another pathetic story."

The victim was found in the wee hours of the morning, around the corner from the Inmate Reception Center on Bauchet Street. He'd just served twenty-three days for driving with a suspended license. He was a small-time bad guy, a music producer who'd screwed his associates, been up on assault charges more than once, and apparently didn't believe in paying child support. When the cops fished him out of the Dumpster, he was still wearing his white plastic ID bracelet.

"Was there another woman?" I asked, finishing my grapefruit juice.

"Naturally."

"Did you talk to her?"

"Can't find her."

"What about the wife? Is she telling the truth about not having seen him?"

"I won't know until I look in her eyes."

The waitress appeared and refilled our coffees. Gambino sloshed his around meditatively.

"What is it?" I asked, putting my hand on his.

"Nothing."

"I love it when you open up to me," I said with a smile.

"Sorry."

Strange. He hadn't touched his bacon.

"Don't be sorry," I said.

Something was wrong. If I knew Gambino, he'd brood for a few more days, then he'd tell me what was going on. But I didn't want to wait. "Is it meeting Richard on Thursday?"

"No. Is that this Thursday? As in tomorrow?"

"Yes! Walt's Baby Headquarters at six thirty. Promise me you won't forget? I need you to make a good impression. They think I'm insane."

He raised an eyebrow.

"You remind me of my father when you do that." My father, who'd never approved of me. My father, to whom I was always trying to prove something. Not that there was a pattern here.

Gambino looked at me across the table. "Look, are we or are we not getting married?"

So that was it. "Of course we're getting married. Why would you think we weren't getting married?"

"Cece. It's taken months to organize a guest list. We've taken dance lessons. We've listened to a dozen wedding bands. We've tasted cakes. Father Joe is ready. But we haven't even set a date. This is getting ridiculous."

"That's not fair. You know the problem. I can't get my mother to say when she's available to come out here. I didn't have a chance to press her last time we talked. She was too busy yelling at me."

"I don't see why it matters if she's there. You can't stand her."

I gave him a look. "She's my mother."

"Listen, I know you're scared, but we either do this thing or we don't. And I want to know one way or the other right now."

"This is ridiculous. You know that I love you," I said.

"That's not what I asked."

"You're giving me an ultimatum? At Hugo's?"

He stood up. "Yes."

I paused for a split second, which was a split second too long. I could see something in his eyes go dark.

"I can't deal with this now," I said, grabbing my purse. "I'll see you tonight."

And I left my fiancé standing there, the wreck of our breakfast all around him.

When I got home, there was an e-mail from my editor, Sally. How's the weather? Your daughter have her baby? Seen any movie stars lately? Just checking in. No pressure. But are you done yet? Have you solved the mystery of why Agatha Christie disappeared for eleven days? Because you're holding up our production schedule. The publishing business isn't what it used to be. Zero tolerance for writer's block. Company policy. Get with the program. Beware self-sabotage. But no pressure. Just checking in.

I did some nervous eating, then decided to walk the dog.

At optimum dog-walking hours (eight to ten A.M., five to seven P.M.), the neighborhood is overrun with creatures of various sizes and configurations wearing studded collars. And you should see the dogs. But that's West Hollywood for you. I quite enjoyed it. Most of the neighbors were pretty mild, actually. The porn star down the block always put on baggy sweats to walk Hubert, his Afghan hound. Lois and Marlene favored bathrobes when out with their 3.5 dogs (the Chow, sadly, was afflicted with a canine form of alopecia). Minnie, the drag queen who owned the thrift store next to the gas station, kept to herself when promenading Prince Pierre, her Labradoodle. There was, of course, the gold guy, who liked to grease his chest up with some kind of sparkling body lotion. He had a good-looking golden retriever named Reggie. And the beagle owner, who had curtain-rod-size rings in his earlobes. Not to mention the seventyish lady from a few blocks over who had a parasol for her German boxer (they are prone to skin cancer). But aside from them, it was your average group of law-abiding citizens. Well, most of them weren't in fact law-abiding. They were creative types with illegal garage conversions, like me. But that wasn't such a big deal. Unless the city inspector came calling.

Buster kept lagging behind me, sniffing the trees more intently than usual. I think it was his way of punishing me for not paying enough attention to him. I bent down and nuzzled him, which seemed to do the trick. He found a nice spot of grass, important duties were performed, and we turned around. At home, I checked my phone messages (none), weighed myself (speaking of self-sabotage), checked the cupboard for food (I'd cleaned us out), and thought about doing some nervous shopping. But I accepted that nervous shopping would only cause more suffering.

Time to face reality.

Gambino needed an answer.

So did my editor.

Ladies first.

CHAPTER 22

Ladies first.

Maybe that was the problem with my manuscript.

I'd been thinking of this story as Agatha's, but stories are bigger than just one person. It was Archie's story, too.

This time, I'd begin with Archie.

Archie Christie was deeply unhappy.

I sighed. Not particularly insightful. Nonetheless, it was a start.

Archie Christie was deeply unhappy. The woman he'd married had become a stranger.

Keep going.

She wanted to talk. He wanted solitude. She wanted to travel. He wanted to stay close to home.

Better.

Then her mother died and her grief cast a pall over the household. Her emotions overwhelmed him. The truth was, he no longer loved her. He'd been seeing Nancy Neele, a twenty-eight-year-old brunette who shared his passion for golf.

It had been eighteen months. He'd fallen in love. He wanted a divorce. He left.

Two weeks later, he returned home. Maybe he'd made a mistake. They had a daughter, after all. He'd try. He'd take Agatha on holiday to Guéthary, a tiny village at the foot of the Pyrenees. It was beautiful there—the sun, the water. Maybe they could turn back the clock. But it wasn't so easy. He was neither able to commit to the marriage nor to end it.

Sounded familiar.

Agatha swore, in any case, that she wouldn't give him a divorce. She threw things. She wrote a short story in which the wife is blackmailed by the other woman and jumps from a cliff side to her death. An obvious pity ploy. At least that's how Archie would have seen it. He had no stomach for drama. He'd told her so from the beginning. There were more rows. Agatha threw a teapot. Archie refused to accompany her for a weekend in Beverley, in Yorkshire, as she'd hoped. She announced she'd go alone. He was relieved the charade was over. But she hurled accusations. Yes, he admitted, he wanted to spend the weekend with Nancy. He stormed off to work. He didn't return home that night.

That was Friday, December 3, 1926.

The first clue Archie had that his wife was gone was a phone call from Charlotte, her secretary. Archie and Nancy were spending the weekend at the home of some friends, the Jameses. Charlotte told Archie the police had arrived at Styles that morning to inquire about Mrs. Christie's whereabouts. Archie had no sooner hung up the phone than a police officer turned up at the Jameses' front door to escort him home.

Of course they thought he'd killed her. It's the husband nine times out of ten, isn't it? All they needed was a body. They already had the car. It had been found early that morning near Newlands Corner, at the edge of a chalk pit on a rutted, twisting dirt track, only six miles from where Archie and his mistress lay sleeping. The police had given him all the details, hoping to intimidate him.

I stopped for a moment, flipped through my notes. I found a quote from *Murder on the Orient Express:* "One cannot escape from the facts."

These were the facts:

The car was in an upright position with the glass screen intact.

The folding canvas roof was still erect and the plastic side screens were in place, though the bonnet was slightly damaged and the speedometer cable broken.

The doors were closed, the brakes were off, the gears were in neutral.

The spare tin of petrol, carried on the side step, was knocked off when the car collided with the bushes, and was found lying in the grass.

There were no signs of skid marks in the soft dirt.

Inside the car was a fur coat, a dressing case, and a license indicating that the owner was a Mrs. Christie of Sunningdale, Berkshire.

But where was Mrs. Christie?

Archie was frantic. He located a recent photo, gave it to the police, and they generated a "Missing" poster. I pulled out a yellow file and from it a sheet of legal paper onto which I'd jotted down the text:

Age 35 Years, Height 5 ft., 7 ins., Hair Red (Shingled), Natural Teeth, Complexion Fair, Well Built. Dressed—Grey Stockingette Skirt, Green Jumper, Grey and dark Grey Cardigan, small Green Velour Hat, may have handbag

*containing five to ten pounds. Left home in 4 seater
Morris Cowley car at 9.45 p.m. on 3rd December leaving
note saying she was going for a drive. The next morning the car was found abandoned at Newlands Corner,
Albury, Surrey. Should this lady be seen or any information regarding her be obtained please communicate to any
Police Station.*

Clues materialized but led nowhere. The police were inept.
Days followed inconclusive days. Searches were conducted,
through woods, streams, ponds, copses, fields. Unreliable witnesses recounted unreliable stories, each of which the press
took up with lightning speed. The papers were ravenous for
news, any news. This was a front-page story, about an almost-
famous writer married to a dashing war hero.

There were whispers.

The parlor maid at Styles slipped up.

She told investigators that Archie and Agatha had had a terrible argument the morning of her disappearance. Archie was
concerned for Nancy's reputation, not to mention his own. His
movements were being monitored now. He could no longer go
to work. His friends were brought in for questioning. Nancy's
name had found its way into the papers.

They knew Agatha had left him a note.

They wanted to know why he'd destroyed it.

He began to crack under the pressure.

Then came the Great Sunday Hunt of December 12, when
hundreds of civilians swarmed the area to comb the under-
growth, looking for Agatha. It was a circus. Members of the
Royal Automobile Club directed traffic. Vendors set up shop to
sell hot drinks throughout the cold winter afternoon. Children
sucked lollipops while search parties set out under police direc-

tion from three major assembly points: Coal Kitchen Lane, near Shere; One Tree Hill, on Pewley Downs; and Clandon Water Works, on the Leatherhead to Guildford main road.

Archie didn't make an appearance that day. The press were already all over him. It would've only fueled their fire.

Dorothy L. Sayers showed up. She looked around for a few moments, declared that Agatha would not be found, then incorporated the event into her third detective novel, published the following year.

Sir Arthur Conan Doyle was likewise intrigued. He obtained a glove of Agatha's and gave it to a medium named Horace Leaf, who insisted that the person who owned it was half-dazed and half-purposeful, but very much alive.

Mystery writers. Archie must've been sick of the lot of them.

On Monday the thirteenth, the papers reported that the Great Sunday Hunt had failed.

On Tuesday the fourteenth, the phone never stopped ringing.

The phone *was* ringing.

My phone.

I dove for it before the machine could pick up.

"Hello?" I said. "Don't hang up. I'm here!"

It was Silvana. I'd left a message for her earlier in the day.

"How are you, darling?" she asked. "You sound a little stressed out."

"Sorry. I'm at the computer. Thanks for calling me back."

"The almost-famous writer? Of course I'm calling you back. How's the book coming along?"

Why did everyone keep asking me that? "It's coming along great. Listen, I wanted to apologize for upsetting you about the lobster."

"I boiled him for lunch. He wasn't as satisfying as I would've liked."

"Speaking of ..." I let my voice trail off.

"Yes?"

"I wanted to ask you something about your second husband, the one who was impotent?"

"That was my first husband. Erectile dysfunction."

"Sorry. Your first husband. Erectile dysfunction."

"You're on your second husband, too, darling, isn't that right?"

I'd never really thought about Gambino that way. "I guess so. Almost."

"We should start a club!"

Agatha could've been a member. She married an archaeologist the second time around. Every woman should marry an archaeologist, she said; the older you get, the more interested he is in you. Probably apocryphal.

"I'm working on Dot now," Silvana went on. "She's coming out for lunch on Friday. I'm going to find her an old geezer if it kills me."

Richard was going to love that. "Listen, Silvana, this may sound a little weird, but did they diagnose your first husband's condition with a test, like maybe a blood or urine test?"

"Ooh," she said, clicking her tongue against the roof of her mouth. "*Now* I get it. Tell me, how long has this been going on with your fiancé, the cop?"

Suddenly, I felt very, very disloyal.

"I'm sorry," Silvana said quickly. "I'm prying. But it's always those law-and-order types. Anyway, let me get to the meat of it, you should pardon my pun. They check testosterone levels. A simple lab test. In and out, you should pardon that pun, as well."

I was staring at the message Dr. R. had left for Ian: "Failure to Perform, 1200/1300, A.V. East Kern W.P."

"You still there, darling?"

"Yes. So what do you think about a level of twelve to thirteen hundred?"

"Twelve to thirteen hundred? Is that what you said?"

"Yes."

"Twelve to thirteen hundred, are you kidding me?" Silvana made gobbling noises. "What I could do with a man like that!"

"Excuse me?"

"He's off the charts, darling. A sexual prodigy! The problem is obviously psychological." Her voice turned low, conspiratorial. "Do you know a store called Trashy Lingerie, on La Cienega?"

I did, as a matter of fact.

Silvana spent the next five minutes telling me exactly what types of garter belts and G-strings I should purchase to help Gambino with his mythical problem. She made me promise I'd call her back and tell her how things had gone.

I hung up, puzzled. These numbers obviously weren't what I thought they were.

I saved my Agatha Christie notes and closed the file. Then I gave it one last shot. I punched the entire message from Dr. R. into Google: "Failure to Perform, 1100/1200, A.V. East Kern W.P."

This was it.

I'd found it.

A.V. East Kern W.P. was not some arcane bit of medical jargon.

It was the Antelope Valley East Kern Water Project.

At last. Something that made sense.

I should have known, of course.

In California, it's always about water.

CHAPTER 23

Every day, after breakfasting in bed with the London newspapers, Agatha took the beneficial waters known as the Cure.

The saline sulfur bath was good for gout, rheumatism, and hepatic disorders.

The sulfur foam bath treated obesity.

The alkaline sulfur bath was used mainly for skin diseases.

The alkaline sulfur electric bath featured constant, interrupted, sinusoidal currents to combat muscle weakness and atrophy.

The thermo-paraffin wax bath eased stiff and painful limbs.

The peat baths addressed lumbago and sciatica.

If you weren't already half-dead, it might be enough to kill you.

The Harrogate Massage Douche was the worst. You'd perch on a wooden stool as a continuous needle spray was directed at your spine and you were massaged by an attendant wielding a warm douche in a flexible tube. Useful for gout, arthritis, and lumbago, none of which she suffered from.

Still, one had to fill the day.

And so she would sit, in the pleated bathing costume and cap *she'd ordered from town, staring down at the intricately tiled black-and-white floor, the water beating down on her back like punishment.*

She accepted the punishment as her due.

She wondered if it meant she were brave.

No. She wasn't brave.

What she was was a bit of a masochist.

Chapter 24

That night I had three surprises for Gambino.

The first was, I'd picked a tentative date for our wedding, four weeks hence. Father Joe was free. Our neighbor Butch gave me his word that the backyard would be done. Bridget wrote the date in her calendar in permanent marker, and asked if she should have a lining sewn into the sheer Greek goddess dress she'd picked out for me (yes). Lael said she and whoever she was sleeping with at the time wouldn't miss it for the world, which was very comforting. Annie was ecstatic. Gambino's partner, Tico, and Tico's wife, Hilda, had no prior commitments. And my mother didn't return my call, which made it perfect.

The second surprise was, I'd paid a visit to Trashy Lingerie. The Cherry Bomb collection worked like a dream.

The third surprise was, I'd rented *Chinatown*, which we put on once we got our second wind, around one A.M.

"Look at that!" said Gambino admiringly.

I rubbed my own nose. "You're a savage."

"Roman Polanski played the thug who cut Jack Nicholson."
Gambino shoved a handful of popcorn in his mouth. "It was
a trick knife. They make 'em with special hinged blades that
only bend in one direction. But if they put the blade in the
wrong way—" He ran his finger across his throat.

"Ssh," I said, grabbing his hand. "You're distracting me."
As if anybody could resist Faye Dunaway in noir-ish widow's
weeds, with penciled-on eyebrows and Cupid's-bow lips. Ali
MacGraw, who was married to the film's producer, Robert
Evans, was supposed to play the part of Evelyn Mulwray, but
she lost it when she left Evans for Steve McQueen, which
actually sounded like a fair trade to me. And when you come
right down to it, who wants to see Ali MacGraw in anything
other than a poncho, plaid miniskirt, and knit cap? I wondered when Bridget had last seen this movie. She'd go crazy
for Faye Dunaway's cream-colored suit with the gray trim.
Anthea Sylbert was the costume designer. This was the second
movie she'd done with Polanski, after their collaboration on
Rosemary's Baby. Anthea Sylbert had been the one who'd put
Mia Farrow in baby-doll dresses, which got shorter and shorter
as Satan's minions closed in on her. But Anthea Sylbert outdid
herself in *Chinatown*. It wasn't just Faye Dunaway. It was the
parched colors of private investigator Jake Gittes's suits, which
made your teeth feel sticky and your mouth dry.

Water.

Chinatown was about water.

After getting his nose cut and following numerous false
leads, Jake Gittes learns that corrupt water officials have been
blowing up tanks, putting poison down wells, and diverting
irrigation water to cause a drought, allowing speculators to
grab valley lands cheaply pending the construction of a res-

ervoir, which would pump water to those lands, driving their value back up exponentially.

Without a steady water supply, the land's worth nothing, he explains to Evelyn.

With water, it's worth tens of millions.

That's Chinatown, Jake.

Which got me thinking about why exactly Ian Christie had received a message from the Antelope Valley East Kern Water Project about a "failure to perform." Maybe Liz saw that message. Maybe she was there the day Ian's assistant received it. Bridget said that Liz had been out to Christietown on several occasions, to prepare for her role in the play. Could she have been blackmailing Ian? Or Dov? About what? What exactly had failed to perform?

I heard snoring. It had taken Gambino all of two minutes to fall asleep. I leaned over him to get the phone and punched in Lou's number. I knew I'd be waking him up (Lou, not Gambino, who slept like a log), but I needed to know if Liz had said anything to him that might shed some light on the situation.

Unfortunately, the line was busy, which was odd considering it was three o'clock in the morning.

CHAPTER 25

Seven A.M. came in the blink of an eye.

My goal for the day was to pretend that everything was normal.

I fed the pets. I made a pot of coffee. I kissed Gambino good-bye. I popped two Advil. I read the op-eds, then flipped to "My Favorite Weekend," which is at the back of the *L.A. Times* calendar section every Thursday.

I am addicted to "My Favorite Weekend" mostly because I find it curious that everybody's favorite weekend—whether they're symphony conductors, sitcom actors, pro-ball players, or indie-band guitarists—is exactly the same. Saturday morning, it's pancakes with the kids; Saturday afternoon, it's biking, hiking, Rollerblading, or antiquing in the Santa Monica Mountains, Venice boardwalk, Griffith Park, or Rose Bowl Flea Market; Saturday night, it's a babysitter and Italian for dinner, followed by drinks at a funky jazz spot. On Sunday, there's dinner with friends and family by the pool, maybe some grilled steaks and scampi. I didn't understand why nobody ever wanted to ditch the friends and family and hang out behind the 7-Eleven. Or gamble. Or set small fires.

Today's subject, however, was a woman with a show on the Food Network who spent most of her favorite weekend in L.A. in Solvang, buying clogs and eating *aebleskiver*. This woman didn't have a pool. On Sunday, she liked to visit a Hindu temple in Agoura Hills.

So much for pretending things were normal.

It seemed like a sign.

I picked up the phone and punched in the number of the Antelope Valley East Kern Water Project.

"How may I direct your call?" asked the receptionist, who'd answered before I'd had a chance to think through my story.

"Hi!" I said too loudly. "How are you? I'm calling from Christietown. I work for Ian Christie." Not a lie.

"Yes?"

"I believe you left a message for him a couple of days ago." Also true. I sneezed.

"Yes?"

Then I coughed. "Sorry. I've been kind of sick."

"Something awful is going around," she conceded. "Hong Kong flu or something."

"Right! Hong Kong flu. Anyway, I've had this Hong Kong flu thing, and then my husband broke his leg, so I've been a little preoccupied and didn't write down the message properly. It's just that my boss is a little skittish, and I don't want to get it wrong."

Pause. "Why don't I go ahead and connect you with Mr. Knight?"

There were a million reasons why she shouldn't go ahead and connect me with Mr. Knight, but that was beside the point because mere seconds later a man's voice boomed, "Teenie? Harry here. How are you?"

Teenie? What kind of name was Teenie? Ian's assistant didn't look like a Teenie. And why were Teenie and Harry on a first-name basis anyway?

He went on, "I was just about to mail you folks the follow-up. It's a whole report, actually. Lots of pages. Are you heading this way anytime soon? Save us the postage."

"Actually, Harry"—the wheels were turning now—"we have a new gal working for us. Great gal. Her name is Cece. Why don't I have her come by for them?"

"Oh," he said, sounding disappointed. "The truth is, I wouldn't mind seeing you, Teenie. It's always the highlight of my day."

I scratched my head. I had a bad feeling about this.

Harry's voice dropped to a whisper. "What about that drink you promised me? Are we still on for next week? You don't need to worry. Whatever happens between us stays between us."

Don't do it, Teenie! You're a married woman and your husband has a broken leg! "Here's the thing," I said. "We don't want to do anything we might regret."

He sighed. "I was afraid you'd say that."

"You were?"

"Yes. And of course, you're right."

"I am?"

"Yes." He cleared his throat. "Guilt is a destructive emotion. I'm already unhappy enough. Do I really need that kind of negativity? I don't think so."

"It's not that you're not an attractive man," I said, immediately berating myself for not leaving things well enough alone.

"No, no. I understand. It's good you're sending Cece. No need to make it any harder than it has to be."

"It's for the best."

"Good-bye, Teenie," he said, his voice breaking.

I'd missed the morning rush, so it took me a little less than an hour and a half to get there. The Antelope Valley East Kern Water Project was located in one of those soul-destroying office parks. Even the shrubbery looked alienated. It was that grayish-green Javier was always trying to talk me into. The security guard gave me a visitor's badge and had me sign the guest register. I caught a glimpse of myself on the video monitor, pen in hand, and had the odd, fleeting sensation that I was watching a cop show, and the tall woman in the clingy navy blue knit dress and matching beret was about to be busted. But I hadn't done anything. Not yet, at least.

My red suede platforms clicked loudly on the polished stone floor as I strode across the main lobby and out the rear door, in search of Building C. In the middle of the wind-whipped quad stood a lone cappuccino cart manned by a tired-looking woman in a parka. As I passed, she called out, "The machine's broken. All we've got is Snapple today." I told her I wasn't thirsty, but thanks.

Building C faced the mountains and the heating and air equipment. The sniffling receptionist had a thick manila envelope waiting for me. There was an awkward moment when she looked at my visitor's badge and noticed that I spelled my name "Cece," whereas the name scrawled on the envelope was "Ceci." I reassured her that surprisingly few people know that "cecis" are garbanzo beans.

Two minutes later, I was turning in my badge, signing out, and fleeing with the contraband. Of course, once I found out what was inside, and who or what had failed to perform, I'd have to hand this stuff over to Ian with some cockamamy story about how I happened to have it, but that was my next problem.

I sat down in my car, turned on the interior light, and pulled out the thick stack of papers. But I didn't get a chance to go through them. Not then at least. My cell phone had started to ring. It was Bridget, sounding upset. She told me to turn on the radio and find a news station right away.

They had just reported another murder at Christietown.

CHAPTER 26

The Vicarage was an unholy mess. Business types in rumpled suits were pacing the floor, looking panicked. Cops were filling out reports and bellowing into cell phones. A pair of reporters from the *L.A. Times* had taken over Teenie's desk. The plasma screens had all gone black.

I marched in looking for Ian, but Detective Mariposa intercepted me like a heat-seeking missile.

"You again," he said. "Keep turning up like a bad penny and people are gonna talk." Somebody called his name from across the room. "Be right there," he answered without taking his eyes off me. "Is that a beret?"

"Can you please tell me where Ian is?" I was trying to keep my voice calm, but he brought out the worst in me.

"Why are you asking about Ian?" Mariposa's beeper went off. He checked the number, then turned on me again. "You interested in who got whacked? You want to know if it was him?"

Asshole. "Yes."

"Classified information, sorry." He thrust his hands into the pockets of his jacket. Probably looking for a pen to suck on.

On the other side of the room his partner, Detective McAllister, was hunched over a phone. He looked pale. Some people don't have the stomach for the profession. Gambino said it's like being a doctor. You have to disconnect from your emotions. If you get too involved, you can't do the work.

Mariposa, following my gaze, said, "He's talking to the next of kin. We always let Pretty Boy break the news. Do me a favor and don't bother people at work, okay?"

Ignoring him, I started across the room but stopped short when I saw McAllister look up and give a nod to one of the reporters, who then shouted into his phone, "That's '*h*,' not '*z*.' You deaf or something? Holtzman!"

Silvana.

My stomach lurched.

Mariposa was on me like a flash. "You knew her?" he asked.

I'd have to tell Dot her Friday lunch date was off. I'd have to tell her that her friend was dead. I didn't think I could do it.

"Yes," I said. "I knew her."

"Come with me," said Mariposa, taking my arm. "I want to ask you a couple of questions. McAllister," he yelled, "I think you might want to be in on this."

He led me into Ian's office and pushed me into the same upholstered swivel chair Dov had. That seemed like a long time ago.

McAllister stood in the doorway and gave me a small smile. "Hey," he said. "How have you been?" Then he shook his head.

"Are you done now?" Mariposa asked, ushering McAllister in and closing the door. "We got a job to do, remember?"

"There's this key," I blurted out. I turned to McAllister. "I don't know what it's to or where it is, but Dov Pick was very upset about it the other night."

"Do you think it has something to do with what happened to Silvana Holtzman?" he asked. "Or Liz Berman?"

Hell if I knew. "I think Dov and Silvana went back a ways."

"Since when is that a reason for shooting somebody?" Mariposa interjected.

Oh, god. This wasn't happening. I squeezed my eyes shut for a moment and wished everything was different, but when I opened my eyes everything was exactly the same. Liz was dead. Silvana was dead. Neither of them was coming back.

"What is it?" McAllister asked.

"Silvana said she and Dov had an understanding," I said, trying to make sense of it myself. "That's a strange thing to say, don't you think? About somebody with a reputation like his?"

"He's quite the ladies' man," Mariposa said. "You seen his girlfriend? The one who looks like Gina Lollabrigida? Boobs out to here." He stuck his hands out in front of him. "Don't know why he'd cheat on her, but maybe he and Silvana had something going. Hey, forget about Dov. Maybe Gina Lollabrigida whacked Silvana!" He turned to McAllister. "Crime of passion, what do you say?"

"What is wrong with you?" McAllister asked. "This isn't a joke."

Mariposa pursed his lips. "Didn't mean to upset you, Pretty Boy. Sorry, okay?"

"Maybe Silvana knew too much about Dov's shady business affairs," I said quietly.

Mariposa's eyebrows shot up. "What shady business affairs?"

The papers from the Antelope Valley East Kern Water Project were still in my car. I didn't know what shady business affairs yet.

"Look, can I go?" I asked. "I have to talk to Ian."

"Be my guest," said Mariposa. "And if you find him, give us a call."

If you find him? Where was he? "Is he a suspect?" I asked.

"Classified information," Mariposa said with a smirk.

"No, he's not a suspect," said McAllister. "We just want to make sure he's okay."

"Is Ian in some kind of danger?"

"Who isn't?" said Mariposa philosophically.

I opened the door and the cool desert air slapped me across the face.

Dot.

She'd become close to Silvana in the past few days.

Was she in danger, too?

Was someone going to shoot her?

No. Dot was fine, I reassured myself. But my racing pulse told me otherwise. I ran out to my car, whipped open the door, grabbed my cell phone from the charger, and furiously punched in her number.

Dot had nothing to do with this.

Why would anybody want to hurt Dot?

My heart felt like it was coming out of my chest until I heard her voice on the other end of the line. She started to thank me for the other evening, but before she could get too far I blurted out the news. I probably should've had her sit down, or made sure she wasn't alone, but I didn't think of those things at the time. In any case, Dot didn't cry. She barely even seemed shocked. She did ask a lot of questions.

How exactly did it happen?

Who did it?

Why?

I didn't know.

All I did know was that I'd never seen aquamarine eyes like Silvana's.

Dot had to go. There was someone at her door. I'd used that excuse before. I was about to pull out of the parking lot when I caught a glimpse of Teenie, walking toward the Vicarage with an empty cardboard box in her hands.

I leapt up, slammed the door shut, and ran her way. "Teenie!" I called out. "It's Cece. How are you holding up?" A diamond on the third finger of her left hand caught my eye. I was glad we weren't going to be cheating on our husband with Mr. Knight.

"Not well," she said.

"I can imagine. Do you need help with that box?"

"I'm fine," she said tersely. "If you'd excuse me ..."

"Sorry. I didn't mean to hold you up. I was actually looking for Ian. Have you seen him today?"

"No." Her face was etched with worry lines I didn't remember from two days ago. "Not today and not tomorrow, if I'm lucky. And not ever again once he pays me the two weeks he still owes me."

"I don't understand," I said. "Are they shutting this place down or something?"

"No, they're not shutting this place down." She put a hand up to block out the sun. "Didn't Ian tell you? Murder is good for business. But I'm done. I'm through making tea for a madman. I'm quitting. I can't take this anymore."

"I have some papers for you at my house," I said carefully.

"They got mixed up with some of my things accidentally. What would you like me to do with them?"

"You can burn them for all I care."

"They're from some kind of water company. In Antelope Valley, I think it was. Does that ring any bells? Some kind of trouble there?"

"Just business as usual," she said bitterly. "To tell you the truth, I don't give a damn."

Teenie was history.

Ian was missing.

Two women were dead, and as far as I knew, all they had in common was Christietown.

It didn't sound like business as usual to me.

CHAPTER 27

Unfortunately, I was not able to reflect upon the day's events as I would have liked because I was stuck on the 14 for two hours and didn't dare lose focus. Lose focus on the 14 and you die. That was no exaggeration. The 14 was home away from home for people who lived so far away from the places they worked that they had to get up at four o'clock in the morning to make it on time. Bleary-eyed, they listened to talk radio and sucked down coffee from commuter mugs in the hopes they wouldn't fall asleep and crash and die and kill you while they were at it. The return trip was worse because everybody was eight hours more tired. The 14 represented everything that was bad about southern California.

I stopped at home for five minutes to get Gambino and to freshen up. We came to a screeching halt outside Walt's Baby Headquarters at exactly 6:28 P.M., two minutes early. Richard was going to hate that. Nothing would please him more than to have us stagger in just before closing smelling like sex and cigarettes—except maybe if Gambino was also wearing a ZZ Top T-shirt.

I'd made him change.

At the moment, Gambino looked imposing in a black three-button cashmere-blend blazer he must've borrowed from another six-foot-four, two-hundred-and-twenty-pound friend, because I'd never seen it before. I, too, was sporting business-like attire: hair pulled into a sleek bun, pin-striped trousers, black sleeveless turtleneck. Of course, the sweater plunged to my waist in the back but Richard wasn't going to know that unless I turned my back on him—and after ten years of marriage I knew better than to do that.

As we walked through the front door, a woman who looked like Snow White (pale skin, black hair) handed us each a checklist and a paper cup of hot cocoa. We downed the cocoas and checked each other for mustaches. Then we heard Jackie's voice.

"Over here, Cece! By the gliders!"

Snow White led the way, telling us how important gliders were for the mother-child bonding experience. Studies show that babies who are breast-fed in gliders—in particular, collectible gliders handmade by Amish craftsmen exclusively for Walt's Baby Headquarters—do better in life than babies who are fed in regular chairs or beds. Gambino started to cough and I pinched him.

"Hi, guys!" Jackie said brightly. The ex-cheerleader made quite a sight, gliding back and forth in her pale yellow Lacoste dress, a patchy-haired baby doll in her arms.

"Hi," I said. "Where's Richard?"

"Using the facilities," she replied. "And this must be your fiancé. I'm Jackie Dehovitz."

"Don't get up, please," said Gambino. He leaned down to shake her hand. "Peter Gambino."

"Would you like to meet 'My Breast Friend'?" She indicated the large foam-rubber pillow in her lap.

Gambino looked at me for help.

"It's for breast-feeding," I said in a low voice.

"Sorry. I think I'm a bit nervous," Jackie said. "This is all kind of strange for me, this blended-family thing. My parents were married for thirty-two years. Never spent a night apart. They were so in love." She blushed prettily.

"That's what we all want," Gambino said, looking at me.

"Well, then," I said. "I guess I'll check out the cribs now."

Gambino sat down on a nursing ottoman at Jackie's feet. "Good idea."

"Don't get up or anything. You just sit there and relax," I said.

He stretched his muscular arms over his head. "It has been a long day."

"Being a policeman must be so rewarding," gushed Jackie.

I left the two of them to their own devices. It was time to get this show on the road. There were at least a dozen models on the floor, several with prices in the four digits. Then you had to choose a finish. I ran my hand across the samples, which were mounted on a pegboard. Their names sounded like flavors of breakfast cereal: honey, pecan, wheat, cherry, summer harvest. Made me hungry. I glanced at the clock over the cash register. Mickey was pointing to the 9 and Minnie was hovering between the 6 and the 7. Where were Annie and Vincent? I hoped they hadn't gotten lost. Annie was going to hate this place, of course. Her version of shopping was to head over to the thrift store in Topanga Canyon, where she and Vincent lived, and grab an armful of anything that didn't have buttons hanging off it. For most of the last nine months, she'd lived in ballet slippers, pajama bottoms, and Vincent's shirts. For parties, she wore an old hippie skirt of Lael's with a drawstring waist. It was apple green with little silver stars all over it. My pregnant pixie.

"How are we doing here?" asked Snow White.

"I'm wondering what the delivery time is on this one." I pointed to a crib that was simple without being spartan. The tiny comforter draped over it was bumblebee themed, yellow and black.

"Four to six weeks is standard, ten percent extra for a rush job. But don't forget, Baby will be sleeping in the bassinet first, next to . . . Mommy and Daddy, is it?" She looked at me for confirmation.

"That's right."

"In this town, you never know," Snow White said, rolling her eyes. "Don't forget, you'll be needing sheets and waterproof pads for the bassinet, in addition to flat sheets, fitted sheets, waterproof pads, bumpers, dust ruffle, mobile, toy cradle, and diaper stacker for the crib. It's all there on your checklist."

Along with car-seat tighteners, car-seat levelers, stroller shields, crib tents, sleep positioners, two-way mirrors, wire-mesh gates, high-chair hooks, nursery monitors, electric bottle warmers, electric baby-wipe warmers, shock guards, drawer latches, hypoallergenic pads for supermarket carts, and entertainment centers, which I think were Baby's version of flat-screen TVs. The *Bambi* mural on the wall didn't fool me. This place was evil.

"This is our top-selling crib," said Snow White, directing my attention to a large structure with Corinthian columns. I noted the straight-from-the-manufacturer price of $1,699.00. "The side rail is supposed to go down to save Mommy and

Daddy's backs." She gave it a delicate little kick with her espa-
drille.

"Sometimes, you have to use force," I said, kicking it for all
it was worth.

"Lovely," said Richard, who'd appeared from out of
nowhere.

"This is my ex-husband," I said to Snow White. "He likes
to sneak up on unsuspecting women."

He crumpled up his paper cup of cocoa and tossed it into
the trash. "Why do I bother? Don't answer that. I'd like a word
with you."

"Fine."

Once we reached the grooming center, he said, "Are you
out of your mind? Did you think I wouldn't notice that you
dragged poor Dot to a murder scene? You live in some kind of
sick fantasy world and I don't want Dot anywhere near you.
And why would you be cozying up to my future mother-in-law
anyway? Answer me!"

"Guess what, Richard?" I was furious. "I don't have to
answer you. You aren't my husband anymore, and haven't been
for years, thank god. So don't try that shit on me again."

"Language, Cece," he said snarkily.

"Shut up," I replied. "As for Dot, I'm sorry I involved her.
Truly sorry. She's a lovely woman, and I never meant her any
harm."

Snow White was back. "Sorry to interrupt, but you don't
want to overlook this." She handed me a small plastic pouch.
Not getting a response, she looked back and forth at the two
of us, then said in a tiny voice, "Number sixty-two on your
checklist? The deluxe oral kit?"

Richard glared at her. "Would you *please!*"

As she made herself scarce, I called out, "You'd have left him, too, admit it!"

"This isn't funny, Cece," said Richard. "The police have been grilling Dot mercilessly. Like she's a suspect!"

"Oh, you mean like I'm a suspect? Thanks for calling my mother, by the way, and getting her all worked up."

"Stop changing the subject," he said. "Jackie and I are livid."

"Jackie didn't look livid."

"That's because she's got class."

"She was talking to my boyfriend about breasts!"

Suddenly, Gambino was at my side. He towered a full half-foot over Richard, who didn't like competition.

"Hey," Gambino said, flinging an arm around my shoulder. "Everything okay?"

I smiled up at him. "Great. Detective Peter Gambino meet Professor Richard Durand."

"I've heard a lot about you," said Gambino with dazzling aplomb.

"Yes, I'm sure you have," said Richard.

"Glad we can all put aside our differences and be here for Annie and Vincent. They're great kids. I'm sure you're very proud of them, Rick."

Richard was suddenly at a loss for words. He shoved his hands in his pockets and kicked an imaginary rock.

"What's wrong, *Rick*?" I asked.

"Look, Cece," said Gambino, taking my arm. "The kids are finally here."

Annie and Vincent were being dragged our way by Alexander, Vincent's three-year-old son by a bad-seed ex-girlfriend. Vincent and Annie had fought for custody and won. I held out my arms and little Alexander flew into them.

"Your back feels cold," Alexander said, burying his face in my shoulder. "You can borrow my sweatshirt if you want."

"Hi," said Annie. "Sorry we're late. This place is a trip, isn't it, Mom? But it does make the whole baby thing seem real." Annie was in her pixie outfit and smiling her beautiful smile. Richard had found Jackie and was holding her hand. I thought I saw a tear in his eye. Impossible.

Alexander scrambled out of my arms and started doing somersaults across the floor.

Vincent said, "This is something I didn't think I'd ever see, all of us together like this. It means the world to Annie." That was him telling us to be on good behavior.

"You okay, hon?" Annie asked Alexander. He'd bumped his head on a jogging stroller and after a moment's careful reflection, had begun to sob. Annie knelt down to kiss him, which isn't easy three weeks before your due date. Struggling to her feet, she tossed the checklist into the trash. "Can't the baby just sleep with us?"

Snow White's hand flew up to her mouth. "Absolutely not! Co-sleeping is frowned upon by the medical establishment."

"What about this?" asked Vincent, holding up a wicker basket lined in checkered flannel. "Let's just get this and go out for ribs. There's this famous barbecue joint somewhere around here. Do you know the place I'm talking about?" he asked Snow White.

"Dr. Hogly Wogly's Tyler Texas Bar-B-Cue," she replied. "It's on Sepulveda Boulevard." She glanced up at a picture on the wall, then looked away guiltily. It was the Three Little Pigs.

"That's the place," said Vincent. "We're done here. We'll take this." He plucked the plastic pouch out of my hands. "And this." He pulled a tiny sheepskin rug off the wall.

"Ooh, soft," said Annie, rubbing her face against it.

"Absorbent, calming," murmured Snow White.

"Jackie's a vegetarian," said Richard.

"Richard," said Jackie. "Don't make a fuss."

"We'll take your top-selling crib," said Richard. I looked over at Vincent, then decided not to argue.

Snow White, visibly gratified, said, "The macaroni salad at Dr. Hogly Wogly's has these little slivers of celery in it. It's delicious. No meat."

Alexander looked at her and asked, "Where are the seven dwarfs?"

"Alexander," said Vincent. "It isn't polite to stare."

I was staring, too, at Gambino and Richard. I could just picture them sitting across from each other in a vinyl booth at Dr. Hogly Wogly's, ripping flesh off bones with their teeth.

"Sepulveda and what?" I asked innocently.

CHAPTER 28

Unfortunately, dinner at Dr. Hogly Wogly's never happened. At Roscoe Avenue, just west of the Van Nuys intersection, Annie started having what she thought were contractions. She and Vincent called her doctor from the car. He'd examined Annie just two days earlier and was fairly certain it wasn't time, but suggested they turn around and meet him at the hospital just to be on the safe side.

Gambino and I took Alexander home with us in case this wasn't a false alarm. We stopped at In-N-Out Burger on the way. Alexander said he could eat two orders of fries, which I found hard to believe considering he was only three, but it turned out to be true.

Annie called us just after nine. They were already home. The doctor had assured them that the baby was staying put for the time being. I was relieved. And grateful about the impromptu sleepover. Having Alexander over defused the lingering tensions between Gambino and me. We took Buster for a walk, played with Mimi, then got ready for bed. While the boys were brushing their teeth, I gave Lou a quick call. The line was busy again.

Alexander was asleep within the hour. Gambino was the next to collapse. I shut the door to our bedroom and snuck out to the car to get the envelope I'd borrowed from the Antelope Valley East Kern Water Project.

It was nice to be outside. The air smelled sweet, like orange blossoms. It was that time of year. The jacarandas would be next, littering the streets with their sticky purple flowers. They say that if you walk underneath a jacaranda and a trumpet blossom falls on your head, you'll be granted your heart's desire. In the meantime I thought I'd wish on a star, but I couldn't see any on account of the massive neon Emser Tile sign up on Santa Monica Boulevard, which shone like a beacon through the night. The Emser sign is actually a cinematic landmark. The first time we see Mel Gibson in *Lethal Weapon*, he is dangling somebody upside down from it.

I unlocked the side gate, made my way through the "dog run" (imagine Buster cracking up right about now), and traipsed out to the office, also glowing like a beacon. I'm bad about lights.

The envelope was big. I opened it and fanned the sheets of paper out across my desk. I was intimidated. Scientific, technical, and legal documents are not my specialty. My eye went straight to the alarming words and phrases: "toxic plume"; "wide-scale irrigation"; "ammonium perchlorate"; "groundwater basin"; "litigious carrot farmers." At least "litigious carrot farmers" made me laugh.

My saving grace was the cover letter.

In a nutshell:

Ian and Dov needed water. The Antelope Valley East Kern Water Agency (AVEK) wanted to provide them with it. AVEK handled state water imported via the California Aqueduct, which would run Christietown only slightly more money than the water they were currently getting from the Palmdale Water Company (PWC), which owned and operated twenty-three wells in the immediate area. AVEK saw an opening for themselves because this January, just four months earlier, ammonium perchlorate, which is a component of rocket fuel, was discovered in one of PWC's wells, located just a few miles downstream from a former Cold War–era munitions plant. In the cover letter, AVEK acknowledged that PMC had announced immediate plans to shut down the contaminated well and clean it up. Nontheless, AVEK's head honcho was concerned that the plume of perchlorlate could be spreading west toward its other drinking wells.

It didn't take a Harvard M.B.A. to get that the people at AVEK were neither altruists nor environmentalists.

What they wanted was a contract.

That part was business as usual, like Teenie said.

But what about the other part?

Poisoned water going from PMC's wells into the pipes leading to the kitchen sinks of every house in Christietown?

Dov and Avi too cheap to change providers?

I kept coming back to the same question: did Liz somehow know about this? And what about Silvana? Did knowing get them killed?

Water, water everywhere, and not a drop to drink.

Now I knew it, too.

I went back into the house and tried Lou again. Still busy. This was getting ridiculous. I had to talk to him. Maybe I could just go over there. It was late, but he obviously wasn't asleep. I wouldn't keep him long. I just needed to clear up a few things. Gambino and Alexander wouldn't even know I'd been gone.

Five minutes later, I was putting the key in the ignition. I even found an old bottle of Diet Coke rolling around on the floor. When you are addicted to caffeine, it's best not to be picky.

On the way I realized what night it was.

Thursday.

If Liz were still alive, Gambino and I would've had our last dance lesson tonight.

The foxtrot.

Lou would've been patient as he took us through the intricate steps.

Liz would've been popping allergy pills and trying to keep a straight face. She turned off the music at ten sharp. Lou never noticed the time. If she hadn't been minding the store, he would've danced all night.

I took a shortcut via San Vicente, swinging a left just past the traffic island with the sculpture of a miner panning for gold.

Midnight in Carthay Circle.

It was quiet.

Everybody had punched in alarm codes, turned on porch lights, gone to bed. This was a nice neighborhood. No loud music, no trailers in the driveways, no stray beer cans in the bushes.

But as I turned onto Commodore Sloat, I saw something that surprised me.

A white VW convertible with a license plate reading BRDGRL.

I'd seen this car before.

Right here, the other day.

BRDGRL. Bird girl.

This was Wren Abbott's car.

Parked right in front of the home of her recently bereaved employer, Lou Berman.

My first thought was, It's a little late for a social call.

My second thought was, Wren is so devoted. The other day she'd been carrying groceries and a box from the bakery for the man in mourning. So sweet.

But Wren is a redhead. Redheads aren't sweet. They're fiery, impassioned. And it's awfully dark in there. Why aren't the lights on?

Ridiculous. Lou isn't the cheating kind. He loved his wife.

I put my car in Park and started toward the house. Then I did an abrupt about-face. All of a sudden I felt uneasy, like I'd be interrupting something if I just walked up there and rang the bell. Something personal.

Maybe I should just bang on the door and demand an explanation. Maybe he'd deny the whole thing while she hid, trembling, behind the shower curtain. Maybe the two of them were just sitting in the living room talking.

In the dark? Who converses in the dark?

In eighteenth-century parlance, "conversation" is something two people conduct horizontally.

Just then I remembered something from *Chinatown*, an old PI trick.

Jake Gittes is tailing Hollis Mulwray, the water engineer. Hollis is parked by the ocean, watching the water. It's been hours. Jake is impatient, but he wants to know how obsessed Hollis is, so he places a cheap pocket watch under one of the tires of his car, the idea being that when Hollis finally drives away, the watch will break and when Jake comes to pick it up the next morning, he'll know exactly how long Hollis sat there.

It was a good plan. Not to mention an excuse to destroy my Eiffel Tower Swatch watch.

I glanced at the house again. Still no lights. No signs of movement. Hurrying now, I unbuckled the watch from around my wrist and bent down in front of Wren's car.

A blue Mazda cruised by. "You got a flat?" the guy called out.

A Good Samaritan. Just what I needed.

"No," I said, smiling. "Just dropped my keys. Thanks."

He moved on.

I fussed over the placement of the watch for a couple of minutes, finally shoving it as far under the right-front wheel as I could manage. Then I made my getaway.

In the morning I'd find out exactly how devoted Wren was.

CHAPTER 29

TWO A.M.

Two forty-five.

Three twelve.

The drummer two doors down liked to practice in the middle of the night. He never woke me up if I was sleeping. Since I was awake, I listened to him play. He was definitely improving.

An ambulance drove by, sirens blaring.

A car backfired.

Two alley cats went at it for a while. Mimi stood by the glass doors in the bedroom, ears pricked. She was jealous.

Love hurts.

I closed my eyes, but I kept seeing Liz and Lou and Wren; Agatha, Archie, and Nancy; me and Gambino; me and Richard; Richard and Jackie.

I curled myself into Gambino's chest. He stirred, then wrapped an arm around me. He was protective even in his sleep.

After that, I think I fell asleep for a while.

At five o'clock, I heard the *thwack* of the newspaper. I got up, showered, fed the pets, and made breakfast, hoping the dizzy, nauseous feeling would soon dissipate. Two cups of coffee and one English muffin later, my head had started to clear. I checked the front page. At least there were no more murders at Christietown.

At five forty-five, Alexander came trotting out in his Power Rangers underwear. I made him a muffin and got him washed and dressed. It was Friday, a school day. I had to get him home. I checked on Gambino, who was still asleep, and Alexander and I got into the car.

Half an hour later, Annie was waiting for us at the front door.

"Hi, big guy," she said. "Thanks, Mom. You want to have a cup of kombucha mushroom tea before you go?" My thoughts on kombucha mushroom tea are unprintable.

"Can't," I said, already back in my car. "Busy day," I called out of the open window. "Love you."

I was back in town by seven.

In front of Lou's ten minutes later.

Wren's car was gone.

I sighed. Of course it was. I must've been out of my mind to think there was anything going on between the two of them. I circled the block once and parked on the side street, just in case Lou stumbled out to get his paper or something. I didn't want him to see me. I'd just pick up my Swatch watch, see what time Wren had left, and be on my way.

The watch was lying there, not far from the curb, in the exact spot where I'd left it. I bent down and checked the time. Seven twelve. Seven twelve? That's what time it was *now*. The thing was indestructible. Not even a scratch. Oh, well. It didn't really matter. Wren had gone home.

Or so I thought.

As I turned the corner, I heard a car door slam. I turned instinctively. And that was when I realized it wasn't just Wren's car that was gone. It was *all* the cars that had been parked on that side of the street. I looked up at the sign posted at the corner: NO PARKING, STREET CLEANING, FRIDAY, 8AM–10AM.

Today was Friday.

Everybody had moved their cars late last night or early this morning to avoid being ticketed.

And there they were, on the other side of the street: Hondas, SAABs, Audis.

And a white VW convertible with a license plate reading BRDGRL.

Lou Berman and Wren Abbott.

They were sleeping together.

Oh, Liz.

Love hurts.

CHAPTER 30

It is a terrible mistake to marry a stranger.

Agatha should have known better. She'd been twenty-four years old and had given serious consideration to three different men before Archie came along on his borrowed motorbike.

All three had been properly educated, with private incomes. All three were deeply in love.

But Bolton Fletcher was too old.

And Wildred Pire, obsessed with spiritualism.

And Reggie Lucy, ever chivalrous, had gone off to India with his regiment, giving her the opportunity to change her mind.

It was a woman's prerogative and, like a fool, she'd exercised it.

Agatha didn't know Archie. She couldn't predict how he would react to a word, a phrase, a look. He was scary, unknown, on a tear through her safe, sane world, and still she found herself drawn to him, like metal to a magnet.

Agatha's mother despaired of her daughter's romantic sensibility. She refused to allow her to rush into the marriage, insisting upon a curative regime of French realist novels, in which the pas-

sionate heroines are hurled inexorably into disaster, degradation, and death. But the cure did not take.

Agatha and Archie married on Christmas Eve.

Scary, unknown: Agatha got what she'd bargained for, and more.

"This thing has happened," Archie said one dark December day. "I must be with Nancy. One way or another I will be."

Fine, then. So be it.

Agatha resumed her handiwork. She'd always been good with scissors. Today she was cutting stories out of the newspapers and pasting them in an album.

One day, they'd be yellowed with age, curled in the places where the paste wouldn't hold. She'd study them and remember. Now their edges were sharp enough to draw blood.

Archie had said in his own defense that everybody can't be happy, that somebody has got to be unhappy.

But why, Agatha asked herself that evening as she slipped on the silver dress and slippers she'd purchased in town, should I be unhappy and not you?

CHAPTER 31

The bell rang while I was doing the breakfast dishes. I opened the door with my pink rubber gloves.

It was Mariposa and McAllister, the former wearing his usual smirk, the latter looking like he was about to be sick.

This wasn't going to be good news.

I had them sit down on the couch while I perched on a wrought-iron chair opposite. I peeled off the gloves and deposited them on the coffee table. The cool air chilled my hands.

"Strange weather," I said, crossing then uncrossing my legs. "Don't you think?"

"Perfectly seasonal," said Mariposa. "Not a native, are you?"

"No, I'm not. Look," I said, "I think we got off on the wrong foot somehow. We're not enemies—at least I hope we're not. Are we?"

"I don't have any enemies." Spoken like a choirboy.

"Why are you here then? Is it Ian?" I asked. "Did you find him? Is he okay?"

"Ian's not the problem," said McAllister, shaking his blond curls.

"Then who is?" Dov Pick. They'd figured it out at last.

McAllister said, "Wren Abbott was arrested earlier today for the murder of Liz Berman."

As I sagged backward, a wrought-iron curlicue dug into my spine. I let out an involuntary gasp.

"Are you really that surprised, Ms. Caruso?" Mariposa asked.

"Sorry. The chair." I sat up straight.

"So you're *not* surprised."

"Well, actually, I am." Everybody knows if it's not the husband, it's the desperately jealous and resentful other woman. Except when it's not.

Mariposa said, "Don't play the fool with us, Ms. Caruso."

"I would never do that."

He glowered at me. "You know exactly why we'd have reason to accuse Wren Abbott of murder."

"That isn't—"

Mariposa interrupted, "What were you doing outside Lou Berman's apartment in the middle of the night tampering with Ms. Abbott's car?"

Shit.

"Yeah, I'm waiting. This ought to be good. Maybe you were getting ready to whack her, so you could be next in line for Loverboy."

I blinked. "You've got to be kidding me."

"Mariposa, come on. Why don't you slow down? Cute dog," McAllister said, bending down to pet Buster. Then he turned his guileless blue eyes on me. "I'm sure there's a perfectly good explanation, right, Ms. Caruso?"

"Yes, there is," I said, standing up. "I was doing the exact same thing you were."

"Oh," said Mariposa. "Silly me. I see. And you were trained in surveillance techniques—where, exactly?"

"My father was a cop," I said. "Both of my brothers are cops. I'm getting married to a cop. I know more than you think."

"You're obviously a smart person, Ms. Caruso," said McAllister. "Maybe you want to tell us how a smart person like yourself can—"

"Act so fucking stupid!"

"Put yourself in grave personal danger," McAllister corrected his partner. "We don't want to see you get hurt."

Sure you don't. Their good cop/bad cop routine was wearing thin. McAllister was as big a phony as Mariposa was. And they were missing the point entirely.

"I want to show you something," I said. "Excuse me for a minute."

"Don't flee the jurisdiction," Mariposa said.

I ran out to my office. The envelope from AVEK was sitting on my desk. I grabbed it and raced back into the living room, where Mariposa was unabashedly leafing through my mail.

"Find anything good in there, Detective?" I asked.

"To be honest, I was hoping for the Victoria's Secret catalog." He put the stack of mail back on the coffee table without a word of apology.

"Just listen to me for a second. There's something you need to know." I stood in the middle of the room, smoothed down my apron, then announced, "Ian and Dov have been pumping water tainted with ammonium perchlorate into all the houses in Christietown." Breathless, I waited for their reaction.

"Now *who* are you supposed to be exactly," Mariposa asked, "Erin Brockovich?"

"No," I said, exasperated. What was wrong with these people? "There's a lot more at stake here than you seem to understand. If word of this got out, Dov and all the rest of them would go under. It's the perfect motive for murder."

Mariposa shook his head slowly. "Hardly."

"Here," I said, shoving the papers at him. "Why don't you just look at what I'm showing you? Take them. Please!" I appealed to McAllister. "I don't want them in my house."

"No thanks," said McAllister, putting up his hands. Finally, he'd abandoned the act.

"Us cops, we're putting our money on Wren Abbott," said Mariposa. "Motive, means, and opportunity. You ever hear those three words?"

"Wren worked with Liz," McAllister said. "She could've slipped foxglove into her allergy medicine anytime."

"So could about a million people," I protested.

"Even you, I suppose," said Mariposa. "Is there something you want to confess to? Guilty conscience you want to clear?"

"Of course not." I picked up the rubber gloves and started fiddling nervously with them.

"There's more," said McAllister.

"Yes?"

"We found some shredded-up foxglove plants in Wren's garbage."

Not good. I put the gloves down. "So what? Anyone could have put them there."

"We're going to find the place she bought them soon."

Maybe she was going to plant them in her garden. Maybe she liked the way they looked when they were in full bloom. Maybe it turned out she didn't have a green thumb and she got rid of them.

"We talked to your gardener," McAllister said, thumbing through his notepad. "Javier Gomez. Wren gave Javier a call last week."

"To talk about the murder-mystery play, I'm sure." I'd given everyone in the cast a complete list of phone numbers so they could get together to rehearse if they'd wanted to. As far as I knew, nobody had, with the exception of Javier and Lael, and that was another story.

"Wrong again. Wren didn't talk to Javier about the play. She talked to him about foxglove. She had some very specific questions about its toxicity."

I paused, floored for the first time that morning. "There must be some explanation. What does Wren have to say in her defense?"

"That's the strange thing," said McAllister.

"She's saying nothing," said Mariposa. "Absolutely nothing."

I remembered Wren bringing Lou that package from the bakery, tied up with a pretty ribbon. I remembered her eyes.

Oh, god.

Of course Wren was saying nothing.

And I knew exactly why.

The blinds were drawn at Le Palais de Danse, but I pushed open the front door.

"Hello?" I called out. "Where are you, Lou?"

The trash hadn't been emptied. The mirrors were streaked with grime. The lightbulbs were sputtering. Lou was the artist and Liz ran the show, but Liz was gone.

And now Wren was gone, too.

Lou shambled forward from the back room. His eyes were black holes. He was unshaven. He smelled like sweat.

"Guess you heard the news," he said, taking a seat at Liz's desk. "Or maybe you're here to get a refund on last night's lesson. Sorry about that. I hope you didn't have your heart set on the foxtrot. It's pretty tricky, even if you're an expert." He made a show of sorting the papers on the desk into piles, but he wasn't looking at them. He was staring into space.

"You must be feeling very sorry for yourself," I said. "Both of them abandoned you. Left you all alone."

He slumped deeper into the chair, like he wanted to disappear.

"Get up," I said.

"I don't want to get up," he said. "I want a cigarette." He reached into his pocket, pulled out a pack of Marlboros, and lit one. I watched him take the smoke in, lean his head back, blow the smoke out. "Today's not a great day for a visit, Cece. I'm really tired."

"I don't care how tired you are," I said. "I want you to get up and look me in the eye while I tell you what a coward you are."

"No." He shifted his weight in the chair. "I know why I feel so bad. I haven't been dancing. Every bone in my body hurts."

His self-pity enraged me. "I can't believe you! How can you sit there complaining while Wren is locked up in some miserable holding cell somewhere because she doesn't want *you* to get hurt? Do you have any idea how much she cares for you?"

"I care for her, too." He stubbed out his cigarette in a dirty ashtray.

"Then how can it not matter to you that she's not saying a word in her own defense?"

"It does matter." He blinked his bloodshot eyes. "I don't get it."

"Don't you see?" I was shaking my head. "She doesn't want to implicate you—her lover, the husband of the dead woman, the most likely suspect. She's protecting you at her own expense."

He turned his head away.

"Listen to me, Lou." I stopped talking until I had his full attention, then I spoke slowly and deliberately. "You have to pull yourself together. And then go down there. And then admit to them that you're sleeping with Wren, but that doesn't mean she killed your wife!" I started to lose it at the end.

He was silent.

"Unless—" I stopped short, took a deep breath. "Unless you think she did kill Liz."

"Of course she didn't kill Liz," he said, lighting another cigarette. "She's a good kid."

Jesus. "You betrayed your wife for a good kid?"

"Look, what do you want from me? I care about Wren, I truly do. But it was Liz I loved. It's Liz I miss. It's always been Liz. Look at this." He yanked open the drawers of his wife's desk. They were stuffed with Agatha Christie paperbacks: *A Murder Is Announced. The Moving Finger. A Caribbean Mystery. A Pocket Full of Rye. Nemesis.* "Even this little play you wrote. Liz researched her role like her life depended on it. I swear, she read every single word Agatha Christie ever wrote about Miss Marple. She didn't want anything to get by her. She didn't do things halfway." His voice started to crack. "I don't know what I did to deserve her."

"If you loved her so much," I asked, "then why did you cheat on her?"

He raked his fingers through his hair. "It's complicated."

"Meaning?"

"Look, Cece. I've talked to the police. I've told them Wren and I have been having an affair. They know all about it. And Wren knows I told them. I even offered to put up my house for the bail money, for a lawyer, for whatever she needs, but Wren won't have it. They're going to stick her with some lousy public defender. I don't know what else I'm supposed to do."

I pulled up a folding chair and sat down on the other side of the desk. "Let me ask you something, Lou. About Liz. I know she went out to Christietown on a couple of different occasions, to work on her Miss Marple character."

"That's right."

"Did she ever mention anything strange she encountered while she was out there?"

"What do you mean, strange?"

"I don't know exactly. Suspicious, maybe. Something she saw or overheard?"

"She never mentioned anything."

"Anything about a key?"

"No."

"Anything about meeting anybody there?"

"You mean Ian, somebody like that?"

"Yeah," I said, trying not to get excited, "Ian or somebody like that."

"She might've met Ian."

"Are you sure?"

"No, I'm not sure. And I really don't know what you're getting at. She never said much of anything about her visits. Just that she had to lay the groundwork. That was it. End of story."

Great. He was no help at all.

"You should move your car, Cece," he said, looking up at the clock. "The valets show up to take care of the lunch crowd around now. They'll have you towed. I'm telling you, they're ruthless."

They, and who else?

CHAPTER 32

Unfortunately for Wren, she got arrested on a Friday. According to Gambino and his cop friends, the weekend judges have a reputation for being hard-nosed. And who could blame them? In any case, there were no visits allowed before the preliminary hearing, which wasn't scheduled until late Sunday. Wren was on her own until then.

In the meantime, I had to find Ian.

The problem was, I didn't have his home address and the only number I had for him was his cell phone, and unfortunately, the mailbox was full. Guess I wasn't the only one trying to locate him. I tried information, but he wasn't listed. I even called Lois and Marlene, thinking maybe he'd given them a different number, but all that got me was yet another recitation of the story of Marlene's near-affair with Omar Sharif. I thought somebody at Christietown might be able to help, but a machine answered and I hung up before the beep. I was tired of leaving messages.

Things were looking bleak.

Until I remembered the "While You Were Out" slips I'd stolen from Ian's trash can.

Sometimes, crime does pay.

My first stop was Showtime Cleaners on Doheny and Santa Monica. I parked in the Petco lot, which was for customers only. It said so in big red letters. I was definitely a customer. I'd spent enough money on chew toys and fancy kibble to last three lifetimes.

"Sorry. Mr. Ian picked up his shirts two days ago," said the woman behind the counter. She pressed an unseen button and a conveyor belt sprang to life, shuttling plastic-swathed garments across the room.

"Yes, I realize that," I said, shouting over the din. "But I think there may be one left. The Tommy Bahama one? It's very cheerful."

She pushed the button again and the conveyor belt shuddered to a stop.

"He likes to wear it on the weekends," I continued. "Maybe you could double-check?" I gave her a hopeful smile.

"No, miss," she said, shaking her head. "I gave that shirt to Mr. Ian myself. It had many stubborn stains. The whole team worked hard to remove them. I am sorry if it is personal, but maybe you can remind him about Mitchum? We recommend it to all our customers. It's an excellent product. We even sell it here. We also sell lint brushes," she said, looking at my sweater. She removed a hot pink dress from the conveyor belt and hung it on the rack near the register. "Customer coming in later," she explained. "Big party tonight."

I acknowledged the ruffles, then invented a missing comforter. "Mr. Ian dropped it off quite some time ago," I said. "I think it must be lost in the system. Can you check back there? It's been getting kind of nippy in the evenings."

"Oh. You are the wife?" she asked.

"Um." I was smiling less certainly now.

"Hold on a minute," she said, heading into the back.

Unfortunately, the moment the woman was out of sight, a tall man in a dark suit came in carrying a pile of pastel-colored button-downs. He looked like a law-and-order type. Foiled again. With a goody-goody like him standing there, I could hardly leap behind the counter, punch Ian's name into the computer, and find his home address.

The woman drifted back on an odoriferous cloud of chemical solvents.

"Any luck?" I asked, already halfway out the door.

Suddenly, she was handing me something big and unwieldy and covered with little blue flowers. "You were right. Smart lady, Mrs. Ian. This comforter has been sitting here for weeks. I didn't know whose it was. No tag. Sometimes we make small errors like that. Sorry, Mrs. Ian."

She presented me with a bill for $45.00.

I had no choice.

While I was at it, I bought a lint brush.

My luck at the gym was no better. They guarded their computer like it was Fort Knox. Maybe they worried about stalkers. The front-desk guy said he hadn't seen Ian in days. He was willing to extend the renewal offer for another week, but that was as far as he could push it. A flame-haired beauty engrossed in a fitness magazine lifted her head up long enough to inform me that her power step class was being moved from Tuesdays and Thursdays at eight A.M. to Mondays and Wednesdays at seven fifteen. She was Gina? Ian was one of her biggest fans? I said he talked about her constantly, and promised to pass on the information.

My last chance was the manuscripts-and-collectibles store on Sunset Boulevard. I knew that if Ian had legs to walk on, he'd stop by to get that Agatha Christie memorabilia. However much it cost him, it would be worth it. A huckster like him could practice copying the Great One's signature and forge some collectibles of his own—for the walls of the Blue Boar Pub, of course.

The tiny storefront was located on the south side of the street. I drove past in slow motion, then turned the corner and cruised down the alley at the rear. The cigar store and coffee shop spaces on either side were full. There was one space behind the manuscripts store, and it was taken by an old black Lincoln with a bumper sticker reading SURFERS DO IT BETTER. Ian would have to park in front. I circled back around to Sunset, looking for a metered spot. No luck there. It was ten to two now. Time to stop pussyfooting around. I had to get into position. I pulled into the Tower Records lot across the street. It had a perfect view of the front door. Now all I had to do was wait for the rosy-cheeked man in the guayabera.

Slowest twenty minutes of my life.

I found an emery board in the glove compartment and did some repair work.

I perused the plastic surgery ads in a stray piece of the *L.A. Weekly* that had been shoved between the seats.

I organized my wallet.

Then I saw Ian pull his car—a green Jag—into the yellow loading zone in front of the store.

At last. I grabbed my purse and whipped open the door,

then stopped short. What was I going to say when I finally confronted him? I had no idea. Was he laying low because he was afraid? Or because he had something to hide? I tended to think it was the latter, but couldn't be sure. Why had Teenie described him as a maniac? Was Lou right in saying Ian and Liz had met at Christietown? I pulled the door closed. Perhaps the most prudent course of action would be to stall until I'd made up my mind. I'd wait until he came back out, then I'd follow him for a while, see where he went. Maybe that would tell me something I needed to know.

Five minutes later, Ian and the bearded proprietor appeared in the doorway and exchanged good-byes. Then Ian emerged into the sunlight, a manila envelope under his arm and a smile on his face, the latter of which didn't vanish even as he plucked a parking ticket from his windshield. Ian got into his car and pulled out into traffic, heading east. Without thinking twice, I swung an illegal left out of the Tower Records parking lot and fell into place behind him.

It was kind of exciting not knowing where we were going.

Mid-Wilshire? Lots of interesting architecture.

Koreatown? I'm a fan of Korean barbecue.

Union Station? The Brits loved their trains.

We turned right at Fairfax and drove past Canter's, where fluffy matzo balls reign; past Farmer's Market, which I tried never to visit after eleven A.M. because you can't get parking; past Johnnie's, the defunct space-age diner; past the beautiful old May Company building with its faded gold ziggurat; through Little Ethiopia, where you get to eat dinner with your hands; past the graffiti-scrawled exterior of Mo' Better Meaty Meat Burger. Block after block of cinder-block apartments followed. Just after the power plant, we merged onto the 10 heading west. The image of Ian in a Speedo flashed suddenly before my eyes. Given the chill in the air, however, ocean frolicking seemed unlikely, thank god.

Being on the freeway was a good thing. Saved me the trouble of worrying about losing him at a light. He was a timid driver, which also helped. No zig-zagging. He'd picked that middle lane and was loyal to it. After National, we approached the on-ramp to the 405, which leads you straight to LAX, but Ian sped on by. He was a man on a mission. At Cloverfield, he moved into the far-right lane. At Lincoln, he exited. I was still only one car length behind him.

WELCOME TO SANTA MONICA read the colorful sign.

I opened the window to breathe in the good sea air, then put it up because it was actually cold. I followed close behind as Ian turned right at the penguin perched on the roof of the offices of Dr. Beauchamp Credit Dentist, and right again at the ten-gallon hat parked in front of Arby's roast beef.

We were on Santa Monica Boulevard now. Up ahead, I could see the palm trees silhouetted against the grayish sky. Below was the blue haze of the Pacific Ocean. We blew past Fifth Street, then Fourth. Were we going to the Third Street Promenade? Maybe there was a Tommy Bahama store there.

At Second Street, just a couple blocks north of the beach, he took a right into an overpriced parking lot and got out of the car, a grubby backpack slung over one shoulder. I pulled in just behind him, but parked on the opposite end of the lot. He couldn't see me, but I could see him. He jaywalked across Santa Monica Boulevard and came to a halt directly in front of Ye Olde King's Head Tavern.

Were we going to get rat-arsed? Watch the telly? Have a natter?

Unfortunately, we'd have to wait until Sunday evening for the big darts tournament.

No, wait, he was walking past the pub, past the Union Jack flying in the breeze. He wasn't headed for the Pawnshop of the Stars. It was boarded up. He disappeared for a moment behind the scaffolding in front of the Mayfair Theatre, which was undergoing renovations. Shoot. He was crossing the street now, over to my side. I ducked behind a bronze fountain so he wouldn't see me if he turned around. Was he going to another pub? There were several in this area, along with half a dozen tearooms where you could munch on buttered crumpets and buy Queen Elizabeth II commemorative mugs.

No.

No crumpets.

I emerged from behind the fountain.

He was heading into 225 Santa Monica Boulevard.

The historic Clock Tower Building, the city of Santa Monica's first skyscraper.

Ian was going up to the penthouse to visit the offices of his friend and mine, Dov Pick.

Chapter 33

There were four art deco timepieces at the top of the building's stepped tower, each one frozen at the hour of twelve. They'd run continuously since the building was erected in 1929, but had been damaged in the Northridge quake several years back and had yet to be repaired. Maybe Dov couldn't find the right person. More likely he got a kick out of making time stand still.

I hovered outside the lobby, still unsure about what I wanted to say to Ian and not at all eager to take on his boss unprepared. But maybe I could catch Ian in the lobby before he went upstairs. I squared my shoulders. No more maybes. I *could* catch Ian. I was sure I could. Pretty sure. Hell, it was worth a try. Switching gears, I tore into the building just in time to see the elevator doors slam shut, and the needle above swing all the way around to the right.

Damn. Missed him.

Life lesson of the day: the early bird catches the worm.

I was just about to leave, dejected in general (about nailing

Ian and/or Dov for the murders of Liz and/or Silvana) and in particular (about the four-plus dollars I'd wasted on parking) when the *other* elevator chimed, signaling that its doors were about to open. Eschewing my usual calm, I took a flying leap and crash-landed behind the unmanned security desk.

"Like I give a damn!" yelled the person exiting the elevator into his phone. "You better have your story worked out by the time I get there. I'm on my way." As he stomped out of the building, I heard the faint but now-familiar echo of Hebrew curse words.

Mr. Personality himself.

I couldn't have timed it better, except for the crash-landing part. I pulled myself up to standing, checked my Bakelite bangles for damage, yanked my sweater back into place, and smoothed down my houndstooth skirt with the kick pleat. It was a miracle it hadn't split at the seams. It was fragile. Okay, and too tight. But you don't find vintage clothing in my size all that often.

I stepped into the elevator.

"Hold the door, please," said a guy wearing a tool belt. He pushed ten. "Nice day," he added, adjusting his hammers.

"Love this time of year," I said. "Lots of work being done in the building?"

"Oh yeah. Twelve is the only floor we've gotten done. We're working on the rest of 'em."

We stopped at ten, but the doors didn't budge. "Elevators are a little temperamental," he said, pumping the 10 button up and down. The door shuddered open. "Guess I gotta deal with that tomorrow," he said, groaning. "You have a nice day."

"You, too."

The penthouse was next. The doors opened onto a bright

and expansive space with huge windows and breathtaking views of the ocean. The far-right wall was painted the color of flesh and branded with the letters "SP." Avi Semel and Dov Pick. Looked like they were sadists as well as control freaks. Underneath stood a brushed-aluminum desk with a complicated-looking phone. There was no receptionist in sight.

I wandered over to the waiting area, and sat down on a woven black leather couch that cut into the back of my knees. Then I got up and walked over to the windows. The waves were crashing against the shore. People on Rollerblades were whizzing along the bike path. It was like watching a silent movie. I tore myself away, peering into one, then another, then another of the glass-walled cubicles lining either side of the cavernous space.

The place was a ghost town.

"Ian? Where are you?" I said out loud.

The phone started to ring. One, two, three times. Then whoever it was hung up. This was no way to run a business. Mr. Keshigian's secretary always answered on the first ring.

At the rear of the space was a large office enclosed on all sides by freestanding walls of glass. Nice metaphor. Nothing to hide, my foot. There was a glass door cut into one of the glass walls. I looked around again. Nobody was there to stop me, so I swung it open.

I wasn't snooping.

I was passing the time.

Inside was a glass desk with two black leather chairs, one on either side, and a bottle of Windex poised below it. On top of the desk were glass card holders, one containing Dov's business cards, the other Avi Semel's.

No phones. No computers. No fax machines.

These guys were Blackberry types.

No, there was nothing in the office—nothing you'd give a second look to, that is, except maybe that big old filing cabinet in the corner.

If it was locked, that would be the end of it. I'd leave.

It was unlocked.

As I glanced back toward the waiting area, which was still deserted, I remembered the corollary to the life lesson of the day: people who trespass in other people's glass houses get stones thrown at them. Then I forgot it.

The top drawer was heavy. Limited-liability corporation filings, workers' compensation claim forms, property tax receipts, insurance waivers, blah, blah, blah. I closed that drawer and opened the one below. I was getting ready to dive in when out of the corner of my eye I noticed a body in one of the cubicles.

A live one, with a Louise Brooks bob and a phone up to her ear.

I was about to go for the tried-and-true tactic of crouching down like a hunted animal but then, from out of nowhere, she looked up and starting waving and smiling at me. Who was this person? I didn't know this person. I waved and smiled back because being polite is always a good policy. Now it was her turn. She pointed to her overflowing trash can in disgust.

Ah.

I understood.

I was the cleaning woman.

I shrugged and went around to the other side of the desk to get the Windex. Tough luck, sister. Take a number. Everybody knows the boss gets preferential treatment. It's a long, hard road to the executive suite.

I whistled to myself as I spritzed Windex on Dov and Avi's desk. Then I waltzed around the room, whistling and spritz-ing, until I was back in front of the filing cabinet. I cast a glance over at Louise Brooks, who was back at her desk. Then I reopened the bottom drawer, and that was when I hit the jackpot.

These were the Christietown files.

Plus, a huge section on Dusk Ridge Ranch.

I pulled out a promotional folder. It had a gold DRR embossed on the cover, and inside, a sheaf of papers detail-ing the fabulous lifestyle you'd be able to have if you plunked down half a million plus to live at Dusk Ridge Ranch. Brand-new schools with state-of-the-art digital production studios for your little Spielbergs, custom-designed parks with horse trails and rock walls and amphitheaters, your own fire station.

DRR.

I looked up with sudden recognition.

Dr. R.

There was no Dr. R.

Oh, my god.

It was Dusk Ridge Ranch—DRR—that had failed to per-form.

This was all about Dusk Ridge Ranch.

Christietown had nothing to do with it.

Frantically, I looked for more.

There I stood, lost in the files, oblivious to where I was, when I heard a strange man's voice.

"I told Dov it was only a matter of time," he said.

CHAPTER 34

A vi Semel strode into the office like he owned the place. Which, of course, he did.

I was pretty sure he knew I wasn't the cleaning lady, but I picked up the bottle of Windex just in case.

"What exactly are you doing with that?" he asked.

Preparing to blind you. Or to use it as a projectile.

"Nothing," I said.

He trained his eyes on mine. His, being brown, were dominant. "So why don't you put the bottle down?"

I gripped it tighter. "I don't know."

He moved slowly, like a big-game hunter. But I was no Bengal tiger. More like a wildebeest. We are scary only in packs. "It's all right," he murmured, taking the bottle out of my hands.

A person would have reason to wonder why I let him do that. Maybe because of his lilting voice, so unlike Dov's bark. Maybe it was the eyes. Nervously, I glanced over at Louise Brooks's cubicle. *Now* she disappears. And I hadn't even had a chance to take out her trash.

Avi leaned against the desk. "You were looking for the key, weren't you?" Before I could respond he said, "Dov was devastated when you left."

Dov hadn't looked devastated.

"He's not very verbal about his emotions," Avi went on, "but he was in real pain, trust me."

"I'm sorry," I said, utterly baffled now.

"Yeah, well." He shook his head. "Look, this isn't fair. I know who you are, but you don't know me."

Oh, I know you better than you think. I know about the dry-cleaning business, the first wife, the nanny, the poisoned wells. I eyed his cell phone. I wanted to call Gambino. I wanted to tell him everything.

"Why don't we make it official?" He cleared his throat. "I'm Avi Semel and you're Valentina. Do you mind if I smoke?"

Valentina? I shook my head.

He leaned back against his desk and pulled a silver lighter from the pocket of his neatly pressed Levi's. He squinted as he flicked the lighter, then took a long drag of his cigarette. He had what in the old days they used to call an elegant throat. Mine was tight with fear.

"Don't look at me like that," Avi said with a laugh. "I'm telling you the truth. But I have to say, you've got rotten timing. You had to pick that day to mess with Dov's head, Christietown's grand opening." He laughed again. "Everything that could've gone wrong that day did. And when you threw the key to his house in his face, well, it cut like a knife. Now you want him back and he's not even here."

Valentina.

Valentina, who wants Dov back.

Valentina, who is not the cleaning lady.

Valentina, who had to be Dov's lady friend, the Gina

Lollabrigida look-alike, the one with the boobs out to—well, you get the idea. I looked down at my sweater in mute wonder, then came to my senses and folded my arms across my chest.

Now it becomes clear.

Valentina dumps Dov. As a parting gesture, she throws his house key in his face. He loses it somewhere, which is tough luck because it means that when she comes crawling back, he won't have it to give to her.

Dov sees me snooping around at Christietown. I stupidly mention a key. He can't even bear hearing the word. He assumes—erroneously—that Ian has blabbed to me about his broken heart and sent me on a search for the unmentionable key. That's why he's so angry.

Okay.

The key had nothing whatsoever to do with the murders of Liz and Silvana.

Fine.

But the papers I'd just found in the filing cabinet sure as hell did.

Mariposa and McAllister couldn't ignore me this time.

"You're absolutely right," I said to Avi, "I'm here because of the key. I made a mistake. I understand that now. I was too hasty. All I really want"—here I'm stifling a sob—"is my old life with Dov." But later. After I got out of here. I picked up my purse and moved toward the door.

"Dov will be so pleased to hear you say that. And look," Avi said, pointing toward the waiting area, "here he comes. You can tell him yourself."

My head whipped around. Oh, shit. And there was no back door.

We locked eyes, Dov and I, and his scowl went from medium to full burn.

He stormed into the office. "What the hell is she doing here?" he asked, throwing his cell phone onto the desk. It skipped across the glass like a stone on the water.

"Cool it, Dov," said Avi. "She's here about the key."

"The fucking key?"

"Show some respect," said Avi.

Dov struggled to stay calm. He turned to me and said between clenched teeth, "What did I tell you about that key? I told you never to mention it again. Maybe you didn't hear me."

"I heard you," I said.

Avi came around and shook Dov by the shoulders. "What is wrong with you, man? You get everything that you want and you're still not happy. You need help."

"I'm leaving," I said, daring to be bold. Valentina was bold.

"Well, if you don't want her anymore, I'm throwing my hat into the ring," said Avi, leering at me.

"I never wanted her," said Dov coldly.

"Could've fooled me."

I was standing in the doorway now. Louise Brooks had returned to her desk. That made her a witness.

"Good-bye," I said. "I have a hair appointment. Extensions, color, the works." Valentina had fabulous hair. I'd seen it. "I'm leaving now."

To my amazement, neither of them stopped me.

Legs shaking, I waited for the elevator and when the doors opened, I tumbled gratefully inside. It took me a few seconds to remember that I had to press a button if I wanted to go anywhere. I pushed Lobby. Nothing happened. I pumped it up and down, like the guy with the tool belt had. Still nothing. Good thing I didn't have claustrophobia. I loved being inside small, closed spaces with possible killers on the other side.

I pressed two.

Nothing.

Three.

Nada.

Four.

Four must have been the magic number because the elevator suddenly started to move, but too bad for me, didn't go very far before jerking to a stop. I waited for the doors to open like they were supposed to. I should have known better. I picked up the emergency phone, but all I heard on the other end was dead air. I pressed the O for operator. She was out to lunch. I pushed the big, red button that said STOP, because it was either that or scream. Then I screamed.

"Help! I'm stuck!"

Did I really want Dov and Avi coming to my aid?

"Help!"

This place was sorely understaffed.

"Help me, somebody! The elevator isn't moving!"

This was a nightmare. I looked up and saw a hatch I could squeeze myself through, like they do in the movies, although I was baffled as to what exactly a person does once she makes it into the elevator shaft. Crawl to safety? Where would safety be? What if the elevator decided to move with me perched on top of it? I'd be squished beyond recognition. I studied the seven-foot walls. How was I supposed to get up to the hatch in the first place? I hadn't thought to bring my suction boots. I pushed Lobby one more time, just for the hell of it, and by some miracle the doors decided to slide open, halfway between the tenth and eleventh floors. I hitched up my houndstooth skirt and with no small amount of effort climbed up to the eleventh floor, where I fell out, beyond relieved.

High heels or not, I was walking the rest of the way down.

The stairwell was on the far end of the space. I picked my way across the raw concrete floors, crawling with red and black wires like veins and arteries. This place had a long way to go before it was ready for tenants. The elevators were death traps. The floors were a mess, the walls were unfinished, the windows were holes in the wall with sheets of plastic hanging over them. You could hurt yourself on all the sharp metal lying around. And what was this, tucked into the corner? Looked like a homeless encampment. And no wonder. There was no security around here. Any Tom, Dick, or Cece could just sashay right in. I peered over the top of the cardboard wall and saw:

1. A hot plate.
2. A cracked teapot.
3. Some teabags.
4. A copy of *Death on the Nile*.
5. A grubby backpack.
6. A crumpled guayabera.

Jesus Christ.

It was Ian.

He was hiding.

And he'd read enough Agatha Christie novels to know that the best place to hide is in plain sight.

I walked down the stairs to my car, got the flowered comforter out of the trunk, walked back into the lobby, frowned at the elevator, and walked back up the ten flights. I folded the guayabera neatly, and laid the comforter down next to Ian's things.

I thought he might need it.

I imagined it got cold up here at night.

Chapter 35

The ride home was frustrating. Call after call led nowhere. Detectives Mariposa and McAllister were out in the field.

Gambino couldn't talk.

Mr. Keshigian was on another line, or so said his ample secretary, whom I had ample reason to distrust.

I decided to pay the latter a visit and see for myself. Of course Friday at five forty-five P.M. is not the best time to pop in unexpectedly on a service professional, but I needed answers.

Liz and Silvana were dead.

Ian was hiding, in fear for his life from the looks of it.

Wren was sitting in a jail cell for something she didn't do.

I was hoping the papers I'd taken from Dov's filing cabinet would put an end to this madness, but I needed some help in translating them.

Mr. Keshigian's office was located in Westwood Village, next door to a restaurant called Noodle Planet, popular with UCLA students and other budget-minded ramen enthusiasts.

I said thanks, but no thanks to the elevator and walked up the three flights. Mr. Keshigian's secretary had her back to the door and didn't hear me come in. She was too busy laughing uproariously into the phone. My mother laughed like that when she was watching *Dick Van Dyke* reruns, but only when they featured Rose Marie. I cleared my throat, and when that failed to get the woman's attention, coughed animatedly, at which point she spun around in her chair and hung up, adopting an imperious tone her fried hair belied.

"Do you have an appointment, Ms. Caruso?" Knowing full well I did not.

"As a matter of fact, yes," I said, smiling.

She buried her head in her date book and came up saying, "Do not."

"I made it last week," I said. "You must've forgotten to write it down. Check again." Now it was my turn to be imperious.

"Your name is nowhere in here," she snapped. "We can make an appointment now if you'd like, for another day. Right now we're getting ready to close up shop." She slammed the date book shut and pulled her gym bag out of a drawer.

"Actually," I said, "I'm pretty busy in the foreseeable future. I'm getting married, and my daughter's having a baby, and I've got a book due, and Mr. K. got me this job that wound up getting a couple of people killed, so I think now is a really good time. I won't be long, I promise. Just buzz him, would you?"

She put away the gym bag and buzzed him.

Mr. Keshigian came out to greet me with his usual pro forma obsequiousness. I could only imagine the bowing and scraping the six-figure earners got. We went into his office and took seats. He put his feet up on the desk and stretched his arms behind his head. I could see my reflection in his shiny Gucci loafers.

"What can I do you for, Cece?" he asked, looking at the clock.

"I'm sorry to keep you, but I need you to help me figure something out." Peering at his instep, I patted down my wayward hair.

"Like I told you the other day, I'm just a number cruncher."

False modesty becomes no one. "Give it your best shot, okay?"

He shrugged noncommittally.

"Remember, you told me that everybody's got problems?" I leaned forward. "Well, I think I found more than I bargained for."

He licked his finger, then dabbed at a tiny green leaf on his shoe. "The *Reader's Digest* version, if you don't mind."

Clutching the papers to my chest, I told him everything I knew, starting with AVEK's findings that the wells providing water to Christietown were tainted with sodium perchlorate and would probably have to be shut down. As if that weren't trouble enough, the L.A. County Waterworks District 35 had indicated that they would not be honoring their prior commitment to supply Dusk Ridge Ranch with water. This was a direct result of the former developer's "failure to perform." That's where I started to get lost.

"You're talking about WindCal?" asked Mr. K. "What, did they renege on a promise to build water-related infrastructure?"

Infrastructure. There was that word again.

I paged through the papers. "Yes," I said. "That's exactly it! Dov and Avi bought Dusk Ridge Ranch after WindCal went into foreclosure, and now I think they are supposed to assume responsibility for a water-banking system WindCal never established."

"Give me those." Mr. Keshigian reached over and grabbed the papers out of my hands. I held my breath as he punched numbers into his calculator. "Hmm," he said, wrinkling his brow. "Uh-huh. Uh-huh. Un-fucking-believable!"

"What?" I asked. "What is it?"

"According to my calculations, Dov Pick and Avi Semel are going to have to shell out five thousand seven hundred bucks per house to ensure a reliable future water supply. You're talking seven thousand houses, that makes—oh, man, that is *brutal*." He closed his eyes, as if in physical pain. "You're talking close to forty million dollars in unanticipated costs."

If news of this got out—the water supply being in jeopardy—nobody was going to buy a house in Dusk Ridge Ranch. If nobody bought a house, Dov and Avi were never going to get a chance to raise the extra money they needed, and the bank was going to foreclose. They'd go bankrupt. Liz must've found out. Silvana, too. Maybe Silvana was blackmailing Dov. Maybe that's why she got away with red curtains.

"It's over," I said. "The whole thing. The Icepick is screwed."

Mr. Keshigian laughed out loud.

"Why are you laughing?" I asked. Maybe he didn't like my mixed metaphor.

"Nice try, but no."

I looked at him blankly. "What do you mean no?"

"Sorry to disillusion you, Cece, but this is no big deal."

I grabbed my papers back. "What are you *talking* about, no big deal?"

He sighed. "First thing they're going to do is sue the Waterworks District to try and prevent them from turning off the tap. I'd be surprised if they haven't done that already. Dov and Avi will argue that they aren't responsible for WindCal's agreements. In the first place, those agreements assume facts that are no longer true. In the second place, Dusk Ridge Ranch has gone forward and become an asset to the community. Jobs, schools, all that means a lot to city officials. Especially in Antelope Valley, which is a mess. The county's not going to be so quick to let them go."

"But what about the water?"

"Lawsuits take years. Dusk Ridge Ranch is going to have water for a very long time. They'll take Christietown's water, contaminated or not, they'll hire somebody to say it's fine, dump some purifiers in it, whatever. Or they'll siphon it from the farmers. Those guys are the ones who are going to get screwed. The water in that area is unadjudicated. That means anyone with a well can get into the aquifer. Agriculture's going to suffer, but what do those guys care about that? Eventually it'll all be decided in court. In the meantime, they're going to line whatever pockets they need to so they can sell every house in DRR. Christietown, too. You mark my words, before this mess ever appears before a judge, they're going to be on to the next thing."

I struggled to my feet. "What are you saying?"

"They're not going to lose a dime."

"They're not going to lose a dime?" I repeated, incredulous.

"Trust me," he said. "Not a single dime."

"This is business as usual?" My voice was weak.

"Business as usual," said Mr. K.

I felt like a washcloth that had been wrung dry.

I had nothing instead of something.

Again.

I gathered up my papers, thanked Mr. Keshigian, said good-bye to his little watchdog, and went down Wilshire to La Cienega, and up La Cienega to Orlando.

I had green lights the whole way, but it still took forever to get there.

CHAPTER 36

Several hours later I heard the key turn in the lock.

"Honey, I'm home!" Gambino called out.

I could see him from the kitchen, throwing his keys onto the coffee table, taking off his jacket, removing his holster. He was tired. His broad shoulders looked like they were carrying the weight of the world. When you're feeling like that, you're supposed to turn to the people you love.

I did.

On the long drive back from Mr. Keshigian's, I made three phone calls.

One to Lael, who said sex always helped her when she was feeling down.

A second to Bridget, who insisted that shopping would do the trick.

A third to Annie, who told me to be thankful for the good things in my life.

Being the greedy sort, I was taking everyone's advice.

"Say it again," I called out.

"Honey, I'm home," Gambino said, laughing.

"Thank you." I opened the oven door and poked the baked potatoes with a fork. Too bad. They needed another half an hour, and I'd already dressed the salad.

Gambino came through the kitchen doorway and let out a whistle.

"This old thing? I found it at the bottom of the hamper." Designed by the eighties minimalist Zoran, who disapproved of long nails on women and feathers on anything but birds, the dress was black silk, cut in one piece, and held together by a single knot in the back. Once somebody undid it, all two ounces would slip to the floor. But that was for later.

"Tough day at work?" I asked.

"Yeah."

"Sounds like you need a martini." I removed the shaker from the refrigerator. I'd made them just the way he liked them: straight up, very dry, very cold, with a twist.

"What's the occasion?" he asked, loosening his tie.

I am thankful for the good things in my life. "TGIF."

"Lucky me," he said, pouring our cocktails. "You. This drink. I must've died and gone to heaven."

I looked at him over the edge of my glass. "You don't look dead to me. Anything but."

His pupils started to dilate. "You're a very bad girl."

"So I've been told."

At that point, we came to a mutual decision that later was now.

After a while, the smell of the potatoes reached us in the bedroom.

"I should get up and turn on the grill," I murmured.

"No you shouldn't," he said, pulling me closer.

"Contrary to the rumors, chivalry is not dead."

He gave me a kiss, then got up and pulled on a pair of jeans. "I'll take care of the rest. You take a shower. You have lipstick all over your face."

I leaned forward and stroked his cheek. "That makes two of us."

Tonight's dinner was a re-creation of Gambino's favorite meal from Taylor's, an old-time chophouse on a nondescript corner in Koreatown, known for its horseshoe-shaped booths and smart-mouthed waitresses. We were starting with a Molly salad, which is iceberg lettuce, tomatoes, and onions, chopped and left to drown in a sea of blue cheese dressing; followed by two steaks charred medium rare (sure to be a challenge on my old gas grill), accompanied by baked potatoes with sour cream and chives in little ruffled paper cups. Green vegetables were superfluous. As for dessert—well, we'd started with dessert.

The phone was ringing now. I'd decided to let the machine pick up, but when I heard Dot's voice I grabbed for the cordless on the nightstand.

"Don't hang up!" I said. "It's me, Cece."

"Hello, dear," said Dot. "How are you?"

"Good." I tucked the phone under my ear so I could pull on some socks. My feet were cold. "How are you?"

"Fine."

She wasn't her usual ebullient self, not that I was surprised.

"I'm going to see you at the shower tomorrow, right?" I asked, settling back against the headboard.

"That's why I'm calling." Dot's voice perked up a little. "I wanted to see if you needed anything. I'd be happy to come early, help you set up."

I told her I thought that everything was taken care of.

"What about party games? Who's in charge of party games?"

I bit my lip. "No one."

There was a long pause. Oh, what the hell.

"Would you like to be in charge of party games, Dot?"

"I'd love to," she said. "I really need the distraction. I've been a little down about Silvana."

"I know," I said. "Me, too."

"At least they've put her murderer behind bars."

"No, they haven't." I paused. "You don't mean Wren, do you?"

"To tell you the truth, I don't even want to say her name out loud. She horrifies me."

"Dot, Wren has nothing to do with *Silvana's* murder. She was arrested for murdering *Liz*."

She made a clucking sound. "I'm afraid you're mistaken. It's just a matter of time, dear, before they add the second murder charge."

This was insane. "You must be confused. Did you talk to McAllister and Mariposa about all this?" Richard had said they'd grilled Dot for hours, but I hadn't believed him.

"Are you referring to the cops?"

"Yes," I said, starting to lose my patience. "The cops."

"I most certainly did talk to them. We had a very extensive conversation. I believe I was quite helpful."

"I didn't realize you even knew Wren."

"Well, it wasn't me who knew Wren. It was Silvana."

"Silvana knew Wren?"

"Honey," called Gambino from the kitchen. "Where do we keep the steak knives?"

I walked toward the hallway. "We don't have any. We use paring knives. They're in the drawer. Sorry, Dot."

"Oh, I'm the one who's sorry. Here I am interrupting your dinner."

"No, it's fine. So what about Silvana and Wren?"

"I can't find any paring knives in the drawer," Gambino called out. "Which drawer?"

"Would you mind holding on for a minute?" I put Dot on hold and padded into the kitchen in my birthday suit plus socks. Wordlessly, I opened the cutlery drawer and took out the paring knives and handed them to Gambino, who said, "Oh, that drawer," then went outside to turn the steaks.

I ran back into the bedroom and took Dot off hold. Unfortunately, she'd had a sudden attack of conscience in the interim.

"I don't know if I'm supposed to be telling you all this," she said, fretting. "I don't want to get anyone in trouble. I should probably hang up right now."

"Did McAllister or Mariposa tell you not to talk to anyone about this?"

"Well, no—no, they didn't."

"Then I don't see how there could be a problem," I said. "No problem at all," I reiterated for good measure. "Wren's already in trouble anyway."

"I suppose you're right. Well, it's not much, when you come down to it. But the officers certainly took note." She cleared her throat. "The day before the play, Silvana was walking from the Blue Boar to her house. She had gotten some scones and clotted cream to go." Dot paused for dramatic emphasis.

"And?"

"And as she turned down her street, on her way home, thinking about the lovely snack she was about to consume, she saw Liz and Wren. In one of the gazebos."

Were they there a day early, rehearsing? They didn't have any scenes together. "What were they doing?"

"Fighting!" She paused again. "Screaming, yelling, carrying on something awful. And—"

"And?"

"Liz slapped Wren across the face."

"Oh, my god."

"That isn't the worst of it." Dot stopped and took a breath. "The worst of it is that after Liz hit her, Wren said—and I quote—'You'll be sorry you did that.'"

Silvana the gossip. She must've eaten it up. I'm surprised she didn't notify the local news. Catfight! Film at eleven! "But anyone could've said something like that," I said. "In the heat of the moment."

Dot sighed. "I really don't think so, Cece. Wren realized Silvana was standing there and had witnessed the entire ugly scene. I suppose she panicked. She was afraid that Silvana might come forward and implicate her in Liz Berman's murder. And now not one, but two people are dead."

Could it be true about Wren? I'd thought Dov or Ian or Avi or some combination thereof was responsible for Liz and Silvana, but, as it turned out, they didn't have anything to hide.

Business as usual is not a motive for murder.

At least everybody keeps telling me so.

I hung up the phone, peeled off my socks, and took my shower. Then I went into the dining room to eat my fabulous dinner, which I could barely even swallow.

Gambino tried his best.

He told me that Butch called him at work yesterday to let him know that the dwarf citrus trees were being delivered early next week and then the garden was done. And that his parents were coming from New Jersey and couldn't wait to meet me.

He put on a Peggy Lee CD and we tried dancing to "Fever," but we kept stepping all over each other.

He thought I might be upset about my Agatha Christie book, so he made me an Editor Sally voodoo doll out of his discarded potato skin and some toothpicks.

He tried to distract me by talking about his case. The dead guy had been found with one thousand dollars in his pocket. Where had he gotten it? And why hadn't the person who killed him kept it? Meanwhile, his wife said it was hers. And his girl-friend said it was hers. What did I think, Gambino wanted to know.

I told him I wanted to talk to Wren.

He stared at me for a minute.

Maybe two.

Then he carried his plate into the kitchen and said he'd arrange it for tomorrow.

And that he was tired and was going straight to sleep.

CHAPTER 37

E veryone thought he was sleeping.

Roger Ackroyd, a good man, the life and soul of the peaceful village of King's Abbott.

But when you are too good—unforgiving, perhaps, of the frailties of others—simply said, such goodness can lead to trouble.

Poor man, dead in his armchair in front of the roaring fire.

First, there is the parade of suspects.

Miss Russell, the housekeeper, disappointed in love.

Major Blunt, the big-game hunter. He'd given the murder weapon—a small dagger from Tunis—to Ackroyd as a gift.

The widowed sister-in-law and/or her daughter, Flora, who hadn't a penny of their own and wouldn't until the death of their parsimonious benefactor.

Ralph Paton, the adopted son, handsome, charming, and plagued by gambling debts.

The young secretary, too good to be true.

The parlor maid with a past.

The lurking butler.

Crime is so terribly revealing. Try and vary your methods as you will, your soul is nonetheless laid bare by your actions.

Indeed it was fascinating, burrowing into other people's minds, trying to unravel the mystery of what makes one breathing, thinking individual so different from another. What makes one bold and the other timid? Why do some people keep secrets and others not? Agatha could busy herself with such thoughts for many an hour. But Archie was little interested in speculation, disinclined to abstractions. So she channeled her curiosity into her characters.

She worked hard on the story of poor, dead Ackroyd. Her new publisher, Sir Godfrey Collins, was delighted with the public reception of the book, though it was indeed a pity he hadn't had the foresight to print more than five thousand copies, which promptly sold out. She'd expected the critics to find the ending audacious, but the News Chronicle *went further, complaining that the book was a "tasteless and unfortunate let-down by a writer we had grown to admire." She'd hardly anticipated that her little story would generate such an impassioned debate about what constitutes fair play in the mystery novel.*

Agatha was, of course, a member and strict adherent of the rules of the Detection Club, forbidding the use by an author of Divine Revelation, Acts of God, or Feminine Intuition as a means for the detection of crime. She placed every clue before the reader. She eschewed tricks. She espoused the principle of fair play.

While she was hard at work on Roger Ackroyd, Archie embarked upon his affair with Nancy, who was young, vivacious, and, like Archie, cared little about other people's secrets. She had too many of her own.

Agatha spent her days writing.

They spent their days planning a future that didn't include her. So who exactly wasn't playing fair?

CHAPTER 38

I t wasn't fair.

I tried everything—a bath, warm milk (with cocoa powder, which probably defeated the purpose), *Us Weekly*, skin care infomercials.

I couldn't sleep.

So I trudged out to my office, spread my manuscript out in front of me, and sat there for the rest of the night, hoping that by some miracle, inspiration would strike.

In the meantime, I sorted papers into meaningless piles, like Lou.

And reread the e-mail from my editor.

And chewed on my pencil.

And made a small detour to Wikipedia where I learned that pencils are composed of graphite, not lead, so no need to worry about loss of brain function.

There went that excuse.

Again:

It is the night of December 3, 1926. Agatha Christie leaves

her house on the border of Surrey and Berkshire and vanishes into thin air. Eleven days later, she is found. The official explanation is amnesia. But things don't add up.

Why does Agatha check into the Harrogate Hydropathic under the last name of her husband's mistress, Nancy Neele?

Is it a coincidence that the Harrogate is not two miles from where Archie and Nancy are having their romantic rendezvous?

Why does no one recognize Agatha, given that her picture is plastered all over the papers?

Why does she not recognize herself?

I suddenly remembered myself in the hall mirror, old and haggard in my Miss Marple costume.

Perhaps Agatha didn't recognize herself because the woman in the mirror was a stranger.

Agatha was striking as a girl, with long, wavy locks and almond-shaped eyes. Her youthful beauty gave her the confidence to draw others to her, even after that beauty faded. Still it pained her that the Agatha Christie the public came to know was, in her own words, "thirteen stone of solid flesh and what could only be described as a 'kind face.'"

I thought of the soft pink lights in Silvana's living room, the magic mirror in her bathroom.

Silvana wasn't going to let a stranger take over her life.

Maybe it was less vanity than self-preservation.

Maybe the rest of us are just masochists.

I mulled that one over for a while. Then I opened the top drawer of my desk and pulled out two photographs of Agatha I'd come across during my research.

Two photographs of two different Agathas.

I laid them side by side.

In the first, Agatha is wearing a knee-length skirt and mannish sweater. She is heavyset and humpbacked. She holds her tiny purse out in front of her, as if she isn't quite convinced it belongs to her. She seems embarrassed by the photographer's attention, a deer caught in headlights.

Interesting that this was the photograph Archie chose for the "Missing" poster circulated by the Berkshire Constabulary. It was plastered everywhere, seen by everyone. A small bit of revenge against the woman who refused to set him free.

The second photograph appeared on the front page of the *Daily Mirror* under the headline "Mrs. Christie's Dramatic Dash to Seclusion!" It was shot the morning Agatha and Archie departed the Harrogate Hydropathic, where Agatha had been taking the waters for the previous eleven days.

Here, Agatha stands straight and tall, the barest hint of a smile playing across her lips. She is wearing a fashionable two-piece outfit (the article states it was pink) with a wide collar; a striped cloche hat; a coat trimmed with fur around the collar, cuffs, and hem; a double strand of pearls around her neck; black gloves; champagne-colored stockings; and sleek black shoes. On the day she was found after the mysterious absence that riveted a nation—her future uncertain, her marriage in a shambles, a victim of amnesia—she looked beautiful, invincible, as if she'd gotten exactly what she'd wanted.

By the dawn's early light, it came to me.

The woman in the first picture—the stranger in the mirror—stole Agatha's life.

The woman in the second picture reclaimed it.

But what does it mean to get what you want?

What if you've made a mistake?

CHAPTER 39

A uniformed guard escorted Wren into the dingy conference room where I was waiting. Visits were strictly against the rules, but lucky for me, I had friends in high places.

She looked like a wayward troll doll, the standard-issue orange jumpsuit hanging on her, her red hair floating like a nimbus cloud.

"Ten minutes," said the guard, who went to stand by the door.

Wren walked over to the long table where I was seated, her pants legs trailing behind her, catching the bits of dust and strands of hair collecting on the cracked gray linoleum. She sat down. Someone had scratched "Life sucks" into the Formica. Tracing a finger over the words, she smiled. There was something green between her front teeth.

"Hi," I said. "How've you been?"

"Fine," she said brightly. "And you?"

"Fine. But I'm not in jail."

She looked up at me. "Are you sure you know where you are?"

"No," I said, taken aback.

She laughed. "Bet you don't even know who you are any-more."

"Excuse me?"

"Relax. I was just thinking about how good you were as Miss Marple."

Not half as good as she was as the kid who could speak to the dead. I wished I'd brought the smoke device. Maybe she could contact Liz and clear up a few things.

"Look, you don't have to worry about me," Wren said. "It's not so bad here. The TV in the common area has basic cable. A bunch of us watched a good movie last night. Woman kills the man who seduced her teenage daughter. Dinner was turkey, mashed potatoes, and Kool-Aid."

Her wide green eyes were opaque. She could've been happy. She could've been sad. Most people don't enjoy spending time in a jail cell, but Wren wasn't most people.

"You have something . . ." I pointed to my teeth.

She picked it out and rubbed her finger on her jumpsuit. "No mirrors. Somebody could hurt themselves on the sharp edges."

I couldn't think of anything to say. I'm sorry? For what? I hadn't done anything. The guilty party is supposed to be sorry. But who exactly was that?

Her voice broke into my thoughts. "You're here to plumb the depths of my soul, right? Find out what I'm capable of?"

That was cutting to the chase. "I suppose so."

"I'm capable of anything," she said.

I still couldn't read her eyes. "I doubt that's true."

"You see?" She shook her head. "You underestimate me, like everybody else. Take my job at the dance studio. I could've helped them. With the important stuff, I mean. But no. Not

Wren. Not the important stuff. Instead, they had me dealing
with garbage all day long." She started counting on her fingers.
"I'm the one who took the brochure down to the print shop
when we were running low on copies. I ordered the toilet paper
and the toilet-seat covers and the paper towels. I cleaned out
the refrigerator once a week. I fixed the CD player when it got
broken. I arranged for ads in the *Santa Monica Breeze.* I swept
the floor and wiped down the mirrors and took out the trash
and ordered the lunches. Anything that popped into her head
Liz wrote down for me on her 'From the Desk of Liz' pad.
Whatever it was, I did it."

At the mention of Liz, Wren's small voice got bigger.

"Did you know it costs the state a hundred and seven dollars a day to maintain each prisoner?" she asked. "That's a lot
of money. I didn't make a hundred and seven a day at the dance
studio. Not even close. No benefits. And my weeks were six
days long. Six days long!"

"You should've quit," I said.

"I couldn't. Things got complicated."

"How so?"

She looked away.

"I never underestimated you," I said. "Maybe they did, but
I didn't. I knew you were good. I could tell right away. But you
aren't onstage now. You can cut the act."

"What act?"

"Lou is worried about you, Wren."

Her cheeks blazed at the mention of his name. "I'm sorry
about that. He should be worrying about other things than me.
I told you I'm fine." She turned to the guard. "Time's almost
up, right?"

The guard looked at her watch and said, "Six minutes."

"He wanted to get you out of here," I continued, "but you wouldn't let him put up the bail money. You wouldn't let him hire a lawyer. He doesn't understand why, or why you won't say anything to anyone. Lou told them about your affair. That's all out in the open now. You don't have to stay quiet about it. The truth isn't going to hurt anyone."

"Since when are you Lou's spokesperson?" Wren asked, not looking at me. She was pinching the soft underside of her arm, studying the flesh, waiting for the red marks to come up. "Anyway, I really don't know what you're talking about."

I reached across the table and put my finger under her chin.

"No contact," said the guard, eagle-eyed.

"Sorry." I put my hand in my lap, chastened. "You know what I'm talking about. And the person who killed Liz is still out there. He's not going to be found if you keep on like this."

Now she was chewing the inside of her cheek like it was gum.

"That must be time," she said.

"Nope," said the guard. "Three to go."

"I understand," I said softly. "You think that as long as you're silent, the case will be closed. If you're responsible for Liz's death, the police don't have to look at Lou."

"No."

"You don't want them to look at Lou because you think he did it."

"No!" she said.

"Because you know *you* didn't do it, and if you didn't do it, then who did?"

"Time," said the guard.

Wren leapt to her feet. "Good-bye, Cece. Thanks for the visit. I enjoyed working with you. Maybe we can do it again sometime."

"Wait," I said.

"She can't," the guard said, propelling her toward the door.

"Please, Wren, stop!"

She hesitated for a moment and I thought I had her, but then she bowed her troll-doll head low and shuffled through the metal door, the guard following silently behind her.

Chapter 40

I got back from the detention center before ten, which was a good thing because Annie's baby shower was scheduled for three in the afternoon and I was completely unprepared. I called out his name, but Gambino was already gone. As I was leaving earlier this morning, I'd told him he'd have to make himself scarce for the day, expecting at least a token protest.

Instead, he'd jumped at the chance to get away from me.

I'd fix it tonight.

Right now, I had to think about Annie. This was her day. I wanted it to be perfect.

Two hours later, even my toilet was aglow. The floors were beautiful. The kitchen counters, a triumph. I'd arranged flowers from the garden in vases. I'd vacuumed up the pet hairs. I could see myself in my dining room table, proving that the makers of Lemon Pledge don't lie, number one; and number two, that I look a fright with my hair in a bandanna.

Lael and Bridget showed up just before noon—Lael lugging the cake, the finger sandwiches, and the tiny antique cradle she was passing down to Annie; Bridget lugging nothing, as is her wont. The two of them accompanied me down to the basement, where we found my silver punch bowl and cups, a gift from my ex-mother-in-law when she still had hope that I could rise above my lowly origins. We polished the silver. We made punch. Bridget went to the market for ice. We moved the big velvet chairs against the wall to make room for the folding chairs Lael had dragged over in her van. We put on classical music. We ate tuna and crackers. Buster hoovered up the crumbs.

Dot bustled in at around two, her arms full. I could make out a metal tube and a wicker sewing basket. Jackie followed close on her heels, a baby doll under each arm: one boy, one girl, remarkably lifelike.

"Hello, everyone!" Dot said. "I'm really looking forward to today!" Richard's accusation about my having put her in harm's way had cut close to the bone. I felt guilty just looking at her. She put her things down on the dining room table, took the dolls from Jackie, pulled a sack of Hershey's Kisses and several jars of baby food out of a brown paper bag from the market, and then marched into the kitchen.

We heard the sounds of cupboard doors opening, the lids of vacuum-packed jars popping, and spoons clinking against china. Then Dot reappeared and picked up the metal tube. She wrestled with the top until it came off, sliding out a large poster.

"Who's going to help me take down the mirror?" she asked, pointing to the only French antique I've ever owned, which was hanging in the entryway, opposite the front door.

Before I could utter a word of protest, Bridget—always happy to thwart me—volunteered to help.

"What are we putting up?" she asked, lowering the mirror to the floor.

"Careful!" I said, trying not to wince.

Dot unrolled the poster, which dwarfed her. It must have measured eight by eight feet. "Pin the Binky on the Baby!"

"Cute kid," said Lael. The baby was lying naked on a bear-skin rug. Its open mouth was larger than my head.

"It's me," exclaimed Jackie.

Perfect. The first thing the guests would see was a huge pic-ture of my ex-husband's bride-to-be with no clothes on.

I excused myself to take a shower and emerged fifteen min-utes later in a sea green shirtdress from the fifties with a twirly skirt and narrow, three-quarter-length sleeves. After careful reflection, I'd accessorized with an armful of pink and gold bangles from Little India and a pair of sky-high, peep-toed fuchsia suede pumps. June Cleaver meets Bollywood was the general idea.

Annie and her best friend from work, Maureen, had arrived in the meantime. Annie was the set decorator on a long-running *Star Trek* clone called *Testament*. She was much ad-mired for her way with sheet metal and spray paint. Maureen was the actress who played Halo, the alien wife of Commander Gow, who saved the world every episode in spite of his meddle-some in-laws. The aliens had zebra-striped hair, which Maureen maintained in real life.

"How are you?" I got each of them a cup of punch and led them to prime spots on the sofa.

"Good," said Maureen. "I'm trying to convince Annie to name the baby Halo. It works for either sex."

"Don't worry," Annie said to me. "I'm naming the baby something very normal. John or Susan."

I plumped up the pillows behind her. "Where are the boys today?"

"At the park shooting hoops," she said. "They probably should've asked Gambino to go. What's he up to?"

"Work," I lied. "Oh, there's the bell." Grateful for the escape, I went to open the door.

Ladies in hats arrived for the next half hour. The house was filled with the sounds of tinkling glasses and high-pitched laughter. Buster, the sole representative of his gender, hid under the bed along with Mimi, who didn't like a fuss unless she was making it. Bridget took the presents and put them on a folding table we'd set up in the corner of the living room. Poor thing had trouble surrendering a Tiffany's bag one of Annie's art school friends had brought. I gave her a supportive pat as I pried it from her fingers. Dot handed out white napkins folded into triangles, instructing the guests to put them in their purses until later. People ate and drank and oohed and aahed over Annie.

"How's Alexander doing?" Lael asked me as we restocked one of the trays with more watercress sandwiches and smoked salmon rounds from the refrigerator.

"He's looking forward to being a big brother," I said.

"That's lovely," she said, wiping her hands on her flowered sundress. She favored prints because they concealed stains. "I remember when I came home with Nina. Tommy told me to take her back to the store."

Dot came into the kitchen and pulled some yarn and a pair of scissors out of her sewing bag. "We're guesstimating the size of Mommy's tummy!"

"If anybody had tried to measure my tummy when I was pregnant," I muttered under my breath, "I'd have decked them."

"You're all bark and no bite," said Lael, who prided herself on being no bark and all bite.

Bridget, who'd come into the kitchen looking for more forks, added, "Doesn't take Hercule Puree to see that."

"Poirot," corrected Dot.

Bridget said, "Everybody's asking when we're opening presents."

"Now?" I asked.

"No, no," said Dot, pushing us out of the kitchen. "We're just about ready for Mommy Is a Juggler. Everybody!" she cried. "Gather round." She turned to Lael. "You have four children, is that right, dear?"

"Yes," said Lael, beaming.

"Four different fathers, too," added Bridget helpfully.

Ignoring her, Dot said, "Then you should have no trouble demonstrating how we play."

The game involved having the mommy in question perform various tasks simultaneously without losing her temper. "First, she will talk into a phone while holding a baby on the same arm."

"No problem," said Lael, taking the doll that Jackie handed her and tucking it in the crook of her arm. Then she propped the cell phone under her ear. "What's next?"

Dot instructed her to bend down and tie her shoe.

"I'm wearing Birkenstocks," said Lael. It was true. Bridget, shod in a pair of Andrea Pfister white suede court pumps with a die-cut instep, which she kept in their original box with the original tissue paper, cringed.

"Pretend," instructed Dot.

Lael bent down and pretended to tie her Birkenstock without dropping the phone or the baby. Good thing the doll didn't need to breathe.

Now Dot set a pitcher of water and a glass on the coffee table. "Have a drink," she said to Lael. By this time, all pretense of a demonstration was gone. The guests were on the edges of their seats. It was Lael versus Dot, winner take all.

Lael secured the doll against her rib cage, clamped the phone down between shoulder and ear, poured herself a glass of water with her left hand and drained it in a single gulp. She raised the glass overhead in triumph. Bridget, Annie, and I cheered.

"Jackie," said Dot, unruffled. "The tray, please."

Jackie hurried into the kitchen and came out with a bag of flour, two sticks of butter, some baking soda, brown sugar, white sugar, a measuring cup, a salt shaker, a bottle of vanilla, two eggs, three spoons, and a bag of chocolate chips arranged neatly on a green plastic tray.

"Everybody loves homemade baked goods," said Dot, an evil glint in her eye. She had no idea who she was dealing with.

Thirty minutes later, Dot was forced to admit that Lael's chocolate chip cookies—sweet, but not too sweet, crunchy but yielding—put all others to shame. Then it was present time.

Annie received little hats, little socks, little towels, a bouncy seat, a mobile, a silver spoon, and, from her friend Maureen, a zebra-striped blanket. Dot had knit the baby a sweater—in yellow, not pink, which surprised even Jackie. In addition to the antique crib, Lael had bought Annie a red negligee trimmed in black lace for a few months hence. Bridget gave Annie a gold locket that had belonged to her grandmother, which made Annie cry.

Then it was my turn. I handed my present to Annie. She ripped the paper off and when she saw what it was, looked at me in disbelief.

"Is this the one, Mom?"

"The same edition. I found it at a used bookstore. Here." I handed her a tissue and she blew her nose.

It was Hans Christian Andersen's *The Little Mermaid*. I used to read it to Annie every night. Her favorite page showed the little mermaid in the window of the sea king's castle, gazing out at the blue-green water, wondering about life up above. It was my favorite page, too. When Annie and I came out to California after the divorce, the book got lost. I'd searched and searched for another copy with the same iridescent pages, the same haunting picture of the mermaid dressed in a golden gown made of fish scales, having given up a life on earth for love.

She doesn't really die, Annie had always insisted. No, I'd reassured her. She becomes a daughter of the air. She lives forever in the sky.

I'd finally found a copy. On the flyleaf, the previous owner had written "Rose Baden, Age 8." Rose was the same age Annie was when she and I started our new lives.

This book was for Annie, and the new life inside her.

"Too bad we didn't have time to play Taste the Baby Food," said Dot, folding up her blindfolds after everyone had gone a few hours later.

"Next baby," I answered. "You were a great help, Dot. Thank you so much."

"What were those little white napkins for?" Annie asked Dot.

We were all outside now, helping Annie pack up her car.

"Oh, fiddlesticks!" said Dot. "I forgot about them. It's a game called Dirty Diaper. I put a chocolate kiss in one of the napkins. The person who finds it is the winner."

"Gross," said Jackie, slamming Annie's trunk shut. "Thank god you forgot."

I burst out laughing. "I couldn't agree more, Jackie."

"I'm so happy Jackie and I are part of your family now," Dot said to me.

Annie started tearing up.

"Hormones," she said. "Sorry."

"Group hug," said Jackie.

The strange thing was, I was happy they were part of our family, too.

Then Richard showed up and spoiled all the fun.

CHAPTER 41

One hour with Richard. That was all I needed. Jackie kindly agreed to let me steal him away (her phrase, not mine). I told him we could walk up the hill to the Sunset Strip in less than ten minutes, but he insisted on driving, then wasted at least double that amount of time backtracking when he turned up Sweetzer instead of Flores, which is where I'd told him to turn in the first place.

I'd picked the Sunset Tower Hotel for its old-Hollywood pedigree. Bugsy Siegel had an apartment there in the thirties so he could be close to the Clover Club and the Trocadero. Howard Hughes once occupied both penthouses and the entirety of the fourteenth floor. John Wayne kept a milk cow on his balcony, currently part of the spa. With its art deco zigzags and white plaster friezes of pagan goddesses, it exuded the kind of Tinseltown glamour I loved and Richard loathed. He preferred boat clubs, faculty clubs, country clubs, golf clubs—any kind of club, as long as it kept people out who didn't wear navy blue blazers and Princeton ties. I was hoping for at least one baby-faced music mogul wearing fat gold chains and drinking Cristal, but I'd settle for a half-clad starlet and her grandpa.

The maître d' led us past the fire to a corner table near the piano. Richard, in characteristic fashion, shoved in front of me to take the brown suede banquette, so I sat down in the chair opposite. Without so much as consulting me, he asked the waitress to bring us two glasses of white wine but I changed my order to a Scotch on the rocks, despite being of the opinion that Scotch on the rocks tastes like cleaning solvent. It was the principle of the thing.

We waited in silence for our drinks. The piano player picked out the sultry notes of "Rhapsody in Blue." I studied the walls, covered with framed black-and-white photographs of long-ago studio hopefuls with their bobs, their Brylcreem, their ready smiles.

The drinks finally came. Richard popped a handful of nuts into his mouth and said, chewing, "I'm glad you called this meeting, Cece. It's high time I established some ground rules."

All those beautiful young men and women. Would-be starlets, leading men, character actors. So many hard-luck stories. Such hope. They came to Hollywood from Tulsa, Des Moines, Phoenix, the hills of Appalachia to make something of their lives. I'd come here to do the same thing. Through the window, I could see the city spread out before me—the palm trees, the flat roofs, the stately old apartment buildings on Fountain, the chilly office towers along the Wilshire corridor. This was my city, my home. Richard was a visitor here. And visitors don't make the ground rules.

"This is a drink," I said, turning to him. "Not a meeting. A drink. If we can just sit at this nice table and have a drink, then maybe there's some hope for us. We haven't managed it before, but with the baby coming, it's the least we can do for Annie and Vincent, don't you think?"

Richard paused. "What is this sudden obsession with alcohol, Cece?"

Jesus. "It doesn't have to be an alcoholic drink. It could be juice. It could be water. It could be soda. Does it really make a difference?"

"I think it does. It makes all the difference in the world. It's a small detail, but small details coalesce into big pictures. It's the way scholars think."

"There isn't only one way to think, Richard."

He smirked condescendingly, which would've given me déjà vu if his condescending attitude hadn't been the defining feature of our marriage. Well, that and his infidelity.

"You seem to be stuck in a place of anger," he said. "It isn't healthy. Are there are some lingering resentments you want to get off your chest? Because if there are, I suppose this is as good a time as any."

"How can you say that to me?" I asked, trying not to lose my temper. "You cheated on me every day we were married!"

"Can we get back to the point of this meeting, please? Excuse me," he corrected himself. "This *drink*."

"Yes, let's do that." I bit my lip.

"The first thing is, Jackie wants the baby to call her Grandma."

"Fine."

"That's it?"

"As long as Annie and Vincent have no objections, it's fine with me. Next?"

He wrinkled his brow. "So the baby will have three grandmothers?"

"The more the merrier."

"You don't think it's confusing?"

Now I understood. He didn't want the baby to call Jackie Grandma. But he wanted me to be the bad guy.

"No," I said. "I don't think it's confusing."

"Does your fiancé want to be called Grandpa?"

"I don't know." I rooted around in the nut dish for a cashew. "*We* haven't discussed it."

"I see."

I waited, wondering if he could control himself.

"If you don't mind me saying so, Cece, your communication skills have always needed work. That kind of problem can sabotage a relationship."

Nope, he couldn't control himself.

"In any case," he said, "the second thing is, I want to pay for private-school education for the baby."

"You should take that up with Annie and Vincent."

"I have. They have a problem with it. I was hoping you could intervene."

"I most certainly will not."

"I should think you would be passionate on this subject, given the way your lack of a college education has hindered you."

I sighed deeply. "Having unprotected sex with a man who seduced me when I was seventeen and then put me to work supporting his education is what hindered me, but I've come out all right in spite of it."

He nodded. "I realize that's the way you see things. I see them quite differently. Why don't we agree to disagree?"

"Why don't we agree that you're an—?" I swallowed the word that came to mind. "No. I am not letting you do this to me."

Eyes wide, Richard said, "Do what?"

"You know what."

"I've had just about enough of you," he said, his face suddenly contorting with anger. "Why don't you get off your high horse? You know what you did."

I raised an eyebrow. "Excuse me?"

"I wasn't the only one to blame. You cheated on me, too."

The room went still.

The piano player stopped playing, the waiters stopped serving, the young couple at the table next to us froze midkiss.

My first impulse was to deny it. I wasn't that kind of person. Cheating went against everything I believed.

But instead I whispered, "I'm sorry."

I whispered it over and over again, until the words were nothing but hollow sounds in my ear.

It was so long ago.

And I was so good at forgetting. Forgetting was easier than remembering.

We were living in Chicago. Annie was in first grade. The marriage was in trouble. I was trying to work up the courage to leave. He was a colleague of Richard's, a young assistant professor. Luke. We'd known each other for years, but had never so much as flirted. He was quiet and serious. I was somebody's unhappy wife. One night, when Richard was away, it just happened. Afterward, I was filled with regret, but Luke saved me the trouble of ending it by suddenly backing off. A month later, he left to take a job in Michigan. I never heard from him again. Two years later, Richard and I were divorced. I'd never dreamed that he'd known.

"Stop saying you're sorry," said Richard. "I never did." He reached for my hands, then dropped them the minute he had them. The gesture was somehow symbolic.

"Richard?"

Now he was running his finger along the outside of his glass, catching the beads of condensation and crushing them.

"Richard."

He looked at me.

"How did you find out?" He must have seen it in my eyes.

He sank back against the velvety banquette. "Luke told me."

Luke? My head started to reel. I had to stand up, to get out of there, but I couldn't trust my legs. No more alcohol. I pushed my glass away so hard it slid across the table and crashed to the floor. The waiter instantly appeared. He picked up the cubes of ice and shards of glass and placed them in a wet rag. The Scotch had already been sucked up by the thick brown carpet.

"Can I get you another one, miss?" the waiter asked.

I shook my head.

"I'll take another," said Richard.

After the waiter left, I asked, "Why would Luke do such a thing? Did you confront him? Did you threaten him?"

Richard shook his head. "I didn't go to Luke. He came to me. He wanted to talk."

"About what?"

"He wanted to know if our marriage was over."

"That doesn't make any sense," I said desperately. "We agreed to keep it to ourselves."

Richard looked down at his lap as he spoke. "He asked me about our marriage being over because he was in love with you. He wanted to be with you. Okay?" He looked up. "Surely you knew that?"

"No," I whispered. "He never said a word."

"Shit," said Richard. The waiter set another drink down in front of him but he waved it away, saying, "Bring it back later."

I took a deep breath. "What did you tell him?"

Silence.

"What did you tell Luke?" I repeated.

He waited a long time before answering. "I told him no. That our marriage wasn't over."

"God!" I shook my head. "You *knew* it was over!"

"No."

"Yes! You were the one who destroyed it."

He looked down at his lap again.

"Did you tell him that to spite me?" I asked.

"No."

"Did you hate me so much that you'd take any possibility of happiness away from me?"

"How stupid can you be? It was just the opposite. I told him the marriage wasn't over because I didn't want it to be over."

"But why?" I asked.

"Because I still loved you."

There was a sudden, deafening silence.

"Look," said Richard, pulling out his wallet. "It's late. I think we should call it a day. We're all exhausted, and Jackie and Dot are waiting for me back at your place." He slapped his credit card down on the thick linen tablecloth. We sat there without saying a word to each other. The waiter took away the credit card, ran it through the machine, came back with a receipt for Richard to sign. Richard signed it and shoved the copy into his pocket. Still, we didn't speak. At the valet station in front of the hotel we waited for the car, both of us staring straight ahead. When Richard's rental appeared, I let him get into it alone.

"I'm going to walk," I said, stepping across the asphalt into the neon glare of the Sunset Strip. Cars cruised by, honking their horns. People crowded the sidewalks. Billboards bore down on them, promising perfect lives if they bought these sunglasses, that CD, that perfume, those jeans.

Just east of the hotel was a set of stairs that led down to a pocket park whose grass never seemed to grow. It was named after the silent screen's first western hero, William S. Hart, whom nobody remembers anymore. I stumbled down the stairs and sat down on a concrete bench opposite a homeless man who was railing against god knows what. He didn't seem to notice or care when I put my head in my hands.

I stayed there until the sun went down, thinking.

About the things I chose to remember.

About the things I chose to forget.

Then it struck me like a thunderbolt.

I'd given myself amnesia.

Just like Agatha had.

CHAPTER 42

Agatha wrapped her fur-trimmed coat more tightly around her. The winds were up, but the cold was a welcome relief from the overheated rooms at the Hydropathic.

Agatha's steps quickened as she walked past the offices of the Times. She laughed to herself about what the clerk had said to her the other day. How quickly he took back his words. She wasn't sure if his demurral was a testament to his politesse or to the efficacy of hiding in plain sight. The latter, she decided.

Good day, said a gentleman, tipping his hat.

Good day, she nodded, daring to look him in the face. What did it matter now? Certainly it had been long enough. It was time.

The windows of the Harrogate shops were festooned with Christmas decorations. Colored string, candied garlands. She drank in the smell of pine and cloves.

She was homesick. Tired.

In front of the photographer's studio she stopped and peered at the black-and-white pictures he'd put up. Other people always managed to look so charming in photographs. A little boy in a sailor suit. A group of friends by the seaside, lined up along the sand. A little girl with dark hair who reminded Agatha of her daughter, Rosalind. How clever he was with the camera—now she glanced up to the hanging sign—this Mr. R. W. Cadgeley.

There were a great number of wedding pictures. Strange, this one of two couples standing side by side. Both of the men were in formal dress, their top hats at their sides. Both of the women were in gowns, carrying sweet peas. The woman on the left was wearing a lighter-hued dress, with some sort of veil spilling off the brim of her hat, but the woman on the right was carrying the larger of the bouquets.

Which one was the bride?

Trick question.

The bride would be the one with the hope shining in her eyes.

Agatha hurried on. It was getting late. One last stop and she'd be finished. The bell on the door tinkled as she entered the small, perfumed space. The saleswoman ushered her into a private room.

An hour later Agatha emerged with the precious package. At last she'd found it: a smart, two-piece outfit with a wide collar and a striped cloche hat to match. She'd wear it with her fur-trimmed coat, a double strand of pearls around her neck, black gloves, champagne-colored stockings, and sleek black shoes.

She'd look lovely in person, and even better in the photographs.

Chapter 43

Amnesia saved Agatha Christie's life.

Only by forgetting who she was—and what she'd done—could she face herself in the mirror.

How well I understood.

I came home, turned on the lights, and took a seat on the living room sofa.

I was waiting for Gambino.

Maybe we could go out for dinner and a movie. It was Saturday night, after all. Romance was in the air. Except that I knew Gambino wasn't coming home. There'd be a message about a late meeting, a department emergency, a new witness who needed to be interviewed.

I rubbed my hands together. They were as dry as bones.

One way or another, I was going to be alone.

I went into my bedroom and took off my borrowed dress. It had to go back to Bridget's first thing Monday morning. I shook it out, hung it up, and wrapped it in plastic. Then I pulled on some jeans, washed my face, and went out to the office.

The Secret Adversary.

I pulled a paperback off my shelf and sat down at the desk.

The Secret Adversary was Agatha's second book, written in 1922, just four years before her disappearance.

The Secret Adversary is about amnesia.

Of course, all mysteries are about forgetting. Clues, suspects, motives, opportunities: the author lays them out before you, then tricks you into forgetting what you know. By the end of the book, with the revelation of the guilty party, your memories suddenly come flooding back. How could I have missed that? How did I not notice her? The answer is simple: you knew there'd be no pleasure in remembering too soon.

The Secret Adversary was the first of the Tommy and Tuppence mysteries.

Thomas (Tommy) Beresford and Prudence (Tuppence) Cowley are two young adventurers for hire. Willing to do anything, go anywhere. Pay must be good. No unreasonable offer refused. Tommy has a shock of slicked-back red hair and a pleasantly ugly face. Tuppence, a black bob and uncommonly dainty ankles. Agatha always complained of people assuming they were idealized versions of herself and Archie.

But art doesn't always imitate life.

It's often the other way around.

Tommy and Tuppence's first case was to find the mysterious Jane Finn.

Poor Jane Finn. She had survived the torpedoing and sinking of the *Lusitania* only to be given the unwelcome task of guarding an oilskin packet containing top-secret papers crucial to the Allied cause. When the bad guys eventually caught up with her (as bad guys inevitably do), they discovered she had substituted blank pages for the vital documents. Fearful of being tortured until she revealed their true whereabouts, Jane Finn came upon the idea of losing her memory.

Jane Finn faked a case of amnesia.

If she didn't know who she was, she didn't have anything to tell.

If she didn't know who she was, nothing and no one could hurt her.

"I think I almost hypnotized myself," she said, explaining her ruse to Tommy and Tuppence. "After a while, I almost forgot that I was really Jane Finn."

Jane Finn feigned amnesia to protect herself from harm.

Agatha Christie feigned amnesia to protect herself from the knowledge of what she'd done.

But wasn't it Archie who had done something to her? Wasn't he the one who had betrayed her?

No.

That wasn't the way Agatha saw it.

She was a woman of her time, a woman for whom love was paramount, a woman who—despite all her accomplishments—had no greater aspiration than that of being some good man's good wife.

She and Archie divorced. Agatha married again. She and Max Mallowan had a happy life together. They traveled the world, they wrote books—Agatha, mysteries, Max, archaeological treatises. But Archie was always the one.

After her death, her writing case was opened and inside was the wedding ring Archie had given her.

If only she'd been cleverer, she wrote in her autobiography, "if I had known more about my husband, had troubled to know more about him, instead of being content to idealize him and consider him more or less perfect, then perhaps I might have avoided all this. I must in some way have been inadequate to fill Archie's life."

Agatha saw the failure of the marriage as her own. She was furious with herself. She needed to punish herself, mostly for the intensity of her rage. She couldn't live with her anger, couldn't bear her dashed hopes.

Amnesia was the perfect vehicle.

She hadn't so much faked it as willed it into being.

There were so many things she needed to forget:

That she'd run away to hurt him.

That she'd appropriated his lover's name to spite him.

That she'd carried poison to threaten him.

And that she'd schemed to look beautiful so that when he finally found her, he'd understand what he was giving up. And maybe—if the stars were on her side—he'd change his mind.

Oh, my god.

Liz.

I was coming to the end of the story, when the guilty party is revealed.

And right on cue, my memories were starting to flood back.

CHAPTER 44

Sunday morning, the sky was dark and angry. Rain had fallen all night and from the looks of it was going to keep falling all day.

As predicted, I woke up alone.

Gambino had called around midnight, saying he had something to take care of out in Orange and an early meeting downtown in the morning. It made sense for him to stay over at Tico's.

I held the phone to my chest for a minute, listening to the rain hammering on the roof, the blood roaring in my ears.

Then I got back on the line.

I told him I understood.

We agreed to meet at Wren's preliminary hearing at five thirty. Gambino knew the judge. She was a decent person, he said. She'd treat Wren fairly. Still, I had my work cut out for me.

I braced myself, then opened my closet door. Half a dozen winter hats, a pair of suede mukluks with rabbit-fur pompoms, and a cheongsam fell at my feet.

A closet like mine is not for the faint of heart.

One good thing: I'd found my eighties fuchsia spike-heeled ankle boots with the barely noticeable scratches.

Also my high-collared Victorian lace blouse, which was back in style, worn with jeans to counteract the Little Bo Peep effect.

Oh, dear, I thought, spying my ice blue satin blazer and matching velvet skirt crumpled in a heap. Would Kim Novak have done that to the suit she was planning to wear at cocktail hour? I think not.

I picked up the woebegone goods and searched in vain for an empty hanger. Hangers were the whole problem. No, the whole problem was the unfortunate confluence between my primitive need to hoard and the puny space I had to work with. I threw the lot on the bed. Focus. My goal here was to remember what I'd been wearing last week when I'd gone over to Lou's to pay a condolence call.

It was a Sunday. Most people dress down on Sundays. Not me. I remember wondering if I should wear black, and then deciding to go the opposite route. A cherry-red tiered dress with a plum cropped wool jacket and matching plum lace-up boots. Edwardian hippie. Bright and cheerful. The life-affirming qualities of fruit. All of which meant—yes!—that I'd carried my black suede handbag with the purple and brown polka dots. And there it was. I grabbed it from the pile and sat down on my bed to go through its contents.

My wallet, keys, sunglasses, and Advil travel day to day from purse to purse, but the miscellaneous stuff tends to accumulate at the bottom of each one until panic overwhelms me and I dump the collective effluvia onto the floor. Most of it winds up in the trash. But sometimes I find good stuff, like forgotten twenty-dollar bills. Well, once I did.

I sifted through the garbage in the polka-dotted purse—pennies, cash-register receipts, eyedrops, cough drops, crumpled tissues, stray magazine subscription cards.

Then I found it.

I brandished the piece of paper like it was a winning lottery ticket.

Liz Berman's to-do list.

Lou had discovered it in the glove compartment of Liz's car. He couldn't bear to look at it, so he'd shoved it at me and I'd stuffed it in my purse.

Many moons ago, I was one of those people who make to-do lists. But I was always so depressed at the end of the day when confronted with how little I'd actually accomplished that I'd started cheating. I'd erase items I'd never gotten to. Or add items expressly for the purpose of ex-ing them out: take shower, feed dog, check messages. It was self-defeating, yes.

Liz used a blue ballpoint pen. Her handwriting slanted to the left, which is the sign of a detail-oriented individual.

The first item on her to-do list read "mani/pedi." Even Bridget had noticed Liz's ratty fingernails when Liz stopped by the shop to try on Miss Marple outfits. But I remembered the blood-red talons from that last day at Christietown. Liz had definitely gotten to item number one.

Item number two was "call Wren." About what? There were all those little jobs Wren had complained about. Or was it something to do with the affair? Liz had slapped Wren; Silvana had seen it. Liz knew what was going on. Was she calling to tell Wren to back off? Or to apologize?

The third item said "Lola's." Maybe Liz had a friend named Lola. Someone she might have visited that last week? Someone she might have confided in? Of course, I had no way of knowing when exactly she'd written this list. Lou had given me the impression that it was recent, but there was no certainty of that. I gave him a quick call, but he was out.

Item number four: "R. Ackroyd." Roger Ackroyd. The one with the trick ending. Lou said Liz had gone through everything Agatha Christie had ever written. Certainly she would have read Christie's most famous book. There were two deaths in this book, which is about the average: a widow dead from an overdose of veronal, and Roger Ackroyd, who'd hoped to marry her, dead the following night, a knife in his back. Nothing in the story, however, is precisely the way it seems: suicides that are not suicides, lovers who are not lovers. Maybe Liz wanted to reread it. Maybe she saw it as some kind of commentary on her own mixed-up life.

Then something occurred to me.

Maybe Lola wasn't a friend.

Maybe Lola's was a place.

There were a million people named Lola in Los Angeles.

But there couldn't be that many *places* with that name.

I pulled out the stack of phone books. I swear that one got dumped at my door every day, each more useless than the next. The one on the top was a White Pages serving "Hollywood, West Hollywood, Los Feliz, and Los Angeles (portions of)," which could mean just about anywhere. I went straight for the Ls.

There was a Layla's Bead Shop on Third Street. A Lolita's on Yucca. A Lulu's Alibi on Sawtelle.

No Lola's.

I went through three more White Pages to no avail, each covering various overlapping subsets of greater Los Angeles. But I wasn't ready to give up.

There was still the mighty Yellow Pages to conquer.

Half an hour and three Yellow Pages later, I'd come up with the following:

Lola's the restaurant.

Lola's the pet groomer's.

Lola's the stationery store.

Lola's the wig shop.

This time, I knew exactly where I was going.

CHAPTER 45

The thing about Los Angeles is, nobody knows how to drive in the rain.

Grown men swerve to avoid puddles, soccer moms inch along like turtles, old ladies gun across three-way intersections, distracted by their windshield-wiper settings. It's enough to make you nostalgic for Jersey.

Sundays are good because nobody's on the road. Even in the pouring rain, it took me less than five minutes to get to the strip mall on La Cienega and San Vicente, kitty-corner from the hulking Beverly Center.

I parked the car underground, then walked up the ramp past the Thai restaurant, the acupuncture studio, and the Payless shoe store until I was standing directly in front of Lola's Wigs.

The rain-spattered window reminded me of Forest Lawn Cemetery, with its Gothic black lettering and dusty garlands of plastic flowers. This was the place old hairdos went to die: Veronica Lake's peekaboo waves; Joey Heatherton's feathery bob; Angie Dickinson's cotton-candy page boy. Inside, you could barely see through the clouds of hairspray. My contacts immediately started to sting.

"May I help you." It was less a question than a statement. A beautifully dressed Asian woman stood behind the counter. An Asian man—dapper, with a thin mustache—nodded his head.

"Thank you," I said. "Maybe in a minute." I went over to the corner, and fished around in my purse for some eye-drops. After making a mess of my makeup, I slipped on my sunglasses.

"Take your time, miss," said the man. "Lots of styles, colors. My wife and I can help you find the one that's right for you. Please put your umbrella over here." He indicated a Hello Kitty receptacle that had two Burberry plaid umbrellas in it already.

I deposited my cheapie collapsible and had a look around. There were many disembodied heads, all staring at me, their wide-open eyes fringed with dark lashes, their lips glossy and beckoning. Join us, they murmured. Liberate yourself from the tyranny of your blow-dryer. A shiny, bouncy life can be yours for a mere $89.99.

I have to admit it was tempting. Platinum corkscrews? An orange-and-yellow-striped bob? Prom queen? Punk rocker? Also short and curly don't-notice-me wigs in various shades of mousy brown. At the back were the men's styles: Elvis, Fabio, Charlton Heston as Ben-Hur.

"We're having a special on falls," the man said. "The Look of Love Pony Express line is twenty-five percent off. You'd look good in a bologne curl."

I had no idea what a bologne curl was, but I was fairly certain I didn't want to look or smell like luncheon meat.

"Great idea," I said. "Can I try one on?"

"Two dollars," said his wife. "We deduct it from the cost of the fall if you buy. Watch out for the bucket over there. Can't get a roofer now, big pity."

I went to sit at a gold-trimmed vanity with hundred-watt bulbs circling the mirror, undoubtedly a fire hazard. Next to me was a heavyset man fiddling with a jet-black toupee. We acknowledged each other, then he swirled spray around his head. I decided to breathe through my mouth.

The wife came over, and gathered my voluminous locks into her hands. "Big hair," she said admiringly. "But more is always better."

The husband said, "Please remove the sunglasses." Then he sprayed something pine scented on my head, which had the miraculous effect of tamping down my hair by at least two inches. Far more effective than the pomade I'd used the other day.

Then the wife handed her husband something that looked like roadkill, which he promptly banana-clipped to the back of my head. He then stuffed my new flat hair into a pocket hanging off the banana clip and stepped back to admire his handiwork.

"Nice," said the wife.

"Very nice," said her husband.

The man with the toupee kissed his fingers to his lips.

I studied myself in the mirror. I looked bald. Bald in the front, with a dead animal in the back.

"I don't think the bologne curl works on me," I said.

Then I saw it.

"That's the one," I blurted out, pointing to a frizzy red-haired number next to a Dolly Parton.

"How come that one is so popular all of a sudden?" said the husband, tut-tutting. "We just sold a nice lady the very same one."

I knew it.

"That was my sister," I said. "It looks so great on her, I want the exact same one."

"Then you can do a sister act," said the wife. "Everybody in L.A. wants to be in show business, right?"

The husband painstakingly de-bologne-curled me while the wife fluffed up the red wig. Then, working in tandem, they stuffed my hair into what looked like a chopped-off pair of control-top panty hose, careful to tuck in the stray pieces. Finally, they put the wig on my head and tugged it into place.

I looked at myself in the mirror.

Wren Abbott looked back at me.

"I'll take it," I said.

As I was paying, I asked the wife, "Are you Lola?"

"Junie," she replied, handing me my receipt. "There is no Lola."

The sky was still blackish and forbidding, but the rain had died down. From Lola's, I took La Cienega up to Beverly, then turned right. At Fairfax, I swung a left and parked on the street in front of a ramshackle orange hut with a sign that had read OKI DOG until the K fell off, long before my time.

An Oki Dog is two hot dogs in a burrito filled with chili and pastrami. The pastrami is what puts it over the top. Only for teenagers and Tums abusers.

I crossed against the light and entered Xotx-Tropico.

Number five on Liz's to-do list.

Xotix-Tropico was a small nursery with foliage crawling up the fence and plants and flowers of every imaginable kind crammed and shoved and balanced on corners and shelves and tables along various skinny, dirt-strewn trails. I could hear the traffic on Fairfax, the honking horns and the screeching brakes, but inside, I felt far away from the city.

The middle aisle led to the greenhouse in the back. It was kind of like taking an around-the-world cruise. Here's the English countryside, with snapdragons and roses in shades of pink, yellow, white, even lavender. Now the jungle, dripping with palm fronds and Mexican weeping bamboo. Finally the desert, with its spiky succulents. One long table was covered with tiny plastic pots containing miniature cacti. Several looked like organs—livers or kidneys. Others looked like pebbles. You could pick up a pretty moon cactus for about the price of an Oki Dog.

"Back so soon?"

I turned around and was face-to-face with a tall man wearing torn jeans. He had the weather-beaten skin of someone who spends his days outdoors.

"Oh, excuse me," he said quickly. He ducked his head and kicked some gravel. "I thought you were someone else."

He reminded me of a bashful cowboy. "I'll bet you're talking about my sister."

He straightened up, studied my face for a minute, then grinned. "I don't know. She didn't look all that much like you."

"Just this crazy red hair," I said, touching my wig, "right?"

"Yeah, just the hair. Maybe the eyes, a little bit. Same shape."

"That's what everybody says."

The air in the greenhouse felt thick, heavy with moisture. I could feel the sweat beading on my upper lip. My heart was pounding.

"She okay, your sister?" he asked.

"Fine."

"Good." He nodded a couple of times.

"Why do you ask?"

"I don't know. She seemed kind of edgy the other day. In a hurry. No big deal."

"Let me ask you something about orchids," I said, changing the subject. I was going to take it slowly. Rushing him wouldn't accomplish anything. I reached out to touch a dark fuchsia flower poised at the end of a long, curving stalk. Its petals were translucent, like stained glass. "Are there any orchids that will grow outdoors?"

"Sure," he said. "We got the climate for it here. Mild nights and all. I'd recommend this one." He took me over to a cattleya in full bloom. Canary green with fringed petals. "Smell," he said.

I bent down. It was crisp, tart, like lemons.

"Biggest mistake people make with orchids is overwatering. You know the trick, don't you?"

"No," I said, shaking my head.

He stuck his hands in his pockets. "Sharpen a pencil so you get fresh wood on the tip. Then stick it deep into the pot and twist a couple of times. If the wood gets dark, don't water. Wait. You gotta be patient with orchids."

"I love flowers," I said. "I don't have much luck with them, though."

"You gotta start small. If you're not an experienced gardener, you might be better off with some daylilies, maybe. We've got

Stella de Oros. Very easy to cultivate. But not for cutting, if that's what you're looking for."

"My sister chose some lovely flowers," I said. "You helped her, right?"

"Sure did."

My armpits were soaked now. My knees were trembling. "Foxglove, wasn't it?"

"That's right."

Jesus.

"Can you show me the ones you sold her?"

"Sure."

We walked back to the front of the nursery, ducking now and then to avoid running into jade vines and kangaroo paws.

Foxglove.

How beautiful they were.

I studied the flowers in silence, hoping he'd say something more.

After a minute, he did. "Your sister is a lot more decisive than you are."

"Oh, I know," I said. "Everybody always says that. She decides what she wants and she goes out and gets it. No looking back. How many plants did she buy, do you remember?"

"Seven—she about cleaned me out."

"Who do you think is taller," I said suddenly. "Me or my sister?" I had to be sure.

He laughed. "I've got two sisters myself. They're very competitive, like you guys. All right." He stepped back, looked me up and down. "You are. But only by a hair."

I was almost six feet tall.

Liz was just about my size.

Wren was a slip of a thing.

I was sure.

"Oh, man, I almost forgot," the guy said, running into the little shed up front. "Your sister left this here. I'm sure she needs it."

He came out of the office and handed me an inhaler.

Liz's inhaler. Another thing she'd lost.

On the way out I stopped in front of the herb garden. I needed to catch my breath. I bent over for a minute, my hands on my knees. I must've looked dazed because an elderly woman picking out some heirloom tomatoes put her hand on my shoulder and said, "It's the angel's trumpet. The smell is very strong. I always need a glass of water after I've been here."

I thanked her for her kindness, then got into my car and checked the messages on my cell.

Lou had returned my call.

I was about to call him back when I saw the hollow-battery emblem indicating that my phone was out of juice. Of course, I couldn't find the charger anywhere. I went back into the nursery to see if I could use their phone, but the guy was nowhere in sight and the office was locked up. So I ran into Oki Dog and pleaded my case to the kid at the counter, who said he wasn't supposed to let people use the phone except in dire emergencies.

I said this was a dire emergency.

Lou picked up on the first ring.

I told him I needed to see him, that it was urgent.

He didn't sound surprised.

CHAPTER 46

I'd have to go down to the dance studio, though. Lou was in the middle of something and couldn't get away.

I looked at the clock on my dashboard. Three fifteen. Wren's preliminary hearing was just two hours away. It would take me thirty minutes to get to Santa Monica, another forty to get to the courthouse downtown. I did the math, then told Lou I'd be there as fast as I could.

Which apparently wasn't fast enough.

By the time I got there, the blinds had been drawn, the door bolted, the blinking PALAIS DE DANSE sign turned off. I rapped on the window but there was no reply. The stoop was awash in soggy take-out menus, one of which had caught on the heel of my boot. It came off in shreds, which I deposited in the trash can at the corner. I didn't have time for this.

Putting my hands up to the glass, I peered through the gap in the blinds. Last time there had been two people embracing behind the screen: Lou and Liz—or so I'd thought, married twenty-two years and still in love. This time there was nothing to see. The lights were off. I wanted to call Lou. I wanted to find out where he'd gone in such a hurry, but there was no pay phone in sight. I couldn't wait much longer. I didn't want to be late. There might be traffic.

Then I remembered the back door.

The alleyway smelled like rotting food. Looming parking structures on either side meant no air, no light. Near the Dumpster, half a dozen homeless men were sitting on pieces of wet cardboard, playing cards. Their perfunctory request for spare change made me sad, like they'd given up twice over.

I smiled. "When I come out, okay?"

"Whoa," said the oldest, also the grimiest. "Pretty lady like you. We should pay you for brightening our day."

"Thanks." The back door had a sign on it reading EMPLOYEE ENTRANCE. I banged on it, then stepped back. Nothing. I turned around at the sound of an approaching car. As it rumbled past, I tried to peer inside but the windshield was too fogged up.

"Something wrong?" the old man asked.

I reached into my purse and pulled out a dollar. "Just looking for a friend. Have you seen anybody go in or out of here today?"

"You got a dollar for me, too, lady?" asked one of the others.

"Shut up," said the first man. Then, turning to me, "Mr. Slick, is all. Came in this morning, been sitting in there all day in the dark."

At that, I started banging for real. "Let me in, Lou. Right now!"

"That ain't no job for a lady," said the second man.

When I nodded, he and his friends clambered to their feet and made a tremendous racket, yelling, pounding, hooting. After a couple of minutes, the heavy fire door creaked open.

The old guy said with a bow, "I give you Mr. Slick."

Lou ushered me inside as the door swung closed behind us. He'd cleaned up a little since the last time, but he still looked like hell.

"Why were you hiding from me?" I asked.

We passed through the narrow corridor leading into the studio, Lou kicking a couple of empty cardboard boxes out of the way. "No reason."

"You knew I was on my way here."

"Sorry."

The light switch was by the music. I clicked it up and down a few times, but the room stayed dark.

"Don't bother," Lou said, tugging nervously on his lips. "City turned off the lights."

"Why?"

"I told them to. I'm not paying for something I'm not using."

In front of the screen was a large red suitcase. I looked at Lou and asked, "What were you in the middle of before, when you were so busy?"

"Just what it looks like. Packing up, getting out of here."

"So that's it? You're leaving? Closing up shop?"

"There's nothing more for me here," he said. "Not without Liz."

I went over to Liz's desk and sat down in her chair. "We need to talk, Lou."

"Okay." He hesitated for a minute, then pulled up a folding chair. He sat on the other side of the desk, drumming his fingers on the cluttered surface. "Mind if I smoke?"

"Go ahead."

He reached for the pack on the desk. There was one cigarette left. He put it in his mouth, then got up to look for matches.

"I found out something today," I said.

He sat down and pulled the brimming ashtray closer to him. His long, thin fingers were twitching in anticipation.

"Wren didn't kill Liz," I said.

"I knew that." He lit his cigarette, closing his eyes as the nicotine flowed into his bloodstream.

"The fact of the matter is, nobody killed Liz. But then, you knew that, too."

He took another long drag, then exhaled. The sound reverberated in the empty space. "I'm an idiot. I don't know anything."

"Don't make me say it, Lou."

He looked at me. It was dark, but I could see his eyes. They were glittering. "Why don't you say it, Cece?"

I didn't want to.

He tipped the ash onto the floor. "C'mon. I dare you."

I wasn't one to back down on a dare. "Liz killed herself."

"Go to hell!" He leapt to his feet and his chair went crashing to the floor. "She wouldn't do that. She wouldn't leave me behind." He made a low sound in his throat.

I got up and walked over to where he was standing, his face turned to the wall. "She didn't want to," I said. "Leaving you was the last thing she wanted to do. But she found out about you and Wren."

"I loved her. We were supposed to grow old together." He was crying now, pounding his fist against the wall. Chips of old paint fluttered to the floor.

"You slept with another woman," I said. "You betrayed your wife. What did you expect?"

"Not this," he said, turning around. "I wanted a chance to explain."

"The thing is, her dying wasn't the worst of it, was it?"

"Shut up," he said, wiping away a tear. "Just go now."

"The worst of it," I pressed on, "was that she didn't mean for it to happen."

"I need another cigarette." He started rooting around the room, pulling things apart, tearing the calendar off the wall, tossing plastic cups onto the floor.

"She wanted you to find her in time. She wanted you to bring her back home."

He went around to the other side of the desk and yanked open the drawers like a wild man. "What is all this? Stupid books!" He threw the drawers onto the floor. Yellowed paperbacks, old bills, tissues, sticks of gum went flying. He knelt down to sort through the chaos. "Where are the damn cigarettes?" In a fury, he grabbed one of the books and threw it across the room. It hit the wall with a smack.

Postern of Fate.

Tommy and Tuppence have acquired a lovely house in the small English village of Hollowquay. They are content. They've grown old together.

If Agatha didn't have it in real life, she'd be damned if she didn't have it in fiction.

If Liz didn't have it, what then? How far had she been willing to go? I knew. Lou knew.

"Stupid, stupid, stupid," he cried. "She read them all so carefully. She was so diligent. Learned her lessons. All about poisons and faking your own death and punishing the people you think needed punishing."

Liz had been a good student, but she'd learned all the wrong lessons.

"It was such a waste, Cece," he whispered.

A terrible waste.

Liz was going to make everyone think that Wren wanted her out of the way, badly enough to poison her. Wren would be caught. She'd go to jail. She'd be out of their lives forever. And Liz, well, Liz would survive. She could survive anything with Lou at her side. He'd come charging to her rescue, like a knight in shining armor. Liz had worked so hard. She'd looked so beautiful. She wasn't going to take any chances. She wanted her husband to know exactly what he was giving up. And maybe—just maybe, if the stars were on her side—he'd change his mind.

Her big mistake had been consulting Javier. What a wonderful coincidence to have a new friend who was a gardener. Pretending to be Wren, she'd chat with him about foxglove and get the information she needed, incriminating Wren in the process. But Javier knew plants, not poisons. He'd thought it took months to kill somebody with foxglove. Liz must have figured out how to distill the leaves and mixed up enough to kill anybody—even a survivor like herself—within minutes. When I'd talked to Javier this morning, he was despondent. The last thing he meant to do was cause any harm.

The truth is like fiction, only badly constructed.

Ariadne Oliver, Agatha Christie's alter ego, a mystery novelist and friend of Hercule Poirot, once said that.

"You've known about this for a long time, haven't you?" I asked Lou.

"Yes."

"You could've saved Wren a lot of anguish."

"That's not true. How could I save Wren when she won't save herself?"

"What you couldn't do was admit you'd failed your wife," I said. "So you failed both of them."

He knew it was true. But was he ready to accept the responsibility for it? Until he did, I had nothing. He had all the missing pieces.

"There's no going back now," he said.

"It's too late for Liz," I said. "But not for Wren."

"She can tell them the truth herself."

"She won't. She's afraid." The words I didn't want to say were the words he needed to hear. What choice did I have? None. "Wren is where she is because she loves you," I said. "Do for her what you can't do for Liz."

And with that, the wall he'd so painstakingly erected crumbled, like the ash at the end of his cigarette. He rose to his feet, walked back over to the suitcase, unzipped it, and pulled out a red wig—the same one I'd bought at Lola's.

"Here," he said, pushing it toward me. He was looking down at his feet. "I found it mixed up with the dancing costumes. That's where Liz must have hidden it."

I checked the clock on the wall. It was 4:30 now.

"Will you come with me, Lou?"

I held out my hand and he grabbed for it, like a drowning man grabs for a lifeline.

CHAPTER 47

We exited the freeway at Temple, entering the evil maze of one-way streets that is downtown Los Angeles.

Looming skyscrapers, sterile subterranean concourses, deserted private plazas, Skid Row to your left, loft conversions to your right. I prayed for clarity. One wrong turn and I'd have to go all the way to Little Tokyo before I could pull a U-turn.

"We're not going to make it," said Lou, tossing his cigarette out the window. "Look at the clock."

It was 5:12. He was right.

"Call McAllister," I said, handing Lou the detective's card. "Tell him we're on our way with urgent information."

Lou punched the number into his phone, waited, shook his head. "Machine."

Wren would be stuck in jail for another night. I slapped my hands against the steering wheel.

If only I'd found Lola's sooner.

If only Lou had opened up the door when I'd first arrived.

If only.

But then we drove past a street called Hope (between Grand and Spring), and I felt something jolt through my veins.

"Oh, yes, we're going to make it," I said to Lou. "Today is your lucky day. I feel it in my bones."

The Clara Shortridge Foltz Criminal Justice Center is a cement monolith on the corner of Temple and Spring, named for the suffragette from Indiana who'd become the first practicing female lawyer. Lou and I gave each other high fives as we pulled into the parking lot next door with less than ten minutes to spare.

"Sixteen bucks," said the attendant, not looking up from the TV. I studied the sign. Three dollars every fifteen minutes; sixteen dollars maximum. No in-and-out privileges. Lost ticket results in death and dismemberment.

"Do I have to pay in advance?" I asked. "We're not going to be long."

"Sixteen bucks," he repeated.

I riffled through my purse, but could find only nine dollars.

The attendant ripped open a bag of chips. "This is a place of business. You parking or not?"

"Do you have any money, Lou?"

He went through his wallet and handed me a five and a one.

"Can you live with fifteen?" I asked, putting the car into Drive. I'd meant it as a rhetorical question.

The attendant shook his head.

I put the car back into Park and turned my purse upside down. I came up with thirty cents and some cracker crumbs. There was somebody behind us now, honking impatiently. "I gotta get to court!" he yelled.

I leaned out my window. "Do you have seventy cents I can borrow?"

"Jesus," said the attendant, who motioned for the guy to go around me.

Lou pointed to the clock. It was 5:23 now.

"Is there a bank machine around here?" I asked, at the end of my rope now.

The attendant pointed to a big, black building sandwiched between two other big, black buildings. "B of A."

"Wait here," I said to Lou, unbuckling my seat belt.

I sprinted over to the bank. There were two machines, one of which had an Out of Order sign taped to it, the other a line consisting of at least a dozen Japanese tourists wearing Disneyland shirts. I was getting ready to take my chances and abandon my car exactly where it was when a tour bus pulled up and honked its horn. The tourists started to cheer, then did a group about-face and left. Now there was only one person between me and my seventy cents. Unfortunately, he was unfamiliar with ATMs. He apologized, explaining that the ones in Norway were different. I looked back toward the parking lot. Lou was getting out of the car. What was that about? I helped the Norwegian get $200, $20 of which he offered me as a tip. I shot another glance Lou's way. Lou was now waving a fist in the attendant's face.

I took the twenty and ran.

After paying the attendant his blood money, we flew up the wheelchair ramp only to be confronted with a security line snaking from outside the building to the metal detector. It was bad. They were frisking people.

"It's after five thirty now," said Lou.

"I'm sure they're running late." I removed my belt and shoes. I hoped my underwire bra was not going to be a problem.

"You're probably right." It was the first halfway positive

thing Lou had uttered in days. "Gum?" he asked, shoving a piece in his mouth. He couldn't smoke inside. I took a piece to be polite.

"Arraignments and prelims?" I asked when we got to the front of the line.

"Check at information," the security guard said.

"Judge Velasquez," said the information officer. "Hoo, boy."

We took the elevator up to the third floor. I scanned the corridor for Gambino, but he was nowhere in sight. My heart sank, then I remembered why we were there. Determined, I threw open the door to Department 35 and shoved Lou in front of me. I wasn't sure he wouldn't hightail it out of there otherwise.

Judge Dina Velasquez looked up, her face framed by a pair of black cantilevered glasses and a spiky crew cut. At the sight of us, she frowned disapprovingly.

"Where's Wren?" asked Lou, slipping into the last row of seats. "I don't see her. When are they bringing her out?"

"I'll find out." I made my way up the aisle. Mariposa and McAllister were seated in the front row, which was reserved for police officers. There were signs everywhere, for those who didn't know how to behave in polite company: TURN OFF BEEPERS, NO SMOKING, NO CELL PHONES, NO GUM CHEWING. I swallowed my Juicy Fruit. Mariposa didn't seem to care about the rules. He was on the phone. Maybe cops were exempt. I tapped McAllister's shoulder.

"Ms. Caruso," he whispered. "What are you doing here? And Mr. Berman," he said, spying Lou in the back.

"Is Ms. Lee here for the defense?" intoned Judge Dina. She'd have made an excellent baritone.

"On her way," said the clerk.

"Ms. Lee is getting exactly ten minutes," the judge said, removing her glasses with a sigh.

The bailiff got up and started jangling keys.

The stenographer adjusted his chair.

The clerk pulled out a thick file and tapped his fingers on it.

"Where's Wren?" I whispered.

Mariposa hung up the phone and turned around. "Zipping up her party dress."

I suppressed the urge to slap him and asked, "Is that the prosecutor up there? What's her name?"

She was in her late twenties, a mousy blonde, skinny. She looked like she was playing dress-up in her mother's clothes.

"A D.A., Clara Webber," said McAllister. "Don't be fooled."

"Ms. Webber," I hissed. "Ms. Webber, I need to talk to you."

"Well, shit," said Mariposa. "You're not kidding. Stop bothering the woman and come with me." He took my arm and marched me down the aisle, McAllister following.

"Join us," I said to Lou, grabbing him on the way out.

We sat down on a wooden bench outside the courtroom.

"This had better be good," said Mariposa.

What a terrible lot of explaining one has to do in a murder, I thought, paraphrasing Christie. "I don't know where to start."

"Contempt charges sound good?" asked Mariposa. "'Cause that's where you're heading."

"Liz wasn't the glamorous type," I began.

"Unlike you," said Mariposa. "Can you do the beauty-queen wave?"

Extend your arm out to the side, bend your elbow to ninety

degrees. Slightly cup your hand. Without moving your fingers or wrist, rotate your hand from the forearm. The point is no underarm jiggle. But why was I letting Mariposa distract me? We didn't have all day.

"On the day Liz was murdered," I said, "her nails were done, her makeup was perfect, her hair was styled, she had on a great suit."

"The jacket had a peplum," said McAllister.

"They don't call you Pretty Boy for nothing," said Mariposa.

"Will you shut the hell up?" said McAllister. "You never know when to stop!"

Mariposa looked surprised. Usually he was the one doing the slapping down.

"She wanted to look beautiful for her husband," I said.

"She was dolled up for the play," Mariposa was muttering. "Opening night, so to speak."

"No," I said. "You don't spend all that time on gorgeous hair when you're about to put on a wig."

A lightbulb went off over Mariposa's head. "No shit?" I nodded.

"She staged the whole thing?" asked McAllister. "She killed herself?"

"She didn't mean to," interjected Lou. "It was an accident. She didn't want to die."

"Lou was supposed to find her before it was too late," I explained. "He had her inhaler. She knew he'd come looking for her. He'd find her, and fall in love with her all over again. Only he didn't make it in time." I glanced at Lou. He was holding up well.

"What about Wren?" McAllister asked.

I told them how Liz had framed her, hoping Lou would lose interest in someone capable of murder. Liz dressed up as Wren to buy the foxglove, then called Javier, pretending to be Wren, to find out about how much to use, dumping the used plants into Wren's trash.

"It's quite a story you got there, but how are we supposed to prove it?" asked Mariposa.

I turned to Lou, who held out the red wig. "I found it in Liz's things. It's what she wore that day."

"It's a start," I said.

"There's more, Cece." Lou stuck his hand in his pocket and pulled out a small brown paper bag.

"What's this?" I asked.

Inside were some broken capsules and what looked like potpourri. "I found a mess in the bathroom that afternoon when I came home from Christietown. Even then, I guess I knew what she'd done. I just didn't want to admit it."

Another missing piece.

Just then, a tall, angry-looking Asian woman came barreling down the hall. "Excuse me," she shouted. "I'm running late. Out of the way!"

I got up and blocked the door. "Ms. Lee, I presume?"

"Yes?"

"Ms. Lee," I said, "today is your lucky day."

Lou said, "Believe it. She feels this kind of thing in her bones."

A few minutes later, a now-jubilant Ms. Lee threw open the door to Department 35. I caught a glimpse of Wren sitting in the front of the courtroom in her state-issued orange jumpsuit. I hadn't realized the other day how close it was to the color of her hair. As the door flew open, she turned around. She didn't react to me, but when she saw Lou she broke into a smile that rippled across her entire body.

Lou returned the smile, if not the depth of emotion.

Still, I hoped they could take care of each other, at least for a while.

After Lou went inside and the door slammed shut, my new best friend sidled up to me.

"So you gonna solve the Holtzman case for us, too?" Detective Mariposa asked.

I looked up at the clock in the corridor.

"That depends," I said. "Can you give me an hour or two?"

CHAPTER 48

The onlookers huddled around the rosy-cheeked man in the guayabera, laughing and joking. He exhaled, steadying his hand. They grew quiet, serious. Taking a step backward, he rotated his shoulder deeper into its socket, then pulled it back sharply, sending his first silver-tipped dart on its lightning-quick path toward the board.

"Bull's-eye!" roared the crowd. "A pint for our man Ian!"

Sunday night. The darts championship at Ye Olde King's Head. The game was 501 up. Each player starts with a score of 501 and takes turns throwing three darts. The score is calculated and deducted from the player's total. Bull's-eye scores fifty, the outer ring scores twenty-five, a dart in the double or treble ring counts double or treble the segment score. The object is to be the first player to reduce the score to exactly zero, the only caveat being that the last dart thrown must land in a double or the bull's-eye.

A woman in a tan gabardine business suit erased the number on the chalkboard and changed it to the number 2. She swiveled around, a look of glee transforming her plain face. "Double one, people. This is it!"

"Piece of cake," said someone.

"For Ian, maybe," said a portly man in blue coveralls, and everyone laughed.

I sat in a corner booth, nursing a pint of bitters. It was warm and flat but I didn't much care. I had my eye on Ian.

His aim was unerring, which hardly surprised me.

Ian, poised for the second dart, spun around to address a beautiful young woman sitting on a bar stool. "You watch out," he said with a wink. "If I make it to Purfleet's Circus Tavern in Essex, you're coming with me." She blew him a kiss.

That was when he saw me.

I hadn't been avoiding him, but still, he'd been unaware, wrapped up in the game. He flinched ever so slightly, then, turning to face the board, let the dart fly. It landed on the black next to the number 1.

A hush fell over the room. The bartender stopped pulling drafts. Patrons stopped chewing on pretzels.

"Too bad," the scorekeeper said, taking off her jacket and hanging it by the side of the bar. "A single." She rolled up the sleeves of her blouse.

"You playing, Sheila?" someone asked.

"No. I'm just warm," she replied.

Ian approached the portly man the way a courtier approaches a king. "What do you say, friend?" he asked. "I find myself in the awkward position of being at one."

The man finished off his beer and perched his empty glass on the bar rail. Studying Ian, he asked, "You really think you can split the eleven?"

"I do," said Ian.

He waved his hand, a benevolent ruler granting a subject's request. "Then have at it, man."

Now the room was silent, the air thick with expectation.

Ian wiped the sweat from his brow, squinted, blew on the dart, rubbed it between his hands. Then, with a flick of his wrist, he sent it on its way.

It landed directly in the middle of the eleven.

The pub broke out in cheers. Ian took a lap around the room, like a prize-winning horse, accepting congratulations, slaps on the back, free drinks.

I looked at the dart trapped between the vertical lines of the eleven.

I saw Ian, behind bars.

He slowed to a stop in front of my booth. "May I?"

"Please," I said, scooting over.

"*Death in the Clouds*," he said. "Do you remember that one, Cece?"

I shook my head. "Not in any detail."

He took a hankie out of his pocket and wiped his face, still slick with perspiration. "The murder weapon is a poisoned dart, with orange and black silk thread knotted around it."

"Ah," I said, nodding.

"The story is set on an aircraft, which is, of course, a clever variant on the isolated country house. All the players are trapped inside. Hercule Poirot, the occupant of seat number nine, is one of the suspects, but we know from the beginning that he's innocent."

"He's the detective," I said. "Despite rumors to the contrary, Agatha always played fair."

But then I remembered that two of the passengers, the Messrs. Dupont, were archaeologists, like Agatha's second hus-

band, Max. At some point in the story, they recount in horri-
fied tones the tale of an Englishman who left his sick wife alone
in a small hotel in Syria. Max had once done the same thing to
Agatha. Was she getting back at him? Was that fair play?

"What are you doing here, Cece?" asked Ian.

"I've been worried about you."

"No need." He studied my face. "Was it you who brought
me the comforter?"

I nodded.

"That was very kind of you," he said, sidestepping the question of why he had needed one in the first place.

"Don't thank me," I said abruptly, pulling something out of
my purse. It'd come in the mail yesterday from England.

They Fly Through the Air.

A history of the circus.

I flipped through the book until I came to the page I wanted.
A photograph of Deadeye Ian, with a trick rifle in his hand.

"'At one time, he was famed around the country,'" I read
out loud. "'Shooting five balloons off an assistant in under a
second, hitting two targets so fast it sounded like one shot,
blasting a target behind him using the sole of his boot to cock
and fire the gun, a dime tossed in the air, an apple once off a
tree and again before it hit the ground, and his *piece de resis-
tance*, the famous bullet catch.'"

Ian's eyes darted furtively around the room. His breath was
coming quickly. I thought for a minute he was going to vault
over me to escape into the night, but then, all at once, he settled back into his seat. Most criminals are relieved when they're
caught. First there's panic, then resignation, and finally, relief.
Agatha Christie had taught me that.

"Everybody's got a secret," I said. "What's yours?"

"It's all in the stance," he said. "You mount the rifle to your shoulder, balancing the front end on either the palm or the web of the off hand. Then you stand, so your bones support the weight of the rifle. Bones don't get tired. Muscles do."

Ian looked so very tired—muscles, bones, heart, mind.

"The trick of the bullet catch," he said, "is wax. You shape the wax just so, then give it a candy coating the color of lead. Nobody ever knows it's not real. They watch you load the rifle and they're never the wiser. The explosion of the charge and the propulsive motion vaporizes the wax. Ta-dah!" He smiled wistfully. "Even then, I never wanted anyone to get hurt."

I took a deep breath. "What went wrong with Silvana?"

He closed his eyes. "Damn mirrors."

The mirrored tiles on her fireplace. The pink bulbs. Silvana wanted to see herself bathed in the soft light.

"She broke the house rules!" he exclaimed. "She knew them inside out and *still* she broke them. You know how thorough I am, Cece, how attentive to details. I go to great lengths to ensure that each and every Christietown resident understands the importance of the bylaws. We sit down together and go over them point by point. But Silvana disregarded me. She and Dov were old friends. She thought that entitled her to special privileges." He lowered his head, dropped his voice. "I just wanted to keep the commotion going, keep the sales figures up. I didn't mean for her to get hurt, I swear it. I am truly sorry."

When he looked through Silvana's window, the rifle poised on his shoulder, Ian didn't see what he expected to see. The room looked like a patchwork quilt. Everything in it was fragmented, reflected, doubled, redoubled. He didn't shoot straight because he couldn't see straight.

They Do It with Mirrors.

That book I remembered.

You always believe the worst, Ruth Van Rydock says to Miss Marple, whose china blue eyes don't so much as blink.

Miss Marple replies: That's because the worst is so often true.

Miss Marple was a pessimist. Agatha was an optimist. Still, the point is not what you think—about the world, about yourself. The point is how you act on it.

"Ian, my boy!" The portly man in the blue coveralls stood before us. "Will we be seeing you next Sunday? My nephew will be here. He once played a game with the great Phil Taylor, or so he says."

Ian looked at me, then said, "I don't think so. I'm going away for a while."

I used his phone to call Mariposa and McAllister. I told them where we were, and that the gun was on the eleventh floor of the Clock Tower Building, among Ian's things. They said to not so much as move, that they were on their way.

"Will they arrest me here, Cece, in front of everyone?" Ian smoothed down his guayabera.

I didn't know.

What I did know was that he was going to jail for an accident.

And Dov Pick and Avi Semel were getting off scot-free, despite poisoning the water supply and looting the aquifer and god knows what else.

Business as usual.

That's Chinatown, Jake.

As it turns out, no place else is any different—not Miss Marple's St. Mary Mead, not Christietown either.

"Ian?"

He looked up.

"You aren't related to Agatha Christie, are you?"

Before he could answer, Mariposa and McAllister had materialized in front of us.

Ian was terrified.

I squeezed his hand and promised him we'd see each other again.

CHAPTER 49

Betrayal by Chambermaid.

In other circumstances, thought Agatha, it might have made for a fine title. Ah, well. So Rosie with the overbite was more astute than she appeared. Agatha couldn't help but berate herself. For a novelist, she'd turned out to be a poor judge of character indeed.

Tipped off by Rosie and then the local police, Archie was in the lobby of the Harrogate, determined to move slowly, as if his wife were a forest creature likely to bolt at the slightest rustling.

He was seated in a wingback chair, his face buried in a newspaper.

But he wasn't reading.

Not about how a medium in Guildford, channeling a twelve-year-old African girl named Maisie, had contacted Agatha through a used powder-puff.

Nor about the hypothesis that she'd driven off in a dark red four-seater with a mystery lover, with whom she was ensconced near Pyrford.

Nor about the most absurd of the theories, that she was living in London disguised as a man.

He knew better than that.

No, Archie wasn't reading.

He was lying in wait.

Superintendent McDowall of the Claro Division was hovering nearby, wondering how this was going to play to his superiors. The twitchy manageress of the hotel, Mrs. Taylor, was pacing the floor of her office, anticipating with no great pleasure the theatrics to come. The esteemed members of the press were massing outside, the chill air biting at their ink-stained fingers.

It was then that an unsuspecting Agatha came downstairs and seated herself in the lounge.

Seeing all he needed to see, Archie signaled Superintendent Mc-Dowall.

Yes, the woman in the pink georgette dress with the silk camellia at her shoulder was in fact his wife.

He'd expected a scene. But when Archie approached Agatha, she acted as if nothing out of the ordinary had transpired. They sat together quietly by the fire. Later, they took a corner table in the restaurant.

She talked. He listened.

She confessed everything.

Afterward, she told him she was deeply sorry.

She whispered the words over and over again until they were just hollow sounds in her ears.

After leaving Agatha in her hotel bedroom, Archie rang Styles to tell his wife's secretary that she'd been found, and that she'd been suffering from amnesia.

That evening, husband and wife slept in separate rooms.

When it was time to leave the following morning, the cameras were poised to strike. Agatha held her head high as the bellboy opened the door of the waiting taxicab, which whisked them to the station.

The railway staff had placed an Out of Order sign on the machine that sold penny tickets, hoping to keep the crowds at bay.

After indicating they would be proceeding to King's Cross station, they switched trains at Leeds, Agatha leading the way through a phalanx of indefatigable reporters.

Westminster Gazette, *the* Daily News, *the* Daily Mail, *the* Leeds Mercury, *the* Daily Sketch.

Agatha and Archie found their seats on the train.

Agatha stared at Archie, who stared out the window.

When he closed his eyes for some much-needed sleep, she reached into her handbag and took out the wedding ring she'd tossed so impulsively out of the car window that fateful night, eleven days earlier.

Before catching the milk train to Waterloo, she'd gone back to find it. In the dark of the night, she'd searched through the leaves, disarranged her hair, scratched her face, blinked back the tears until she'd seen it, half-buried in the underbrush.

"I know of no other experience which confers so much grace as loving and being loved by one person."

The words she'd once written came to mind, and to her surprise, she still believed them.

Archie began to stir and Agatha slipped the ring back inside her purse. As she zipped it closed, she could see the gold glinting in the dying light.

After that, she remembered absolutely nothing of her time at the Harrogate, nor of the long and terrible night that had preceded it.

When it came to the story of Agatha Christie's life, that chapter was lost forever.

CHAPTER 50

"Cece! Where are you?" Gambino shouted into my ear.

I was in the foyer of the King's Head inside one of those old-fashioned fire-engine-red British telephone booths with a gold crown at the top and seventy-two individually beveled glass windows. Not that I was going to tell him. Not with that attitude.

"Where are *you*?" I yelled back. "You were supposed to meet me at the courtroom hours ago."

"I've been trying to call you. And I'm not the only one."

Two young women with Princess Di hairdos and tiaras were rapping on the phone booth now. They pointed at their camera. They wanted to take a picture. I held up my index finger and smiled. Apparently, they didn't want to wait. Nor were they in a smiling mood. "I have to hang up in a second," I said. "Sorry you couldn't reach me. My phone's been dead all day. What's the big emergency?"

His voice softened. "Are you sitting down?"

"No," I said, feeling suddenly faint.

"Is there a chair nearby?"

"No. What is it? You're scaring me."

"Don't be scared. It's good news."

Turned out Annie was having her baby a little bit ahead of schedule.

I flew out of the phone booth, nearly mowing down the Dianas in the process. The one with the bigger tiara yelled, "Screw you," the other gave me a hand gesture that would've made the Queen Mum blush. You could tell right off the bat they were frauds.

The folks at Cedars Sinai were more polite, with the possible exception of the valet, who looked askance at my unwashed Camry, which even I had to admit stuck out like a sore thumb amid the luxury vehicles swarming the underground parking lot. Annie's water had broken this afternoon at four while she and Vincent were having a predinner corned beef and cabbage snack at the Farmer's Market. The Farmer's Market was on Third and Fairfax, and Cedars was about two minutes away. That's how they'd wound up at the most expensive hospital west of the Mississippi. At least she'd get a private room and good drugs.

The lady at the information kiosk had seen my type before. After giving me a pat on the back and a booklet about anxiety disorder, she sent me to the maternity ward. On the way up, I became aware of a jackhammerlike pounding in the vicinity of my heart. I brought my hand to my chest, which seemed to alarm the man standing next to me, who breached elevator etiquette to reassure me that the cardiac-care unit at Cedars was world-class. I explained that I'd been stuck in an elevator recently, plus my only child was having a baby. Then I started to weep. That earned me another pat on the back. I watched the numbers light up on the monitor: 2, 3, 4. At last, the doors opened.

"Cece!" cried Lael. "Finally."

"You're here?" I asked.

They were all there, assembled in the mauve-accented waiting area: Lael, Bridget, Gambino, Richard, Jackie, Dot, with little Alexander on her lap, and Vincent, who was as pale as I'd ever seen him, but grinning from ear to ear as he rushed up to give me a hug.

"I've gotta get back in there," he said. "I just wanted to say hi."

"Can I see her?" I asked, clutching the hem of his T-shirt like both our lives depended on it.

Vincent shook his head. "It's really important to Annie that it's just the two of us in there. Please don't take it wrong. It's a bonding thing."

"Tell her I love her," I said as he walked away.

"She knows," said Gambino, putting his arm around me.

When Annie had arrived several hours ago, she was 100 percent effaced but less than one centimeter dilated. Her contractions were weak and were spaced fifteen minutes apart. The doctor had decided to give it three hours, but if there was no change, they were going to induce labor. Annie balked, but only until being informed that it would reduce the risk of a cesarean. The three hours were up thirty minutes ago. They'd gone ahead and administered Pitocin. Despite being informed that the contractions brought on by induction would almost certainly be severe, Annie was refusing an epidural.

"No drugs?" I asked, weak at the knees.

Lael shook her head regretfully.

Bridget's comment was, "I hear the Deluxe Birthing Room has a Jacuzzi." Then, "The gift shop is very well-stocked."

Jackie and Dot were pacing the shiny faux-tile floor.
Richard was reading the *New York Times,* a box of cigars at
his side. It reminded me of the day Annie was born. Richard's
father had brought a box of cigars to Asbury Park General
and forced his son to have one. Richard had promptly
thrown up. I never knew if it was from the tobacco or the
shock. He was twenty-two, I was barely eighteen. We knew
nothing about life, less than that about raising a child. Still,
Richard had been there for Annie. She'd spent summers and
holidays with him, he'd flown out for graduations and special
occasions. Not much in terms of time, but he'd given his
love unsparingly, and it was a big part of what made Annie
good and strong. Twenty-one years later he was still there, a
newspaper in his hands. He'd always been better with words
than with people. Just then, he looked up and caught my
eye. I nodded at him. He nodded at me. It was the best we
were going to do.

"So now we wait," I said to Gambino.

We sat down next to each other.

"What's new?" he asked.

A trick question. "You first," I said.

Gambino told me he and Tico had run into a brick wall
with their murder investigation. It was obvious that the guy
had been dealing drugs from prison, and that whoever had
whacked him wasn't enthused about the idea. It had to be
someone higher up on the food chain. They'd left the thousand bucks on him deliberately. It was a show of power. But
there was no forensic evidence. And thus no real suspects.
What about the women? I asked. The wife and the girlfriend?
They'd given up on him long ago, said Gambino. They were
smart enough to know he wasn't worth life behind bars.

Then it was my turn.

I told him about my visit to the wig shop and the nursery, and Lou's and my mad dash for the courtroom. Mostly, though, I talked about Ian. We'd had a few minutes together after I made the phone call. It had been awkward. I'd put him between a rock and a hard place. He wanted to do the right thing; he wanted to run as fast and as far as he could. But we both knew there wasn't anyplace he could run where he'd be able to forget what he'd done, regardless of how many larkspurs and hollyhocks and snapdragons were lining the path to his front door.

Was that when McAllister and Mariposa showed up? asked Gambino.

No, I said. That was when Ian reached into his pocket and pulled out his brown leather billfold. From between two twenties, he extracted a thin piece of yellowed paper with frayed edges. There was a gold monogram at the top: *A.M.C.*

Agatha Miller Christie.

Ian unfolded the piece of paper and placed it on the table in front of me. He watched my face for a minute.

Did I know about the note Agatha had left behind for Archie before she disappeared? he asked.

Of course I knew about the note. Archie had destroyed it.

Was I so sure about that? Now Ian's eyes were sparkling.

Yes, I was sure. It was full of recriminations about Archie's affair with Nancy. Archie destroyed it because he didn't want anyone to see it.

Ian shook his head.

I looked down again.

The note was written in a shaky hand I recognized.

Where did you get this? I asked.

Family heirloom, he replied.

You picked it up at the memorabilia shop, didn't you?

He didn't answer. His eyes had filled with tears.

Oh, Cece, he said. Life is such a mystery, isn't it?

That was when Mariposa and McAllister appeared.

And now it was Vincent who was standing in front of me. I leapt to my feet. "How is she?"

"Do you mean Annie," he asked with a smile, "or my gorgeous new daughter?"

"A girl!" Richard cried from across the room. He reached over to hug Jackie. "You've got a sister!" he said to Alexander, who was jumping up and down. Alexander was always jumping up and down, but this time there was a reason.

"Congratulations, man," said Gambino, pumping Vincent's hand.

"Is Annie okay?" I asked him anxiously.

"Your daughter is radiant," he said. "Like every day." He embraced me, then said, "I am the luckiest man in the world."

"Do you have a name yet?" asked Dot.

"Radha."

Jackie gave Richard a sideways glance.

"How exactly do you spell that?" Richard asked.

"R-A-D-H-A. She's a cowherdess who gets transformed into a goddess through love," explained Vincent.

I looked at Gambino, who whispered, "Don't worry. We can call her Hot Rod."

After a long pause, Richard said, "I like it."

"Me, too," I said. "Radha. It's beautiful."

"Annie would like to see you both," Vincent said. "To introduce you to your granddaughter."

Richard and I stayed for an hour, fussing over Annie. Lying in the bed, with her daughter in her arms, she'd never seemed happier. And Vincent, well, he was beside himself. His smile, normally beatific, was otherworldly. Richard had forgotten all about the cigars. Instead, he snapped pictures of the tiny, perfect newborn. I was content just to stroke her skin. It was so velvety, like Annie's had been. Baby back, Richard and I used to call it. The softest skin imaginable.

Annie and Radha would be spending two nights in the hospital, just as a precaution. Once they returned home, the only thing the doctor was recommending was keeping the baby away from crowds for several weeks. It would give her immune system a chance to kick in. Would Gambino and I consider, Vincent asked as he walked us back to the waiting room, postponing the wedding for a few weeks so they could all be there?

I laughed and told him it wouldn't be a problem. I wouldn't consider having a wedding unless Radha could be the flower girl.

Gambino and I took Alexander home with us so Vincent could stay at the hospital with his wife and new baby. We fed the pets, had a midnight snack of orange juice and Oreos, and went to sleep.

Sometime around dawn, the screeching of a siren woke me up. After tossing and turning for a while, I gave up the fight. I went into the bathroom, washed my face, put on my robe, and tiptoed out to the living room, a yellowed piece of paper in my hand.

I know of no other experience which confers so much grace as loving and being loved by one person.

That's what it said, the note Agatha wrote to Archie, the

note Archie claimed to have destroyed, the note that Ian had given to me for safekeeping.

Bull's-eye.

The words hit me like a knife to the heart.

I looked down at the beautiful ring Gambino had given me, and thought about the wedding we were supposed to have, the one I'd postponed without so much as asking him.

I know of no other experience which confers so much grace as loving and being loved by one person.

Loving and being loved by one person.

If you don't get it right the first time, you might get another chance.

Some people take it, others run from it.

Sitting there alone on my living room couch, the early morning sun streaming in through the window, I wondered, not for the first time, if I was the kind of person who took it, or the kind of person who ran.